P9-DVB-102

The Consequences of Desire

Winner of the Flannery O'Connor

Award for Short Fiction

The Consequences of Desire

Stories by Dennis Hathaway

The University of Georgia Press

Athens and London

Published by the University of Georgia Press
Athens, Georgia 30602

Designed by Erin Kirk
Set in Sabon by Tseng Information Systems, Inc.
Printed and bound by Thomson-Shore, Inc.
The paper in this book meets the guidelines for
permanence and durability of the Committee on
Production Guidelines for Book Longevity of the
Council on Library Resources.

Printed in the United States of America

96 95 94 93 92   C   5 4 3 2 1

Library of Congress Cataloging in Publication Data

Hathaway, Dennis.
    The consequences of desire : stories / by Dennis Hathaway.
        p.   cm.
    Contents: Counting Mercedes-Benzes—Lost in Rancho Mirage—I
like Rap, don't you?—The night of love—The girl detective—
The apocryphal story—Space and light—The consequences of
desire—Bésame, bésame—Sawtelle—The chosen.
    ISBN 0-8203-1475-7 (alk. paper)
    I. Title.
PS3558.A7385C66   1992
813' .54—dc20   92-8947
                                                                        CIP

British Library Cataloging in Publication Data available
"Bésame, Bésame" first appeared in The Georgia Review (Fall 1992).

To Laura

Contents

Counting Mercedes-Benzes

Marshall counted his first Mercedes-Benz as he turned from Doheny onto Sunset Boulevard, at that spot where the Sunset Strip is swallowed by Beverly Hills and all becomes green and silent. A cream-colored 450SEL sliding languidly past his window and prompting him to note, in order, a missing piece of chrome, a female driver with horsey yellow hair, and a license plate that read 14ME2B. Distracted by the enigmatic legend of the plate, he failed to notice a pickup overloaded with hoses and rakes and other paraphernalia, and had to hit his brakes to avoid collision. The driver of the pickup gave him a baleful look but not the gesture one might reasonably have expected, and in gratitude Marshall bared his teeth and waved, an apology that the driver acknowledged with a compact nod of his dark Latin head. Feeling suddenly lucky, Marshall punched a button on his radio, looking for music with a stronger beat. The pickup swerved into a street where nothing could be seen but hedges and jacarandas, and he said the word "*hombre*" aloud, just able to hear his own voice above that of a rapper proclaiming, as nearly as Marshall could understand, the virtues of real leather shoes.

"*Trabajo,*" he said, aware of compound failure: he hadn't rolled the "*r*" and his "*b*" was much to explosive, the latter a failing especially painful to the tutor who came once a week to teach him this simplest of languages. He could come out with either "*b*" or "*v*" but not the hybrid that she wanted. What did it matter, anyway? He was only trying to pick up enough to carry on a rudimentary conversation with Geneveva, his mother's maid. He loved the way she pronounced her name—"Henna *vay* va"—and he particularly liked the way she looked in the uniform his mother forced her to wear, even though he had chided his mother for imposing such a requirement.

He turned the music up to a volume that transported him backwards in time to a throbbing womb of noise. The traffic raced and lurched and halted, and at the stoplight he watched in an upper corner of the windshield gray trunks of palms swaying as if in incantation over the scene below. He had grown up just a few blocks from this intransigent signal and he and his high school friends had convinced themselves that they were in Hell. "When we die as sinners this is where we will have to spend eternity," they had said, needing no further excuse to drive up high in the hills above and drink vodka and Mountain Dew until it all, suddenly, became bearable. When Marshall was seventeen his family moved west—albeit to a neighborhood, if anything, more silent and excessively green—and he considered himself lucky to have escaped. The new neighborhood was closer to the chaparral and a fire that had burned hundreds of houses, some on the very street where their new house stood, but this was before he was born and therefore history, a tedious and irrelevant subject.

The 450SEL was shortly followed by a white 300D with a handsome middle-aged female driver and a license plate with a random combination of letters and numbers. Marshall recalled a childhood impression that all Mercedes-Benzes were gray. "*Dos*," he said aloud. His father had recently purchased a burgundy Jag which complemented the claret-colored Cadillac Marshall's mother had gotten after the divorce, on a trade-in for the Audi that she had been allowed to keep in the settlement.

"Dad," Marshall said, when he saw the Jag, "did you and Mom consult on color?"

But Marshall's father saw nothing funny in the question—the word "Mom" was thoroughly dyspeptic.

"Why doesn't she do something—take some classes? It's not the money, for Christ's sake. If she was trying to become independent, hell, it would be worth it. I don't even care if she sleeps with these young Lotharios . . ." He actually used the word "Lotharios." "If she would just get out of the hay in the morning and make some use of her time. Jesus."

His father was a man who made excellent use of his time, on the cellular phone in his Jag in morning traffic, pulling together a deal to put up a building on some underutilized property out in Santa Monica. "Dammit, they've finally got a sensible zoning board," he said, allowing that the system still had life, despite the violent perpetrations of regulation. Marshall's father, however, was no reactionary: he was into Greenpeace, and had recently told Marshall about how he insisted that his current interest—he used that term, "interest," at first confusing Marshall with the other kind—get rid of her furs. "She says I can go jump in a lake," he said. "I mean, we're talking, hell, a whole bunch of dough. But I say, 'It's me or them, Snookums,' and the next time I'm at her place she takes me to the closet and shows me, yeah, they're gone. Every one of 'em. What do you think of that?"

Marshall's father didn't really want his opinion, Marshall harbored no illusions on that point. The woman—his father's "interest"—could have put the furs in storage, given them to a friend to keep, stuck them under the sink, in the laundry chute, anywhere out of sight. He didn't ask his father what became of the furs—were they burned, sent to the dump, taken out of circulation permanently? In truth, he admired his father, speaking up for Greenpeace in circles where anything to the left of the Rotary Club might be seen as sinister. His father even defended their tactics.

"I'm opposed to interference with a person's right to use his own property in a lawful manner," he said. "But when you're killing dolphins or clubbing baby seals, dammit, it's time to draw the line."

As Marshall drove west, toward an invisible horizon, into the light from an invisible sun, he thought about the legend of the plate—14ME2B. It made sense, grammatically, but on an emotional and intellectual level it had no shape. He tried a few different combinations, at the same time counting another cream-colored Mercedes whose model number he could not catch, and a red 380SL with black top and driver of indeterminate sex. The plate read IPDCSH.

"Geneveva!" he could hear his mother cry. In her mouth the name he found so musical was dull and heavy, a weight.

"First she's late. The bus, she says. I say, 'Take an earlier bus. Get up half an hour earlier.' Then she says something I can't understand. She can understand everything I say, if she wants to. If she wants to get off early, she can say that too, in perfect English. If she wants twenty dollars in advance, she can say that so that I have absolutely no problem understanding her. But if I try to explain to her why she can't put plastic in the dishwasher she doesn't understand, I don't understand that she doesn't understand, and the plastic melts and I have to throw perfectly good things away."

Five, six, seven, all in a row, going the other way.

He was in love with Geneveva, in some unstatable manner. His father, who had a direct way of looking at things and drawing conclusions, said, "You'll never get yourself headed in any direction until you find the girl you want to settle down with. You can't keep your mind on business while you're sowing your wild oats. Find the girl you want, but don't make the mistake that I did. Marry a girl who's got ambition—who wants to be independent. If you make the mistake that I did, you're going to wake up one morning and find you've got nothing to say to each other." His father favored women's rights. "The world is full of people who are tickled pink to get the job of taking care of the house, hauling the kids around. You don't have to marry a woman to do all that. That's crazy. That's the past."

His father advised him to get an apartment, unaware that such a thing would be unendurable, the separation from Geneveva. On a recent morning, after his mother had left for the country club to meet her tennis partners, he had invited Geneveva to go swimming. He was home because he was supposed to be sick, but in fact he was only bored with his job momentarily. He tried to make her understand, but she only blushed. He got into his trunks and dived into the water, which was not as warm as he expected, and when he climbed out his arms and legs were thick with gooseflesh.

"You," he said, gesturing at the pool. She was just inside the open patio door, vacuuming. "Shut it off a minute," he yelled. Dripping, he came inside, followed the hose to the wall and poked the button. She stared at him, perhaps a little fearful, perhaps because he was shivering. He had until that moment been entirely circumspect with her, even while feeling tenderness and lust and other sometimes confusing things.

"Want to swim? Come on."

"No," She shook her head. Her straight brown hair was pulled tight and tied old-fashionedly at her neck, so that a broad tail hung to the small of her back. She was short, soft, with skin neither light nor dark, and widely spaced brown eyes that agitated him. Her uniform was too tight, and revealed a plumpness, not unpleasant, around her middle. Her calves were also plump and curved drastically to thin ankles and tiny feet. Her body seemed ripe, about to burst out of the starchy dress, and he imagined that he could liberate her, not only from this uniform but from some larger confinement. Her tongue wet her plump, uncolored lips and he shivered.

He concentrated. "It's—*esta bien*. I am . . ." He drew a breath from this exertion. "*Soy el* . . . it's okay . . . in the *agua*." He waved at the open door, the brick, the white table and chairs and lounges, the green pool, the eucalyptus hanging as if in disapproval above. "To wear . . ." He indicated swimwear by drawing his hands across his pelvis and chest and she winced and looked away.

He had solemnly promised himself, somewhere in the weeks past, that his dealings with her would be entirely respectful and honorable. Not that he wasn't capable of aggressive behavior with a woman when the situation called for it, he just was sensitive enough to understand Geneveva's position, coming from a different culture, having a job that was important to her, not wanting to do anything to jeopardize her opportunity. He dreaded above all else the possibility that any demonstration on his part would drive her away, that he would never see her again, because he didn't even know where she lived, didn't know anything about her, couldn't quite imagine meeting her under different circumstances. He noticed that she gripped the wand of the vacuum as if to keep from being swept away, staring into the kitchen where the dishwasher could be heard churning and cycling.

"It's okay . . . *bueno. No problema.*" He backed away, retreated at the same time that a hot and incautious urge afflicted him. He ran across the patio and flung himself into the pool, dove deep, and swam in a circle at the bottom until his chest burned and he was forced to surface. He gasped, treading water, and in the distance the vacuum roared like a taunt.

Another 380SL, brown on brown, scooting past a truck so quickly that its plate cannot be read. Not a gray one yet. His father knew women Marshall ought to like. His father called them girls, and tried to fix him up. He telephoned from the Jag to say, "There's a girl you ought to take a stab at. She just got out of law school, works for Hank. You remember Hank? He was here that time I had you over for dinner with those Arabs. Who have you been going out with, anyway?"

For his father's benefit, he named a name, the daughter of a friend of his mother's. He took her out to dinner once and then drove to Malibu and back and dropped her in front of her condo at ten o'clock.

"Forget that stuff," his father ordered. "She'll spend all your money on Rodeo. That type plays tennis all morning and shops all afternoon. Listen to me. Find a professional woman. Lawyer. Architect. There are good-looking women in these professions now, believe me. Believe me, these debutantes, after the sex wears off you'll have nothing to say to one another."

His father's reference to the dinner invoked a memory of two men and a woman, impeccably and formally dressed, all wearing lots of jewelry, speaking perfect English, telling him in detail of their plan to rescue the Shah, who hadn't died at all but was being held by the United States government somewhere in the Caribbean. He recalled that his father had listened respectfully, even nodding in sympathy now and then, but as soon as a break in this litany came he began to tell them of the desirability of putting their money into the development of commercial real estate.

"The climate's right," he said, "zoning, depreciation, you can't go wrong. Listen . . ." He had an effective way of lowering his voice to get attention, and it seemed as if the three guests visibly cocked their heads. "Forget your Shah." He dismissed protest with a semaphoric motion of his hands. "He's history. It'll take another twenty years for those people to run the country into the ground, and he'll be dead by then. I'll make you a deal." His father gave him a look that could have been conspiratorial, a way of saying, "Watch this!" or simply a look of evaluation, a wondering if the son would ever be capable of such maneuvers. "You give me two million," he said to the men and woman, "and in a year I'll give you three." The complexities of his father's business, which Marshall had never tried to understand, seemed almost lurid in this simplicity.

A 190E and a 300E, both silver blue, both captained by classy looking females, one of them with a companion who held a cigarette up in direct line between the hood ornament and her nose. His father, who went to Shick three times, who tried acupuncture and hypnosis, who once asked his son to hide his cigarettes and then offered him a hundred dollars to reveal their whereabouts, quit on his own when his "lady friend"—who liked to do all kinds of things in bed, he had divulged—refused to kiss him. His mother, conversely, took up smoking after the divorce, a necessary step, she said, to keep from overeating. He had never seen Geneveva smoke, although he suspected that she might—there was something spirited about her, undocile, some nerve possessed in common with the sassy Latinas he saw now and then walking in their tight, short dresses below his office window.

"Quit that job," his father said. "Go to work for me. Or Phil Dexter. Phil's looking for a sharp young guy. He's got five buildings out of the ground right now. He needs somebody to keep on top of the superintendents—if you don't they'll go to sleep on you and the first thing you know the materials are fouled up and the subs are sitting on their hands and nothing's happening, nothing except that Mr. Vice President over at the bank has got his hand in your pocket looking for his, and you're saying, Shit, why don't I just go to Hawaii or Mexico or someplace and just forget it, it ain't worth the trouble?" His father appeared to view his son's work, which had some connection with computers, as an extension of the rebellion that began when Marshall traded the Mustang that was a sixteenth-birthday present for an orange Checker Marathon and three boxes filled with disk drives, motherboards, monitors, and what was purported to be thousands of dollars worth of software, although that was in no way verifiable, at least not to his father's satisfaction. Marshall had loaded the Checker with his computers and computer parts and left for Santa Cruz, having failed, despite both his mother's and father's exhortations, to apply to USC. On his second day in Santa Cruz he started a conversation with a Eurasian girl in front of him in an orientation line and, mesmerized by the red dot on her forehead, fell in complete and hopeless love.

"Geneveva!" his mother called. "*Venga aqui!*" With surprising ease she had absorbed the lessons of *Spanish to Speak to Your Do-*

mestic Help and he felt like a third party, a man without a country. The tutor who came on Tuesday nights at exactly seven-thirty and scooped up her flash cards at precisely nine o'clock seemed irritated by his lack of facility with what she apparently regarded as a childish language. She had yet to accept his offers of coffee, soda, wine, fruit juice, or the little chocolate cookies his mother liked so well. She was blonde, thin, in her twenties, and appeared to be an art student or aspiring artist since she always took a pad from her bag and sketched while he struggled with the sentences that she assigned him to write during the last half hour. She dismissed his interest in what she was drawing as efficiently as she rebuffed his attempts at hospitality.

He followed a black 500D with a plate that read "SEA ME" through the Bel-Air gate. He said "*diez*" just for practice, since he had quit counting even before the street began to rise and fall through the shadows of eucalyptus that he had gradually come to see as excessively dense and concealing, like curtains drawn to deny the curious a view of something morbid. "Don't talk that sixties crap," his father said, when Marshall alluded to the privilege that had accrued to him despite the absence of any particular effort or virtue. "That's history. There's no revolution coming. Get with the times, will you? There's nothing noble about being poor. Never was. You want to help them, you put up a building. You've got your carpenters, your steel workers, your cement men, your sheet metal men, your masons, your electricians, your plumbers; you've got your laborers, your plasterers, your roofers. When it's done you've got your maintenance people, you've got offices which employ people, you've got taxes going to help out the so-called underprivileged you're worried about."

He stopped at the gate that his mother had hired a company to install after his father left, poked his card into the slot, and grinned at the video camera hidden in a bush, feeling both confident and uncertain, as if the resolve he had manufactured was but a layer of self-delusion. His mother, who had embarked upon an apparently complex redecoration of the house, sat at the dining room table, which was deep in fabric and carpet samples, magazines and sketches made by the decorator on sheets of salmon-colored paper. He got a beer from the refrigerator and sat on a chair opposite his mother and told her, in what he intended to be a matter-of-fact tone, that he was in love with Geneveva.

"She's real," he said, looking a little past his mother, trying not to imagine a look of horror on her face. "Not plastic like these other women."

"Plastic?" his mother said, in a slightly clotted voice. "What is that supposed to mean?" She twisted a swatch of violet fabric in her fingers, the veins bulging on the backs of her hands and the skin going white between. She seemed to be trying to wring something out of this cloth. "Have you told your father?" Questions, he had come to understand long ago, were primarily rhetorical devices for his mother and did not require answers. "I suppose he approves." She suddenly pushed away the things in front of her as if in disgust with so many choices and stared for a moment in turn at the buffet, the chandelier, the sculpture, the other things in the room.

"Bring me a Southern Comfort," she ordered, now embarking upon an inspection of her nails. "I'll have to let her go, of course. You know how difficult it is to get someone . . . God knows she's not perfect, but she comes every day, she's *reliable* . . ."

Marshall placed the glass of Southern Comfort on the table and put his arms around his mother's neck and buried his nose in her hair, a need for reconciliation threatening to overwhelm his previous resolve. She didn't react. He sat across from her and watched her drink a little eagerly, but with a sophisticated tilt of chin.

"Things are changing," she said with a little sniff that might have meant something or nothing at all, an allergy. "It's not the same anymore. All these people . . ." She swept her arm in the air as if these people were lurking just outside the French windows that opened onto the garden. "When I was a girl . . ." He knew this story already and his attention began to wander; he began to listen for any sign of Geneveva. When his mother was a girl they had a maid named Josephine, who watched television with his mother when all the programs were black and white and the screen was nine inches wide, who cooked and cleaned the house and was never surly and uncommunicative like Geneveva.

"Madeline Spencer hired this Guatemalan girl," his mother said. "She doesn't have any papers. I said to her, 'Madeline, you could be murdered in your beds at night. You don't know what kind of people they come from.'" She looked at Marshall with an expression both combative and resigned. "If you had pledged a fraternity you would have met some girls of your own background." With a shocking abandonment of her former grace she gulped the whiskey, and he was startled to see that the bitter look on her face was not so remarkable; it was not so different from how she looked every day. Her lips puckered in the same way when she claimed that his father had left her because he had become excited by younger women, that he had gotten the best of the settlement because he could afford a more expensive lawyer, that many things said in the course of the divorce, while plausible, were bald-faced lies. "What's her beef, for Christ sake?" his father had said in the presence of Marshall. "Market value of the house is what? Two million, two and a half?" He wouldn't let her have the condo in Rancho Mirage, though. "She doesn't care about golf," he said. "All she ever did was sit around and play bridge with these women who complained about their husbands making stupid moves in the market."

Marshall believed both of them, a consequence of choosing not to take sides. He loved his mother and admired his father, and these emotions that he felt, if different, were equally profound. He loved his mother enough to be affected powerfully by a sadness which seemed to spill out from her like an intense, bathing light.

In silence he refilled her glass. He remembered seeing her drunk only once, and that was when he was in junior high, and he guessed that she was maudlin, although he didn't possess a term for it at the time. He remembered that there was a party and that she threw up in the bougainvillea that spread like a disease all over the backyard of the old house in Beverly Hills. Where was his father then? He tried to construct a tableau out of dusty remnants of memory, but only the odor of vomit and her repeating over and over something about her checking account prevailed with any clarity. Perhaps she had bounced a check and his father had lectured her. She couldn't stand his father lecturing her, and he couldn't abide the fact that she never balanced her checkbook. In the living room of his place in Century City, which had a view all the way downtown in one direction and to Palos Verdes and Catalina in the other if the air was clear, he urged his son to keep a tab on her finances.

"It's the biggest mistake I made," he said. "Not teaching her to be independent. Not *forcing* her." He drank club soda, with ice made from filtered water. He rattled off the amounts she had gotten, the checking account, the mutual fund, the bonds, the stocks. "I don't care," he said. "Screw money. The whole thrill is in the chase, if you know what I mean. But dammit, I'll feel like crap if she fritters it all away. Don't laugh . . ." When he was particularly serious he peered out over his reading glasses with his dark gray eyes. "Out at the office in Santa Monica, there's this woman who sleeps in the doorway. They're attracted out there, you know, the government is liberal. Anyway, she's asleep there in the morning, behind one of the planters. She's got a cart full of— hell, who knows what it is—cardboard, rags, that kind of thing. Don't laugh . . ." he warned again. "I can see your mother there, somebody who can't take care of themselves, who once had it all, then frittered it away."

To Marshall this scenario was indeed implausible, but then again his mother, her face bright with sorrow, did look vulnerable. He knew that she had an accountant in Westwood who sometimes summoned her to his office in urgent tones—he knew this because he had heard her play back messages from him on her answering machine.

"I want to marry her," said Marshall. "Then she won't have to demean herself this way."

His mother shut her eyes.

"Your father would disinherit you," she asserted after a long moment of silence, smiling slightly as if the thought amused her.

"Huh?" Marshall's conception of his own future had never, unlike that of some of his high school friends, revolved around the thought of how easy life would become when his parents died. He had even considered, while in Santa Cruz, asking them to leave their money to famine relief, to the ACLU. His mother looked sly now, as she might have looked when he was in the sixth grade and she had hit upon a bribe to get him to finish his homework.

"Besides," she said, "you couldn't marry her even if you were silly enough to try. She's already married."

"What?" Marshall's mind for a moment was frozen. "That's not true," he said, even as his brain unthawed and began to scour through what little he knew of Geneveva.

"She's married," said his mother, the alcohol thickening her speech, imparting a slightly smutty sound. "She has a child even. Down there." She gestured vaguely. "It's with her mother. Or her grandmother. She sends money. Why do you think she has to leave early every Thursday?" She gulped again the Southern Comfort as if to cool something that burned her throat. "She has to go to a place to send money."

She's too young, Marshall wanted to say, even as he groped for some reason to suspect his mother of lying, and wondered what this information, true or false, meant about his relationship to Geneveva. Where was she? Somewhere in the house, doing something, working or avoiding work, perhaps even eavesdropping on this conversation. He felt himself blush. He had entertained a fantasy in which her family—about which he knew nothing, but surely included a parent or two, brothers, sisters—would come to the United States and find work, perhaps with the help of Marshall's father. How did his mother learn these facts, if indeed they were facts and not the product of some pathology? Contempt stirred up briefly like indigestion. His father was right, she was pathetic. He got up to go. He would find Geneveva, and somehow ask her.

"She's going back, as soon as things get better," said Marshall's mother, the mild bit of grief now superseded by an air of detachment, as if her son's foolishness bored her. "You can't blame them," she added, now in a tone of annoyance, with him or with some larger circumstance. "It must be horrible, having to leave your children . . ." She drank again and Marshall recalled, momentarily, her dead weight and loose rag-doll form as he pulled and pushed her up the stairs that night long ago. He wondered, suddenly, why he had rebelled, why he had traded the Mustang, why he hadn't gone to USC, why he had spent so much time constructing an image of himself at odds with what he had always been, what he had even now, despite himself, become. He thought of a child, small and dark-eyed and black-haired, somewhere in a village, in an overgrown but otherwise indeterminate landscape, and a woman, old and withered and tired but not distinct enough to be an individual, only a photograph in a *National Geographic*, a thing and place that he could look at but never know.

His mother muttered a name as he got up to leave the room, a name he knew from high school, a woman he had seen a few weeks before in his bank, a tan young woman who told him in their brief, desultory conversation that she had just gotten back from a trip to some other part of the world and that it was wonderful as long as you didn't let the poverty bother you. She had just bought a Mercedes—used, of course, she couldn't afford a new one—and they had joked about how many Mercedes-Benzes one might be able to count in a square mile of Beverly Hills. "Call me" she had said, but he hadn't, and now his mother was invoking her name.

"I'm going out," he said. Surrounded by her samples, his mother seemed safe enough. The number of the woman he had seen at the bank was probably still in his wallet, written in a neatly ornate hand on the back of a deposit slip. His mother's voice followed him out the kitchen door and faded as he crossed the garden to the driveway. He thought he heard another voice, the familiar yet forever foreign cadence, and he got quickly into the car, as he might in the dark on a badly lighted street, in response to some sound or movement suggesting a malevolent purpose. He waited impatiently for the gate to slide open and pressed the accelerator going downhill, causing the tires to squeal through the curves. He turned east on Sunset, let himself be sucked into the flow, fifteen miles an hour above the limit, tucked in with a sensation of solitude and ambiguous comfort behind a gray Mercedes with windows tinted so darkly he could not see the driver. "Twelve," he said. "Fifty . . . five thousand." He would call the woman he had met in the bank. He would drive to a bar he knew and call from there; he would ask her to meet him for a drink and then find out if she was a debutante, as his father put it, or an independent woman, a lawyer or an architect, a woman with a profession. He saw Geneveva's eyes, black and inward looking, but he turned the radio up loud and the image did not persist, it faded into the dim and irrelevant past.

Lost in Rancho Mirage

Nobody approved of Jill. Not Denton's mother and father, not his sister Claire, not even his best friend Mark, who said that even if times had changed in most respects a man without an appropriate wife was still a stray dog, something that would only get scraps and leftovers, a creature that you would feel leery about getting close to. "What about David Felter?" Denton wanted to know, thinking the dog metaphor not only inappropriate but lacking imagination. "It's okay to be gay," Mark asserted. "It can even be an advantage, as long as there aren't too many of you. But a bachelor . . ." He shook his head remorsefully at the utter unfortunate sadness of the idea.

Denton's father said that marrying a previously married woman was like buying a used car, you could never be sure how well it had been taken care of. "It's almost the twenty-first century, Dad," said Denton, suspecting that his father knew nothing beyond what he read in certain sections of the *Wall Street Journal* and the quarterly reports of companies whose stock he was thinking of buying or selling. "Nobody stays married to the same person all their life anymore. Besides, you can't compare a woman to a car."

"Why not?" Denton's father lit his pipe in defiance of any new conventions that might presume to displace the old, the perfectly serviceable, the tried and true. "Some are fast and some are slow." He smirked through eddies of smoke. "Some don't cost you a penny, while others bleed you dry, like your mother . . ."

"What in the world are you talking about?" Denton's mother's tone lifted to a high enough register that Denton could imagine a scene he didn't want to be anywhere near the middle of. She didn't approve of Jill either, not because of the previous husband and child, but because of the fact that the child lived with the father, not with Jill. "I don't care what you say," she said, in response to Denton's explication of this arrangement. "A normal, balanced woman is not going to give up her child under any circumstance. You would have to be a mother to understand."

Denton decided to call Claire. He said, "They assume that anyone who isn't rich is after money," and Claire said, "Yeah, well . . .," as if she agreed. Claire had met Jill when Denton and Jill stopped at Monterey on a trip to San Francisco, and Jill had irritated Claire by complaining at length about the weather that had turned gloomy during their drive up the coast and rendered what she had expected to be the stunning vistas of Big Sur into gray, sodden disappointments. Jill, who had grown up in the Midwest, loved the perpetual sunlight of L.A., while Claire, who spent her first twenty-one years there, professed to hate the city and all of its inhabitants.

"Why is it that you have to have their approval, Denton?" she said. "They're dinosaurs. They're not on the verge of changing."

"What do you think?" Denton imagined a familiar scowl of impatience on his sister's face.

"It doesn't matter what I think, Denton. Do what you want to do. You're an adult."

"I guess I'm not 100 percent certain," Denton said.

"What do *her* parents think?" Claire's tone flipped up a little red flag in Denton's head. "Do they approve of you?"

"We haven't met," said Denton. "She hardly ever mentions them. I don't think they know about me."

"I'd say she's conflicted," Claire said.

"What's that supposed to mean?"

"She wants to be independent, but she's carrying around all this baggage—her background, her kid, the fact that her husband was abusive, verbally and physically . . ."

"What?" Denton felt that he had just walked into the middle of a movie. "Do you know something?"

"Yeah," said Claire. "We talked."

"She didn't tell me," Denton said, uncertain of what to blame for his feeling appalled, the fact that Jill had kept things from him or that she had been a victim of something tawdry.

"I'm a woman," said Claire, with a declarative assuredness that further sank Denton's self-regard and confidence. "We understand one another."

The sun predictably appeared each day until the week after New Year's, when, without sound or fury, the sky turned a rubbery gray and blessed the earth with cold, mechanical rain. Jill told Denton in a rueful tone that wind and lightning and thunder were the only midwestern phenomena for which she felt nostalgia. She acknowledged an ongoing state of irritability brought on by the weather, and he began to think about the condominium that his parents owned in the desert. An image of its red tile roof and sandstone stucco walls transformed into a picture of himself and Jill stretched out on the patio lounges beneath a curative sun. By habit, his mind turned to logistics: a real estate deal had bogged down at the bank and he could safely leave town; Jill did clerical work out of an agency and could get off when she wanted, so that if they left on a Friday afternoon and returned at the end of the following week they would have time, between eating and making love and lying in the sun, for a trip to the mountains to ski. He might give her lessons in golf, or tennis, neither of which she had ever attempted. They could hike in the desert, ride the tramway, sneak out late at night to swim naked in the pool, watch movies on TV. The prospect glowed like sunlight through the wet, dispirited sky.

Jill had more or less moved into Denton's place, although she kept things in the apartment that she shared with another woman, an apartment in a building that allowed children and was perpetually defaced with graffiti. She had gone to the apartment to get a certain sweater and Denton waited with growing impatience for her to return. Without reflection upon possible consequence, he dialed her number. She sounded sleepy, and in a mumbling, childish fashion told him that she had lain down to rest and the very next moment discovered herself the victim of a nightmare in which a telephone rang and rang and rang, an instrument of torture. "Now I can hear somebody's stereo," she complained. "Like it's in the next room." Not wanting to dwell upon Jill's annoyance with cosmic circumstance, Denton described the imagined trip to the desert.

"I'll think about it," she said, indifferently.

"Wow," said Denton. "I really sold you on this one."

"I'm tired," she said, her tone defensive. "And Jenny called."

"Yeah?" The flat, resigned invocation of this name implied that something unpleasant was involved.

"She said her father won't let her eat pizza because the cheese is crammed with cholesterol and will clog up her veins."

"Jeez," said Denton. "She's seven years old." Jill's ex-husband was a chiropractor, unreasonably obsessed, it seemed to Denton, with matters of health. He lived with Jenny in Indiana, a state that Denton had never set foot in but that he guessed to be like the agricultural parts of California, entirely flat and green. The denial of pizza struck him as a form of abuse. He said this to Jill, with the possibly defective expectation that she would laugh, or at least giggle.

"Denton," she said, in a tone that warned him to be careful. "It isn't funny. The poor baby. I feel like such a heel." The thickening quality of her voice meant that she had either begun or was about to cry, and Denton suddenly felt self-conscious, as if the telephone in his hand had turned into an embarrassing revelation. He heard her sniffle.

"I'm glad that he cares about her." There was shuffling, rustling, then a blowing of the nose. Denton rummaged his mind for an appropriate remark.

"Maybe I should go back," she said. "Maybe I could work at the turkey plant. They're always hiring. I could take her horseback riding on weekends. My best friend in high school married this guy and they live out on the edge of town where you're allowed to keep horses."

"Jill," said Denton, not because he had a response to this but because he felt themselves, the two ends of this electronic connection, fading in opposite directions. She had arrived in L.A. with a commonplace desire—to become an actress, to get into movies, TV. He had met her when she was working for Mark selling real estate, a job that couldn't have lasted, Mark explained to Denton later, because of her unfortunate propensity to offer clients her honest opinion of the houses she showed them. When Denton first met her he told her that she looked like Meryl Streep, although he didn't know then about her aspirations. As it turned out, she didn't consider Meryl Streep the least bit attractive, so it hadn't been the perfect thing to say.

"There's a jacuzzi," he said. "There's a thirty-six-inch TV. We can rent all the Bette Davis movies."

"Oh Denton." He heard in her voice a softening, a yielding. He felt suddenly giddy.

"We can go dancing." Jill had a thing about ballroom dancing, and although Denton found everything but the Samba boring, he was fairly light on his feet. "It's still the fifties there, Jill. Everyone drives around in Cadillacs."

"Denton," she said, "my big goal in life at this point is to play Mother Courage. Do you think that's unrealistic? Silly?"

"I don't know." Questions like this, impossible to answer, tended to irritate him. Jill was undeniably attractive, and possessed an unselfconscious ability to draw attention to herself, but thinking of the variety of circumstances, accidents, coincidences necessary for her to actually become a successful actress made him almost dizzy. With dogged persistence she went to auditions, called up agents, concocted schemes for getting into invitation-only events, but Denton regarded as midwestern naivete the belief that she would succeed if only she worked hard enough. Telephone one more agent, run out to one more casting call. Denton's father once said, "If hard work was all anyone needed to get rich, then the guys who pick up the garbage would be millionaires." Denton might, himself, have been picking up garbage or digging ditches if his grandfather hadn't left his father a piece of real estate that turned out to be directly in the path of a freeway. "You got to have luck," Denton's father said. "Your mother and I were going to live in that dump, but instead I had this dough in my hand and I thought, I ought to do something with it. Invest it. Buy another piece of property. That's how it all got started."

"The condo," Denton said, trying to divest his voice of a tone he knew to be impatient and unappealing. "It's in this place called Rancho Mirage. Right on a golf course. You can sit on the patio and watch the golfers go by in their carts."

"Mother Courage," Jill sighed. "And Cordelia. 'If for I want that glib and oily art . . .'"

"Jill." Denton squeezed the phone, frowning, trying to summon her attention. "The sun shines every day. It never rains. There's a sauna. There's an exercise room with a rowing machine. What more could you possibly want, Jill?"

"Money," she said, her voice now floating on a cloud above the tawdry details of the present and real. "Fame. Love."

"I love you," Denton said.

"Yes," she said, in dreamy affirmation. "I know you do."

She adored the TV and pool, hated the exercise room because the carpeting gave off an odor, and found the plush green of the golf course to be, in some inexplicable way, annoying. "I could never spend my time like that," she said, staring from the living room window at a pair of middle-aged women in visors gliding down the fairway in a cart. Denton wanted to sleep in the guest room but she refused, on the obvious grounds that the master suite was larger and more luxurious. The idea of making love in his parents' bed made Denton a little queasy, although he didn't say so. They sat in the jacuzzi at night, under a cloud of stars such as she hadn't seen since she left Indiana. She slept until ten or eleven and then spent the afternoon on the bed, flipping channels between three or four soap operas with a P. D. James as thick as a dictionary in her lap. "If that woman's an actress, I'm the Duchess of Kent," she would comment, or things to that effect.

Even though he had bought her a racket, she decided that tennis would be impossibly difficult and therefore boring. She was irritated by the golfers, who could sometimes be seen or heard stirring around in the rough outside the windows, and a populist inclination seemed to be awakened by the sight of Cadillacs and Mercedes-Benzes and women wearing what she described as tons of jewelry in the middle of the day. "If I were you," said Denton, feeling helpless, "I wouldn't be so quick to judge things just by appearance," but of course she said that wasn't what she was doing at all; she didn't even expect him to understand, having had a Mummy and Dad with oodles of money, and never anything serious to worry about.

On the morning of the third day he left her asleep in the fading darkness of dawn, drove his car beyond the golf courses and condos, and found a spot where he could pull off the road and hike a short way into the desert. He climbed to the top of a flat rock and sat staring at the glow of the impending sunrise, wishing that Jill were with him, snuggled against him in the air so chilled that when he opened his mouth a cloud of vapor blurred his view. He waited, shivering and impatient, and finally an arc of liquid orange appeared above the ragged line of distant mountains. He had almost begged her to come but she had emphatically declined, saying that getting up at such an hour was entirely inimical to her idea of vacation. The arc grew into a half-circle and then a complete disk of radiant heat and light that dissolved the darkness of the sky, making Denton feel like a witness to a miraculous event that would never be repeated, at least not in his lifetime. He watched a lizard dart between two twisted pieces of vegetation that may or may not have been alive. His eyes followed the rim of the mountains and descended to a sea of roofs all white and glittering in the shower of oblique light.

"Just think," he had said to Jill when they first descended into the valley, into a long irregular shadow the mountains cast over the habitation. "A hundred years ago there was nobody here but Indians." The change inspired him to think of his business as invested with the power and significance of history. He was involved in nothing less, he thought, than transformation. He wanted to say as much to Jill but feared that she would find him pompous. She seemed to find people who spoke too freely of their own accomplishments pompous—a peculiarly midwestern trait, Denton suspected. And perhaps she was right. After all, he thought, as the perceptible ascent of the sun began to drive the chill from the air, I have been involved only in the transfer of some pieces of property, the construction of some buildings devoted to purposes of minor importance. Of the millions in the city, Denton reflected, only a few hundred enter these buildings, and perhaps a handful know my name, or care who I am. As the shadow of the mountains retreated, exposing more of the sparkling gravel of identical roofs, his exultation expired and he felt depressed and hungry.

With the sun like a nosy eye in the rearview mirror he drove back to the condo where he made coffee, ate cereal from a box, and got out his tennis racket and took some practice swings in front of the sliding glass door that opened onto the patio and the verdant, deserted fairway. The chance of meeting someone looking for a partner on a weekday morning was highly unlikely, and he practiced spinning the racket on his finger for a few minutes before letting it drop to the floor. He opened a closet and stared at his golf bag. He took out a putter and ball and stood in the middle of the living room, trying to smooth out his jerky, unconfident stroke. He returned the putter to the bag, the mute heads of the clubs speaking the truth that golf attracted him only as a social event—some badinage with friends, some harmless gambling, now and then the conduct of some piece of business. He was typically inept and unlucky, and the idea of scouring the rough for his ball or endlessly putting while others waited impatiently behind was distinctly unappealing. He gazed with a sentimental longing at his skis, which leaned above the golf bag. Jill had not expressed the slightest interest in waking up early enough to get to the lifts at a reasonable hour, and while Denton was not opposed to going by himself, and in fact found the imagined solitude of cold and height and descent acceptable, some elemental fear or need to encircle and protect made him loathe to abandon her.

He lay on the sofa, thinking of a golf ball nestled like an egg in grass, and he fell asleep, to be awakened from a vaguely sensual dream by the cascade of water in the toilet and then the steamy hiss of the shower. He got up and went into the bedroom and lay on his back on the mussed-up bed, staring at the vaulted ceiling upon which unfolded a hazy vision of a future—Jill, older and plumper; children of indeterminate sex and number; a house with trees and grass. The bathroom door clicked and from a mist emerged a miracle—Jill, wearing only a towel wrapped into a turban about her head and flowing like a cape to the small of her back. She saw him and smiled a prim, girlish smile that made her look innocent and somehow inviolable.

"Denton," she said, her voice perking up as she spoke, "do you think I should cut my hair?"

He thought a moment, but the lingering confusion of sleep rendered him incapable of visualizing what was beneath the towel. It was almost eleven o'clock. She waited for him to answer and an idea blew like a gust of desert wind into his head.

"I made coffee, Jill. Want some?"

"Thanks" she said, "I'm tired of my hair."

"I don't want to talk about your hair," said Denton.

"Oh. Okay." Silence was threaded with a faint, electronic hum, and far away, the resonant whack of a golf club. "You'd look good with a beard, Denton. Cover your chin."

"What's wrong with my chin?" He had begun to feel a swarmy, feverish desire.

"Nothing's wrong with it. It just recedes a little. With a beard it would look stronger."

"Jill." With a shock of adolescent fervor he almost said, "I want us to get married, Jill," but he stopped himself, because he had already decided upon the accoutrements to a proposal—the particular restaurant, the kind of wine, the shirt and jacket he would wear, the moment within the afterglow of the meal when he would lift her hand and gaze into her eyes. It's true, he thought, about my chin. Juvenile longings to the contrary, he knew that he would always resemble most closely his father, not Richard Gere. He had once grown a beard but it had looked unclean, a smear of charcoal on his cheeks, and after enduring a few weeks of comment he had shaved it off.

"I watched the sunrise," he said, delving for suitable adjectives to bring alive this phenomenon. But she did not find his description remarkable enough to comment upon. His passion began to leak like air from a punctured tire. He left the bedroom to get her a cup of coffee and when he returned she had put on a robe and was sanding her nails with the P. D. James open once more in her lap, and when he bent to kiss her she offered her cheek and not her lips, which were pursed in thoughtful, enigmatic speculation.

"I want to go out," he said. She turned her head as if on cue and produced a smile that Denton felt was meant not only for him but for some larger audience. "This babe is in a different world," Mark had said, shortly after Denton and Jill had been introduced. Denton suspected that an actor or actress might sometimes have trouble distinguishing between the artifice of the stage or set and the reality of the everyday, but when he tried to say as much to Mark he got a condescending look in return, along with the suggestion that Denton give a certain female architect that they both knew a whirl. The architect's face passed like a shadow through Denton's mind. His desire to play tennis or ski had been displaced by an urgent need to drink a martini in a bar with low smoky light and the tinkle of a loungey piano, but he knew without asking that Jill would decline—she had resolved to lose five pounds and therefore alcohol, along with butter, potato chips, even pizza, was forbidden.

He left the bedroom and walked down the hall and through the door into the garage, where he started his car and backed into the street without a clear idea of destination. The sky was a faded blue, completely free of clouds, and he drove for a few miles, listening to country and western music on the radio. *My man's gone off somewhere to play, and left me with the bills to pay,* a woman sang in a voice that reminded Denton of Jill's imitation of Patsy Cline. He began to think that perhaps he should have turned left instead of right, or vice versa. The street became a highway that seemed to lead toward the open end of the valley, but he felt loathe to stop and turn around and gradually the houses and condos receded in his rearview mirror like a fading dream. "She's got a nice pair of bazookas," Mark had said of Jill, as if little else about her merited observation. The highway of diminishing width bored onward through a landscape absolutely flat and empty save for groves of palm trees and an occasional roadside stand that advertised dates for sale. "She's beautiful," Claire had said, in a tone not of admiration but rebuke, as if the unremarkable features she possessed in common with Denton had been held up to ridicule by the presence of Jill. Denton pulled the visor down against the inquisitive glare of the sun. He felt a need to articulate to himself all the reasons that he loved Jill, but before he could begin a sign appeared, implying the existence of civilization, and then the road abruptly curved and he was on the main street of a town, a town of an entirely different nature, a place where a scattering of dusty vehicles sat at various angles against a curb that wasn't a real curb at all but a strip of gravel interrupted here and there with tufts of yellow vegetation.

Denton drove slowly, staring at buildings that all seemed to be in a mild state of dilapidation. He saw the word BEER in blocky, unlit neon in front of a window framing a murky scene of backs at a counter, a tableau that promoted a sense of having arrived in a new and possibly dangerous country. He parked beside a truck that appeared to have just brought someone from the deepest recesses of the desert, a Power Wagon the color of the dirty gravel without any top, with a single seat nearly bereft of upholstery, a dirty windshield with a spider's web of cracks that led in diminishing concentric circles, he observed with a little bump of fear, to a hole the size of his finger.

He stood inside the door, trying to size up the unfamiliar situation. He was glad that he hadn't changed clothes after his hike to view the sunrise—his Levi's, his boots, the jacket that he had bought at a place that sold backpacks and sleeping bags, made him feel that he belonged. He looked around at men who all seemed to be wearing cowboy hats or caps with bills. He smelled cigarette smoke and the fermented odor of beer. No one appeared to stare, or even to notice him, as he walked to the far end of the bar that formed a narrow horseshoe in a long room lined on opposing walls with wooden booths. The booths appeared to be empty, but nearly all the stools at the bar were occupied. Denton wondered where these people lived—the town had seemed no more than a handful of buildings and houses scattered without any sense of order, as if blown there by the desert wind, by accident.

He felt both wary and excited by the strange surroundings. He sat on a worn and polished stool between a heavy young man and a much older man with jowls and forehead so ruggedly crevassed that his face didn't look entirely human. Neither man turned his head to look at Denton. The younger man was systematically going at something on a plate in front of him, while the older man held a glass in both hands and stared intently into it as if the liquid contained a vision of compelling grandeur or complexity. Denton looked at the double row of bottles reflected in the mirror, the cash register of an obsolete style, the faded signs dispensing aphorisms and a sort of humor that he considered rustic and unfunny. A woman in jeans and T-shirt knotted above her waist appeared and waited indifferently for him to speak, and unable to make up his mind conclusively he asked for a common brand of beer, thinking that in this place, perhaps, he might be able to discover something authentic. She didn't pour the beer, but merely pushed a glass and bottle toward him. It was lukewarm. In the city, he thought, in another sort of place, he would refuse it, but then he confirmed for himself that he wasn't in the city, he was somewhere in the desert, possibly lost, possibly in some sort of trouble that he had yet to perceive. In the mirror he saw himself, and the barmaid, who looked bored, and the magnitude of the distance between this place and the bars that he found himself in from time to time caused him to feel, in successive little jolts, exhilaration and fear. He heard a voice. For a second he thought it was Jill, doing another of the imitations she was fond of; for a moment he did not know where the voice came from, or that its lascivious message was intended for him.

The voice droned loudly on and then abruptly stopped, as if controlled by a switch. Denton felt that everyone's eyes had lifted from the ardent attraction of the liquid in their glasses or bottles to fix upon him. He tried to maintain an aloof and consciously bemused expression. The voice belonged to a woman seated at the opposite end of the bar, a woman with brassy hair and a face puffed up as if by gas, with bloody eyes that gazed at him with infantile directness. Denton guessed that she was drunk, and that no one would expect him to take her seriously. He briefly imagined in general detail the melodramatic elements of a life that would permit her to get drunk in the middle of the day, to humiliate herself in front of what he guessed were acquaintances, to offer herself to a total stranger. The beer, the stale odor of the place, the smoke, made him feel slightly ill. The barmaid, he observed, was the only other female in the place, and as he stared at the slightly flaccid girdle of flesh between her jeans and T-shirt he wondered why she hadn't said anything, hadn't attempted to divert the other woman's attention, tell her that she already had enough, that she ought to go home, lie down, sleep. Denton observed the wale of a scar just to the left of the barmaid's deeply hollow navel, and with a mildly nauseous unease he imagined blood and tissue and a circle of hot white lights above an operating table. He wondered why no one else had spoken. The silence seemed dangerous, evil. He decided to leave, immediately, even though he hadn't finished the beer. An impulse he didn't reflect upon led him to put on the bar an overly generous tip, and he sensed with a little tug of trepidation that the men between whom he sat had watched him delve into his wallet, had guessed at the amount of money in it, had suspected this amount to be considerable, and had arrived at some conclusion and possibly even an idea.

The slatternly woman's voice switched on again as the heat and light of the outdoors embraced him, and he desperately hoped that she would not get up and follow, create a situation from which he would have to extricate himself. He walked back past the Power Wagon, hurrying, and with a snap of elemental fear he saw that his car was gone. He was suddenly transported back to the condo, back to bed, where he had tossed the previous night in the turgid, sweaty grip of a nightmare. "Jill," he had moaned, unable to reach the solace of her heat and form. He blinked. The windshield of the Power Wagon was intact, there was no provocative series of cracks, no portentous hole. The color of the vehicle, in fact, wasn't exactly right, and instead of the springs and tufts of gray sticking out of the seat there was a worn green blanket. He heard a crack of indeterminate cause and location and spun in a panic to see, in gradually reassuring detail, an identical vehicle, the one with the hole in the windshield, and beyond it, a section of the bumper and grille of his car, a sight so reassuring that he smiled, then chuckled, then laughed aloud. In a rush to escape a complication so minor that he could already laugh about it he had turned the wrong way, been momentarily disoriented. No one had followed. He heard a murmur of voices and the click of a glass. Jill appeared in his mind, as she was when she emerged from the shower, a conglomeration of genetic accidents so sublime as to inspire awe and worship, and Denton felt happy, even as he knew that it was her languor that had brought him to this alien place. He peeled off his jacket and threw it into the backseat of the car as the sun poured its blessing freely down upon his head.

Bored with soap operas, Jill had put a movie in the VCR. In three nights they had worked their way from *All About Eve* to *Deception*, with Jill murmuring certain lines and pointing out how a sudden drop in register could convey an infinite volume of meaning. "Did you see the way she lifts one shoulder?" she would say, excited by discovery. They would then have to rewind, play the scene two or three times. "God," Jill said softly. "Was she a brilliant actress or what?"

Denton didn't know. He didn't know what constituted a brilliant performance, only what he liked and didn't like, and he knew that despite occasional tugs of interest he found what he saw to be dated, a vestige of a distant, irrelevant past. He stared with indifference at what seemed unhappy goings on. He looked at Jill's knee, a promise exposed by a parting of her robe. He saw Bette Davis nearly swoon into the arms of an actor he did not recognize, and the sight of their heads together awakened a thought that glided to his tongue.

"Did you ever do a scene like that?"

"Of course." Jill pulled both her knees up to her chin, causing a flutter in Denton's chest.

"Did you feel anything?"

"Huh?"

"I mean, kissing a stranger. Does it make you feel anything in particular?"

"Well, he wouldn't be a stranger, exactly." Jill stared straight ahead, studying the scene as if she expected to be quizzed upon it later. "It would be somebody you had rehearsed with. It might be somebody you knew real well."

"I was just wondering," Denton felt compelled to explain, although he was in fact uncertain of what he was actually digging for. "I was wondering if you get turned on doing scenes like that."

"Sometimes," said Jill, in a disinterested voice. On the screen a door shut, locations changed, Claude Rains appeared. Jill stretched out her legs and leaned back against the headboard. "Sometimes not. I don't know. It depends."

"On what?"

"Huh?"

"What does it depend on?"

"I don't know. The guy." She leaned forward and the front of her robe sagged open, freezing Denton's mind with a vision of smoothness and curvature and a deep, mysterious divide. "There was this guy one time who was really great-looking. I mean, totally gorgeous, but kissing him was like kissing a rock." The memory caused her to frown, then giggle. Denton laughed, too, and Jill suddenly clutched the robe, as if aware of her exposure and Denton's leer, a liberty improperly taken despite the fact of their intimacy. Denton thought of the savagely handsome actor and despite her description of his stonelike lips he felt a small tongue of jealousy lick at the edge of his ardor.

"Jill?" he said.

Her throat made a slight humming sound.

"You don't really look like Meryl Streep. More like Faye Dunaway." With a shudder of fear and expectation he slid a hand between the halves of her robe, a hand which encountered an efficient, virginal reflex. She wasn't flattered, amused, anything—she had reentered the gray screen and stood next to Bette Davis, so overwhelmed with awe that she couldn't speak. Denton rolled away, in a paroxysm of need and despair.

"Faye Dunaway is old," said Jill, without turning her head from the apparently climactic moment. The acuteness of his desire caused Denton to groan at the same time she said, softly but distinctly, "I'm trying to figure out exactly what it is she's doing."

Denton swung his feet over the side of the bed and tested the carpet. He saw himself tiptoe away, then run, flee through the sliding glass door and down the center of the golf course, startling a cartload of women identically dressed in pleated skirts and visors and tasseled shoes. He stared at Jill's hair, revealed now, a woodsy damp confusion of brown that he thought, yes, should be cut very short, so that her oversized ears, one of her most unattractive features, would be revealed and mitigate the oppressive perfection of her eyes and nose and mouth. He had commented once on these ears—a serious mistake. He thought of her body, rendered shapeless by the robe, and then of her mind, a discrete and separate entity like something electronic on a shelf, with gauges and dials, something that could be tuned and adjusted.

"I want to go back," he said, reaching for the boots that he had kicked off. The simple verities of passion burning like gasoline in the engine of their togetherness, Denton thought, had transformed into ashlike elements tiny and lost in a vast and unknowable universe. His love, despite his belief in his own maturity, was puppy love, an adolescent crush, nothing more. He felt distraught, embarrassed, angry.

He put on his jacket, giving her time to respond, but she just lay on the bed, clutching her robe beneath her chin as if on guard against any more improper advances. He stood unhappily between the bed and door, the beer slightly gaseous and sour, rising to his throat. She turned to look at him, her eyes shaded as if from sunlight by a long, slender hand that terminated in vermilion nails. The opal ring he had bought for her on the trip to San Francisco, he noticed with an irrational little shock, was still on her finger.

"Why? I thought we were having a good time. I mean, I'm having a good time. Is it still raining in L.A.?"

"I don't know," Denton said, even though he had heard on the radio that the sun, indeed, was not yet expected to appear. His lie was a means to avoid the complication of discussion, of deviation into subjects mundane and therefore suggestive of normality, a world immutable and unchanged. The imaginary sunlight bathing Jill, he realized, was a microcosm of a world in which she would always be the center; he would always be standing a little off, in a shadow, where he belonged. He did not want to be in this shadow, and yet the sun was far too hot and bright. "I want to leave, Jill," he said.

A glimmer of possibility stirred in him, an image of some past moment sublime in his bedroom, in a sailboat, in his car, at a party, on the street. Perhaps they were lost, he thought, and once they found their way back everything would return to the way it was before. Indeed, there was something artificial and disheartening in this place with its relentless heat and sun and people diligently engaged in such pursuits as golf and tennis rather than going to work, pumping gas, reading meters, delivering mail, selling, buying, arranging, detailing. It was a place for his parents, who in spite of their incessant quarrels seemed more firmly bound together than Denton could imagine being with Jill, or any other woman that he had met, or known. A place where nothing extreme would ever happen, where if you got lost it didn't matter, you wouldn't even know it. Like the incident in the little town and bar, any dislocation would flatten out and quickly fade from the mind.

"I'm afraid," she said softly, shutting the P. D. James in her lap.

"Of what?" Denton attempted with partial success to feign disinterest.

"Jenny's father." With her perfectly white, perfectly even teeth she bit her little finger. "He wanted to buy this house, out in this subdivision, but I said I wouldn't move. I mean, Jenny liked her school, and where this house was there weren't any trees or anything, just these cornfields."

The transparency of a tear beside her nose caused Denton to feel a loss of freedom, a sense of being caught in the net of her emotion. Small, ungallant remarks came to his mind.

"We were arguing about whether or not I would move to this house and he told me to shut up or something and when I didn't he hit me." She sobbed suddenly, turning her head away from Denton, seeking some solace or comfort that he was obviously incapable of giving. Then she sat up straight, stiffened herself into an attitude of exaggerated dignity, and rubbed a fist in her eyes. "What if he hits Jenny?" she said in a plaintive tone.

"Did he ever?" Denton managed to say.

"No. I mean, she would have told me." She sighed deeply, looking up at him as if she had just then noticed him, contemplating him with an expression he felt to be evaluative. "I guess he gave her a swat on her bottom once in a while. I mean, *my* father did that." She puckered her lips and planted an exaggerated kiss on the air.

What did that mean? Denton thought.

"If you ever hit me, Denton, I'm not kidding, I'll call the police." She glared at him with huge wet eyes, as if he had already committed this crime. Then her voice dropped to an introspective murmur. "I should have called the police." The tips of her long fingers brushed her cheek. "There's still something wrong with my jaw." Her mouth opened wide and slowly closed, a gesture that beckoned him against his will. "Sometimes there's this catch. And a pain . . ." Distracted, her mouth opened again to hint at the soft mysteries within, she seemed even more desirable than ever. But Denton, who could not remember the last time he had lost his temper, who believed that violence directed toward women or anyone else was an evil deserving of harshly punitive measures, managed to resist the charm that wafted like the odor of perfume from Jill's agitation. He sat down on a corner of the bed, an undeliberated action that did not immediately suggest another. He felt confused by the mixture of grief and ardor that hung in the air, and after a moment in which the silence threatened to expand and engulf them he reached out and touched her arm. "I want us to get married," he said. The words poured out of his mouth so suddenly that he was stunned, and if she hadn't turned her head and raised her damp, inquisitive eyes he might have been able to convince himself that the idea had simply been whispered in the dark captivity of his mind.

Her lips parted slightly and her tongue glimmered, causing a nerve in the back of his neck to tingle. He decided that if she responded at all she would say, "I'll think about it," in the same indifferent tone with which she had reacted to his idea of this vacation, but just as he was about to surrender to humiliation and despair her body suddenly melted, one arm flopped over his leg, and her long hair brushed his face and hand as her head descended to his lap. A murmur arose from his thigh, a neural dance made the skin jump on the back of his head. A river of details flowed through his mind. Details concerning change—alterations of furniture, decoration, perhaps of the very place where they would live. He imagined once more the house, Jenny coming to stay, some legal action concerning custody, a newer car for Jill, a honeymoon in Hawaii, Europe, Japan. A squirmy, childish excitement made it almost impossible for Denton to sit still. He took a deep breath and inserted his fingers into the unbrushed wilderness of Jill's hair. He stroked this miraculous hair, wondering how it would look if cut, if styled differently. He wondered if he would be able to approve.

I Like Rap, Don't You?

Annie, once Ann, named Anna after the tragic heroine of what her father called the greatest novel ever written, wished that she had been named Emma after the Madame whose equally unhappy demise seemed in its Frenchness somehow more sublime. Annie was part of her own defenestration of a self-constructed character whose ego gave her permission—compelled her, actually—to swallow or smoke almost anything, to loathe her parents, to develop a queer antipathy towards food. That her father continued to call her Anna in spite of the miracle of her metamorphosis and her own desire, sometimes stridently proclaimed, was a lapse that only he could be forgiven. She knew her father to be a genius, and while secure in her belief that he loved her more deeply than anyone else, she recognized that his mind was also perpetually enraptured by matters of beauty and truth and couldn't be expected to encompass the everyday, the jejune.

At dinner one evening, an unruly ball of spaghetti halfway to his mouth, he lifted his eyes from his normal abstraction to gaze at her. His expression was puzzled, as if he wanted to address her but couldn't quite remember her name; then a spasm of recognition jerked the long skin of his forehead, a wave that coalesced into a ridge that became the inverted image of a cunningly prescient smile. "You're beautiful," he said, his eyebrows arched as if he had been startled.

In addition to his duties as a teacher of English to people who couldn't speak it, Annie's father wrote poems and stories, and behind the ridge of surprise and admiration she imagined a dance of adjective and metaphor. He said nothing further. Her mother said, "Of course," in a disappointing, noncommittal tone, confirming, despite the content of her remark, nothing. Annie felt cloaked by a dreamy silence into which a desultory conversation between her mother and father failed to intrude; she finished eating, excused herself, and made her way, in stages of deliberated nonconcern, into the kitchen for a peek into the refrigerator, out of the kitchen and into the living room to open a magazine and gaze at an ad, out of the living room and into the den to aim the remote control at the TV and allow perhaps five seconds for each of a dozen channels, out of the den and casually down the hall and into her own room, where she collapsed on her bed and stared up at the familiar imperfections of the ceiling for what seemed like ages before throwing herself abruptly to her feet and planting herself in front of her full-length mirror.

"You're beautiful," she repeated, at random moments over the next few days. She caught herself twice, suspecting that she had uttered this declarative aloud in inappropriate surroundings, but no one seemed to have heard, or if they had heard, to have cared. Inexorably stuck in the eleventh grade, with the unhappy sense that time not only had come to a halt but was possibly moving backwards, she endured the grim logic of education with a stiff upper lip while embracing a childish fantasy of herself asleep in a fairy tale, awaiting the kiss of a prince who, in her consciously modern version, didn't have to possess a male form but merely needed to symbolize rescue and escape.

She had given up obvious friends, but instead of a rush of satisfactory replacements, boys and girls both appeared to avoid her, without the logic of category that one would expect—the dull and intelligent, the handsome and ugly, the boisterous and the withdrawn, all of them keeping a distance as if her emergence from the squalid had made her invisible. She moved like a ghost through the school day, arrived at home and undertook chores with an industrious cheer that her mother seemed unable to quite believe, ate dinner free of acrimony, then locked herself in her room and gazed into her mirror, where suddenly her father's portentous voice and her own pallid repetitions blinked from the depths of the glass in bright neon letters spelling TRUTH. She felt breathless at first, then so nervous that she began to hop and twirl about, the idea of some action suggesting another almost immediately—she read half a page of her history assignment, worked part of a physics problem, put on her Aretha Franklin tape and listened to "Chain of Fools" while trying to decide what to do next, read another chapter of her father's unpublished novel or open the window and call her cat. The state proved to be temporary, however, expiring with a nearly audible hiss, like air from a collection of party balloons, a signal to clean up, to go home. She sat cross-legged on her bed in reflective fatigue, thinking of her father making his way through a crowd with his shirttail flowing and his hair on fire and his carrotlike nose and rabbitty teeth stuck out in front like the ornaments of a fifties car—the very fact that he could recognize his daughter's sudden, inexplicable beauty confirmed that his mind traveled a plane above the banal and everyday. As for her mother, well, her mother was her mother, a utilitarian fact that precluded further judgment.

The stuck quality of time was jarred ever so slightly by the appearance of a boy named Justin, who, taking note of her physics textbook open on the concrete bench outside the school entrance one afternoon, attempted to lure her into the question of how, if the physical world has been governed by the laws of mechanics since the inception of the universe, there can exist such a thing as random, unpredictable activity. Annie said she didn't know. She stopped herself from adding that she didn't care either, because in spite of an awkwardness in posture and speech and a shaggy sort of grooming the boy had a sensitive, even sensual face. He was the sort of boy, she thought, who might be kept indefinitely interested through the grant of minor favors. He was the sort of boy who would blame himself when things inevitably went awry. His earnestness, she thought, a quality she once found deadly, might be just the thing to palliate her recently growing need for long discussions of matters pertaining to the self.

"Justin," she said. She disliked the name, it seemed to coat her tongue. She invoked the name of the Roman antecedent and like an unwary fish he rose to the bait, set off on an expository flight requiring nothing of her beyond an occasional nod and murmur. A bore, she decided. But she wouldn't hold that against him. Although she couldn't recall ever having seen him before, they kept running into each other between classes, before and after school, one day at the minimarket where she had gone to buy film for the family camera that she intended to use in the creation of an artistic series of self-portraits. The very sight of Justin made her drowsy, but she stifled a yawn and asked him if he was familiar with a certain foreign film that she wished to see in order to hear the speaking of French. He admitted to having once liked French films, but now found only the work of certain Czechs to engage his imagination. Everything French, he said, was concerned with surface, while the Czechs had succeeded in peeling away this outermost layer to expose the reality of the core.

A note of self-confidence in the splattering rush of his voice defeated her desire to utter a clever antiquity like "Piffle." She considered her own regular and acute attacks of uncertainty that had a palpable leveling effect—made hamburger taste like filet mignon, made Top Forty sound like Bach, rendered *Hamlet* indistinguishable from *Cheers*. Her mind paused at a door closed upon the entrance to an infinite chamber of doubt. He wasn't who he seemed. She stamped her foot, but he was too occupied by his dissertation that had strayed from film making into art and political theory to notice. He wasn't who he seemed, she thought, but then, who was?

He invited her to go with him to the art museum, and Annie murmured her assent while staring through glass at glossy hot dogs turning on a spit. In the days leading up to this journey her romantic and pragmatic selves engaged in debate upon the subject of a kiss, and she had decided, finally, to permit a single, informal but circumspect conjunction of the lips, avoiding excessive pressure, moisture, or time, but at the same time allowing a quantity of each sufficient to leave an impression, to create suspense, which in Annie's mind was the belief that in the vast, unfathomable future at least one thing of interest would happen. He arrived at her house an hour late in an unwashed Volkswagen Bug, and her approval was only slightly tainted by the fact that her mother and father appeared to like him on sight, possibly because of his polite, relatively articulate, earnestly self-effacing manner so vividly at odds with what they had come to expect and dread. He even called her father "Sir" and bowed as he took her mother's hand, creating in Annie's mind the dreadfully embarrassing expectation that he would lean even farther and plant a kiss on her mother's knuckles that were black with dirt from the garden. Justin and Annie's father managed to slide from an exchange of pleasant formalities to the scratchy buzz of a discussion in which such words as "narrative" and "preliterate" and "Faulknerian" poked her like a playground pest, and she heard a shrill tone in her voice, a tone that she thought she had modulated to a throaty murmur of factual disengagement, almost a purr. She felt like a leaf in a breeze, turning this way and that, reflecting light in different quantities, changing color, yet at the same time stuck, always attached, unfree.

Amidst the riotous strokes of the Fauves and a well-kempt mob that had waited in line to admire them, Annie asked Justin if he thought she was beautiful. Her intention had been to complain that the colors made her dizzy, and to insist that they take a walk in the sculpture garden, a place she remembered coming to as a child with her father and finding herself unable to take her eyes off a figure she knew to be an enormous insect even though her father assured her that it was meant to represent a human being. She remembered the sculpture as the most profoundly ugly, most horrifying thing she had ever seen, and how her father, responding to her antipathy, had embarked upon an explication of the concept of beauty, using words that she didn't understand, like "perception" and "expectation," words that made her irritable and sleepy.

"Do you think I'm beautiful?" She suspected that Justin wouldn't answer at all, think the question beneath discussion, for he had already professed to find all the popular norms of culture to be the antithesis of his own independently worked-out system of values. Would he say something tiresome like "Beauty is in the eye of the beholder"? He cocked his head as if to listen for an echo. She was appalled, suddenly, momentarily, by her own sense of self, so acute that she felt the collective stare of the crowd to be reflected off the walls and transformed into an intense, inspecting light that she could not escape, that would pursue her everywhere, unclothe her, make her feel like that figure in the sculpture garden, exposed to ridicule, misunderstanding, analysis.

An urge to flee made her feel shrill and breathless as she repeated the question. The act of contemplation twisted Justin's mouth in a way that made him look like Steve McQueen. He was preposterous, she decided. They both were. So was the crowd, and the whole idea of painting, of the museum, of art. Odors rose like mists from the swamp of absurdity in which she stood—breaths, some stale, some minted; laundered cloth, leather, the conditioned mass of air about their heads, with its metallic hint of having been manufactured deep inside some dark piece of machinery; and the staleness that lingered about Justin, a mixture of cigarette smoke and sweat and a glandular male odor that she could recognize but not describe. She hoped, briefly, without imagining the details of any possible intimacy, that Justin's body would not prove to be covered with hair.

"Of course," he said.

"What?" She had already abandoned him for an uncle whose voice wheezed like a bellows, who was perpetually attached by means of a transparent tube to a tank with gauges and dials. Smoking together outside the minimarket, she had said, "It's really disgusting what this does to your body," and Justin had constructed in some detail his idea of a world in which people do whatever they please and then are allowed, after the age of forty, to go to a hospital and commit suicide. "The whole thing from the beginning has been for the human race to self-destruct," he had said. "When you understand that, all the rest begins to make sense." She had never quite grasped philosophy and wondered if what he propounded was existentialism.

"You *are* beautiful," he said, with such a ponderous look that she felt the urge to giggle. "I'd say it's the way your eyes . . ."

"Don't analyze me!" A frigid chill of panic rose from her toes to the top of her head and beat noisily into the air, like a raptor risen from a pile of bloody fur. In the edge of her vision a child flapped the empty arm of a coat, a semaphoric signal of boredom. She arranged upon her face a sweet, deliberate smile, seeing for no possible reason other than her proximity to Justin the steamy cover of a novel she had stared at on a rack at the minimarket checkout stand, a cover of shiny, lurid red upon which the scanty dress of a woman she assumed to be southern slid in two directions, up a swollen thigh and down an inflated bosom. The shirtless man who lurked above the woman possessed the sort of ludicrous muscles she hoped that Justin didn't have, and she decided that if she could somehow displace the woman she would either scream in terror or succumb to a fit of hilarity. She attempted but failed to exchange these cartoonish figures for her father and mother. She incautiously opened her mouth and a nasal fit of giggling erupted. She looked at the little boy who had reinserted an arm into the coat, and wondered if it was he who had actually made this inappropriate noise.

They sat outside a little café in the museum courtyard, drinking cappuccinos.

"If I'm beautiful . . ." she began, and he clicked a spoon annoyingly in his cup and interrupted.

"They're just value judgments," he said. "Beautiful, ugly . . ."

She didn't wish to argue, because she knew that she would end up feeling that she had lost no matter how brilliantly she might expostulate something, but she did feel diminished and undervalued. He was thinking, she knew. He seemed to enjoy thinking, while her own journey into fevered states of pure sensation had been catalyzed by a desire not to think, to simply move, stretch out, prowl with the same random rhythm of instinct as her cat. She didn't care about the Fauves, she decided, or anything else in the museum, or anything that Justin might have to say about an Olmec figure that he began to describe with what she thought was excessive detail. She didn't want to see this figure. She had already told him that she hated history and wished to totally ignore the past, a statement that had prompted him to propose what she felt was a labored concept of time in which the past, present, and future were all indistinguishable, like discrete things thrown into a blender and churned into a soup.

"If I'm beautiful, then why are my parents—you know . . . ?" She thrust this question into a pause that may or may not have concluded the dissertation on Pre-Columbian sculpture.

"Maybe you're adopted," he said, in a careless tone untypical of him.

"No." Belief was solid, massive, a quantity almost visible.

"Maybe they never told you."

"No!" She rapped their table with her fist and liquid slopped from his cup onto his hands. Fortunately, he had talked so much that it had cooled. He wiped his hands on his shirt, an act that charmed and softened her, made her feel like succumbing, entering the cover of the novel and letting the desire in the man's eyes pour over her like chocolate syrup.

"I don't want to talk about it," she said, even though he hadn't spoken. In fact the expression on his face was empty, vacuous. She considered the possibility that despite his impressive command of facts and vocabulary he knew nothing of any value; that all of his theories and conclusions were utterly useless. Unlike other boys she had known, he did not appear to be in the grip of a hormonal frenzy, and the only time she could recall him even alluding to sex he had said that celibacy stimulated the mind, or something to that effect. Perhaps he was gay. Her physics teacher was thought to be gay and two or three girls in the class believed that the mediocrity of their grades proved that he hated women. She recalled in imperfect detail Justin proposing a theory that people contain in equal parts opposing qualities—masculinity and femininity, gayness and straightness, goodness and evil. He had said to her that he was as much a woman as she was, and vice versa, despite the obvious elements of difference that he considered of no more relevance than the shape of the teeth or color of the hair.

"It's all just a random collection of accidents, anyway," he said.

"What is?"

"Appearance. Everything. Just bits of energy bouncing around inside of atoms."

"I don't know what you mean," she said, feeling stubborn. Her physics problems seemed to imply the very opposite, that everything happened in obedience to one law or another. She imagined her father and mother making love, but the particulars of this made her tense and squeamish, so she directed her mind to a textbook view of a sperm wriggling toward an egg. Theorems and postulates meshed and clicked like the gears in an obsolete adding machine, and out came a strip of paper upon which could be read not only the sum but all of the parts: cells, membranes, follicles, tissues, all particles of the whole that was her beauty. She noticed that Justin looked morose. She felt like a virgin, despite the violations that Anna or Ann had allowed, even encouraged; she suspected that it was a private part of her mind and not her thighs or breasts that he wanted to curl his long, sensitive fingers around. She felt the intense, momentary fear that arises from ambiguous noise or movement in the dark, and she demanded in what she recognized as a shrill, impatient voice to be taken home.

She saw Justin's lugubrious figure in the hallway just outside her physics classroom, and after a moment of frozen hesitation she turned and headed in the opposite direction, ending up in an annex far from her intended destination, out of breath as if she had run for miles. A pair of boys who knew her intruded with possibly salacious remarks and she screamed, an alarm that awakened a sluggish process that eventually transported her to the vice-principal's office, a green entrapment filled with stale air and questions that made her dizzy. "Do you want me to call your mother or father?" The question accused her of unknown crimes she knew that she must have committed—why else would she be imprisoned, denied the beauty of history, the truth of physics, the sublime revelations of PE? She had been in the office another time, at the inconclusive end of a journey that began in a classroom where she had called a teacher a stupid fart, but then she had known exactly how to sneer and maintain in the face of all argument to the contrary that everyone and everything in the school was utterly dumb and useless.

When Justin called she clenched her teeth and banged the receiver down the moment she heard the word "Freud," a moment arriving after the utterance of perhaps a dozen words. She lay on her back on the floor with her eyes tightly shut, thinking of a female name to go with each letter of the alphabet—Anna, Barbara, Connie, Deborah, Ellen, Frances, Glenda, Hannah, Iris, Jane, Kelly, Laura, Meredith, Nancy . . . she could not think of a name for the letter O and felt the muscles tighten in her face. She finally decided to skip it, murmured the name Patricia and immediately encountered the difficulty of Q, a quandary so profound that she began to cry. She dragged a pillow from her bed and sobbed into it until her ribs ached, then got up and stared at the titles of the books and other things on the shelf above her desk, her gaze eventually coming to rest upon the porcelain face of a doll, a geisha that her father had brought her from a trip to Japan. The face looked first impassive and then full of grief, and Annie sat down, opened a drawer, and set up a little mirror and tubes and brushes. The telephone rang again and she took the receiver off the hook and pushed it away so that it fell and hung, dangling and eventually beeping, toward the floor. She stared for a long time at her face, and then at the face of the geisha, and finally she picked up a brush and a tube and began to reproduce the ivory cheeks and crimson mouth and azure eyelids of the doll, observing the disappearance of her self with a feeling that swung wildly back and forth between ecstasy and despair.

At the dinner table her father's asymmetrical eyebrows rose and fell, and her mother's mouth opened and shut at least twice, but neither could bring themselves to comment. The pretense of normality, the please pass this or that, the discussion of what was wrong with the transmission in the car, the silence in which the noise of mastication rose to horror-film intensity—these things added up to a ritual so grotesque that when her mother asked in an innocently hopeful tone if she was still seeing Justin she got up abruptly and carried her plate to the sink and dumped the contents into the disposal and flicked the switch, creating a din that drowned out all but the first two words of her father's commentary. "My dear . . .," he said, a form of address she once found charming but no longer could abide. She fled to the darkness of her room and flung herself to her bed, and after the passage of what might have been seconds, or minutes, or even hours, she sat up and stared out her window that looked upon the backyard, at the cloudy mass of a tree, the black shape of the garage, the squares of yellow light that added up to a window in the house across the alley. The word "Opal" blinked in her head like a beacon. The word a piece of fruit in her mouth, a small plum or a grape, round and smooth and slightly sweet.

"Opal," she said aloud. It was the name of the old woman who cast a momentary shadow upon the squares of yellow light, and Annie saw herself—a girl of eight or nine—dash across the alley and pry open an arthritic gate and sit at the old woman's table and drink a glass of tea with a taste so new and exotic that she felt herself transported to a foreign and much more desirable country. She switched on her light and looked around her room. She decided that she would get rid of everything. There would remain her bed, her desk, her stereo, but nothing on the walls, nothing on the shelves but her schoolbooks, nothing cluttering the floor. She looked at her face in the mirror with objective disinterest. She would break the mirror, accidentally, and tell her mother and father that it needn't be replaced. She dragged a sweater she hated from the bottom of a pile in her closet and pulled it over her head. On her way out of the house she smiled sweetly and said, "I'm going to Meredith's house to study," even though she carried no books and knew no one by that name. Her father cleared his throat but the door banged shut upon anything he might have been prepared to say.

"Anna?" The old woman answered her door, peering at Annie with the gray, watery eyes that Annie had once used in the construction of a poetic metaphor involving stones on the beach. She had visited the old woman regularly when communication with her parents had regressed to a prehistoric level of shouts and grunts, but in the becalmed period preceding Justin and her father's recognition of her beauty she hadn't felt the need to listen to the old woman's voice, which in its grainy lack of urgency was soothing, almost hypnotic. She found the system of folds and creases that covered the old woman's face and neck and arms to be a map of some exotic, alluring country. She could only recall this sound and sight, and not a single word of anything they had ever talked about.

"Do you like music?" Annie asked. They sat at the old woman's lace-covered dining room table in yellow light that seemed ancient, as if the bulb in the cloudy ceiling fixture had been burning for a hundred years. "Do you ever listen to music?"

"Oh my goodness," said the old woman. "I have my favorites . . . let me see . . . Vaughn Monroe . . ."

"I bought this tape," said Annie, who had never heard that name before. "It's rap. Do you know what rap is?"

"Why, yes," said the old woman uncertainly. "I should say I ought to."

"My mother found the tape and played it and said it's demeaning to women." Annie was certain that she had never complained about her parents to the old woman before, and the fact of doing so now made her feel queasy, as if she had poked her finger into something of uncertain origin and texture. "I don't really care. I honestly don't."

"Well," said the old woman, twisting her crosshatched lips this way and that as if to get a good taste of this information. "I'm opposed to censorship."

"So am I," said Annie. "I believe that people ought to be able to read or see anything that they want to. I mean, what's freedom for, anyway?"

"Yes," the old woman said, the positive as full and drawn out as a phrase or sentence. "You are certainly right. I remember when . . ."

But Annie did not wish to have the old woman's attention deflected into nostalgia and she interrupted with a question that the old woman pondered with a complex animation of her face, a show of twitches, tics, folding and unfolding, a blinking of faulty eyes.

"Yes," she said finally, with the same roundness and fullness of diction. "Our son was killed . . . in the Korean war . . ."

Annie thought that she ought to interject a condolence, but by the time a suitable form of this expression came to her it seemed that too much time had passed, and the old woman's voice had begun again to rustle, like something alive but invisible and possibly scary beneath a pile of leaves.

"I have a daughter . . ." Annie hadn't observed any tears in the old woman's eyes, but her crooked hand rose out of her lap and proceeded with deliberate speed to a box of tissues. The daughter, Annie heard, her attention beginning to be distracted by regrets of her own, seldom took time to visit or even call on the telephone. Annie dimly remembered sitting at the lace-covered table in the grasp of something hysterically funny that the old woman had said. The funereal aspect of the present made her feel cold and much older than her years. She saw herself, briefly, shockingly, behind the withered mask of the old woman's face.

"I can't see that anything makes any difference at all," she interrupted.

"Well, yes," the old woman said. "That might be so . . ."

"Everything might be just the opposite of what it seems," she said, uncertain of herself and aware of borrowing a tone from Justin. "I mean, I could be beautiful or I could be ugly."

She waited for the old woman to say, "Of course. You're beautiful." But this approbation was not forthcoming, Annie saw with both dismay and curiosity. The old woman's gaze seemed to have taken an inward turn, to have folded back into a past too distant and hazy for Annie to make out any detail. She would revert to nostalgia, Annie guessed, and then Annie would have to excuse herself and make her way back across the intense darkness of the alley and backyard and enter the impossible reality of her parents' house, where, if she wanted to listen to her tape, she would have to keep the volume so low that the desired effect, the transportation into a state of pure sensation, would be impossible. When Justin had reached to change the station in his car on the way to the museum she had said, "I like rap, don't you?" and he had looked at her as one might look at an irritating little brother or sister, with supercilious scorn. He didn't want to be seen as ordinary in any respect, she thought, with a shiver of panic at the thought of the thick darkness of the alley in which persons could sometimes be seen rummaging through the garbage cans or sleeping against the fences. He had constructed himself as the antithesis to what was considered normality around him, and she suddenly perceived him to be foolish, even stupid. He had more or less said the same thing as her mother, about this business of demeaning women. She decided that they simply didn't understand, neither of them. It's just music, she had said. It's just noise, she had said, sensation.

She said, "Do you know a woman's name that begins with the letter *Q*?" but even as the rugged relief of the old woman's forehead configured itself into a pattern of utmost seriousness Annie remembered a girl she had known in grade school—Quincy . . . Quincy Potter. The androgyny of the name bothered her a little as she saw a dark girl with a single braid of hair and lips that turned a juicy red when she opened her mouth, like the inside of something freshly peeled.

"Well," said the old woman, "let's see."

Annie nodded. To herself she said, Rebecca, Sarah, Tanya, Eunice . . . she stopped, doubt curling like smoke into her eyes still tender from her sorrow. She tried to get into the line of the old woman's inward slanting sight. "Do you know the name Eunice?"

"Eunice?" The old woman's teeth appeared like yellow apparitions beyond the mysterious wrinkle of her mouth. "Oh my yes. My sister-in-law's name was Eunice."

"How do you spell it?" Annie asked.

"Why yes." The old woman laughed, a sound that seemed to originate from deep within her body, like an echo from a well. She carefully pronounced the letters, as if in a spelling bee.

Annie frowned. "Do you know any girls' names that begin with the letter *U*?"

"Well." The old woman carefully moistened her upper lip with a tongue so pale that it was almost gray. "Let me see . . . I knew a woman named Uta . . ." She gave the name what sounded to Annie a foreign pronunciation, the *U* drawn out like a string of lowercase *o*'s. "She was a German lady who I did housework for."

"You did housework?" Annie had never imagined the woman as anything other than what she was, a slow, wrinkled entity sitting at her table or moving with utter lack of urgency between the table and her stove, her refrigerator, her cabinets. "You mean, as a job?"

"Yes. It was before the war." Although her eyes were open, the dreamy look made her seem asleep. "We lived in an apartment then."

A scratched reel of history turned in Annie's head. The war. It had a prehistoric sound. "Vera," she said, moving her lips. One of her father's favorite authors, she recalled him saying, had dedicated all of his books to his wife, whose name was Vera. "Wanda, Xenia." She tried to see the latter in her head, but it was obscured by some sort of shadow. She said it uncertainly aloud.

"Is that a name?"

The old woman repeated the name and it sounded somehow different, less exotic, like the name of something common. "It's a town," she said. "In Ohio. I grew up in Ohio, you know."

"A town?" said Annie, unable to conceal her disappointment.

"It could be a name. Goodness sakes, yes. I imagine I've heard it as a name."

"What about *Y*?" said Annie, beginning to feel indifference pressing at her like an unwelcome question from her parents, from Justin. "And *Z*?"

"Well let's see . . . there's Yolanda." The old woman's unemphatic manner made Annie wonder if this were true—she had never heard such a name. "There was a woman named Yolanda who lived right down the street, that house with the pepper tree in front. There's a young couple there now. She died, oh my goodness, it must be twenty years now."

Nostalgia in the air felt worn and thick, like the upholstery of the furniture that Annie could see through a wide doorway, furniture upon which she had never sat and which looked like accoutrements to a diorama such as she had seen in a trip with her parents to another museum. In Annie's mind the old woman's languid voice picked up speed, threatened to race, to become reckless, to derail.

"Then there was Zelda Finney, who was in my club before she died."

The old woman's voice trudged onward through the past as Annie began to wonder if she had ever been beautiful, if her skin had been as smooth as glass, if her teeth had been perfectly straight and white, if her body had possessed a shape entirely different from the present undefined heaviness that seemed to flow from her neck to her feet. Her imagination would not shake free of the present in which she felt trapped and forced to view the lumps and spots and crooks of an antiquity that would never change. There were photographs inside the curved glass front of a cabinet opposite the table, but Annie had never been interested in looking at them. Now she stared, with an almost feverish desire to know who these people were, trapped in frames of varying sizes and material, in varying degrees ornate and old-looking. She got up in the middle of the old woman's declaration of regret over the fact that her club no longer met and stood close to the glass and peered inside. Her eyes moved along a shelf, stopping at a tarnished frame within which a dark-haired woman sat on a stool or chair rendered invisible by a dress that fell in silky folds to the floor. "Is that you?" she wanted to know, aware suddenly that all of the time she had spent in the room, a thick block of time that must have constituted many hours, had simply been time in which she had warmed herself in the encirclement of the old woman's attention. "Can I see it?"

"Why yes," the old woman said. "Bring it here." Annie opened the door that creaked and reached inside a little gingerly. The old woman held the frame in her bent fingers and moved it back and forth to bring the portrait into focus. "This is my mother," she said. She let Annie look again. "When I was that age we wore shorter dresses."

"She's very beautiful," Annie said, uncertain what the tinge of emotion in her body constituted—admiration, empathy, jealousy. She wanted to know what the beauty of the woman in the photograph meant, but she didn't know how to articulate this curiosity.

"I was always plain," the old woman said matter-of-factly. "My mother was beautiful but I was plain, goodness knows why."

"Did she have trouble?" Annie asked. "I mean, because of being beautiful."

"Oh my." The old woman's wet eyes shut for a moment and her dry lips pursed. "She used to say what a nuisance it was to have so many beaus."

"Bows?" Annie saw in her mind a satin ribbon tied about Quincy Potter's long black braid.

"That's what we called young men," the old woman said, with a chuckle. "It's what you call boyfriends nowadays."

"Oh," said Annie. "Beaus."

"She had the most terrible time making up her mind who to marry."

Annie nodded, although she couldn't quite imagine this predicament.

"She decided on my father even though he was far from being the most handsome man. She decided on him because she thought he had the best prospects."

"Prospects?"

"Some of her beaus didn't seem like they would be able to hold a very good job."

"Oh," said Annie. This visit, she could see, was not going to give her what she wanted, which as nearly as she could tell was some kind of revelation. She felt cold, indifferent, and even a little hostile. As soon as the voice came to a pause she said, "I've got to do some homework," and shook her head in response to the old woman's offer to make hot chocolate and bring out cookies she had just that morning baked. "I've really got to go," Annie murmured, and slipped out of the house, crept across the alley and through the yard to her front door, holding her breath, trying to draw as little attention as possible, trying to become invisible.

In her room she put on the tape, with the volume low; she attempted to listen to the voice, but the drift of her mind turned the words into repetitive noise so annoying that she abruptly shut off the machine. She stood in front of her mirror, taking what felt to her like a final look. The makeup on her face looked slapdash and absurd, and as she stared at it she saw a corpulent tear form at the blue rim of her eye and slide down through the white that was like the stale icing of a cake uneaten, left over from some forgotten occasion. In order to smash the mirror she would have to go into the garage and get a hammer from her father's tools. She decided to undertake this task when alone in the house, perhaps the following afternoon. The tear deformed at her lip and spread and she tasted it with her tongue, its salty taste along with the sticky taste of her lipstick. The old woman hadn't commented upon her appearance, she realized, because the old woman was nearly blind. This knowledge felt like a pressure inside her, a pressure that squeezed forth more of the tears, produced a flood that streaked the brittle icing of her face, dissolved her eyes, her nose, her brilliant vermilion mouth.

The Night of Love

Anderson read in the newspaper, nine months after the earthquake, that the local hospital was swamped with women giving birth. He imagined a mob of these women, all in labor, pushing and shoving to get in the hospital doors, and he remembered Coral's refusal to sleep in the bed—how they had sat up talking for hours before collapsing together on the rug in front of the fireplace, where an aftershock arrived with uncanny timing at the climax of their lovemaking, a shiver normally unsettling but rendered almost subliminal by the intensity of their endeavor. He imagined couples scattered throughout the surrounding hills, all in the sweaty grip of ardor, as if in thrall to the same dark fantasy of apocalypse, a splitting of the earth to swallow them and deny them another chance to experience this earthbound passion. He smiled. The unexpected increase in population, the pressure on schools, on public services, effects of a force so reckless and unforeseen as to be miraculous.

Coral, with her literal mind, preferred to think in boring terms of geology, while Anderson sailed off on a voyage of irony in which the mysterious power of nature mocked the genuflection of humankind before the altar of technology. Irony, he decided, was the mischief of an evolution that had blessed and damned him with the ability to feel and think at the very same moment, conflicting activities as inseparable as the smoke that mingles above different portions of a fire. To the lower forms of life, he thought, what *is* simply *is,* has nothing to do with what might have been, what could have been, what is illuminated not by the sun but the light of intellectual fervor. Thus, the general destruction had made him happy, even as specific reports of loss had twanged an empathetic string, squeezed his throat, and stung his eyes.

"Coral," he said, having digested the newspaper item and enjoyed the attendant fantasies. "I've got to get somebody out to fix the chimney." Nights had lengthened and grown colder; rain would soon arrive, producing the chill that only a decent conflagration in the fireplace would keep at bay. The bricks from the section of chimney above the roof had produced a thunderous symphony in their tumble and slide across the shingles to the eaves, from which they had plunged in a staccato of thuds to the rosemary bed below, their fleeting shapes across the window creating in Coral's hyperactive mind the idea of bats. Anderson regretted that he hadn't witnessed this spectacle. After convincing himself that all was stable he had collected and stacked the bricks, but when he called up masons he discovered that the few not busy for the rest of their lives were proposing to charge a fee just to come out and view the damage. Coral, whose embrace of feminist principles did not encompass any desire to be involved in such matters, had agreed with his decision to wait until things settled down, until most of the damaged chimneys around were rebuilt and the masons affronted by the idea of one more job would be happy to estimate the work for free.

Anderson regarded her with the eager reserve of a teenager, thinking of the hiss and flicker of a fire and her body unwrapped like a gift in his arms, but outside in the dusk he felt a silly, irrational panic. The earth was molten, he realized, with the uneasy feeling of having failed to grasp, until that moment, the actual breadth of a fact he had always known. The ground was simply a floating crust and for a moment, walking the perimeter of the house and gazing up at the ragged stub of the emasculated chimney, he felt a jiggling sensation, as if the ground wasn't even substantial enough to be called a crust but was the skin of a colossal pudding. He reached the stair to the deck that hung outside the living room, level with the tops of trees that leaned against the steep slope of the hill, and he felt, on something human-built and unnatural, safer.

"I talked to Pete," he said, referring to their neighbor whose house was out of sight but not of earshot to the southwest, directly at the spot where the sun in its slow southerly collapse now disappeared. "He says I ought to take the chimney all the way down, because it may be damaged and unstable, even though it looks okay."

She wanted to know how much this would cost. Her interest in his finances, beyond what information could be inferred from descriptions like "okay" or "so-so" or "getting better," had recently taken a turn toward the inquisitive, and in some way Anderson felt but couldn't defend in so many words, judgmental. They sat on the deck in familiar if not entirely comfortable silence, watching the sun sink through the redwoods that blackened the ridge above Pete's roof. "I can use the money I was saving to buy a radial-arm saw," said Anderson. The expectation of routine—the preparation and eating of dinner, the watching of an hour of TV, the reading of a book or magazine before getting ready for bed—made him feel relaxed and content. But the silence had perhaps begun to coagulate, to gel, and when Coral finally spoke up with the question "When was the last time they gave you a raise?" the sound was jarring, discordant, and iced with a glazing of portent.

The question, Anderson thought, contained within it as a matter of tone the alternate formulation, "When was the last time you asked for a raise?" A frozen moment of guilt and paranoia took hold of him like the prelude to a sneeze. He knew the answer to both, but like the guilty party that he was, he knew better than to blurt out the truth, at least without consulting counsel, in this case himself. "Why?" he wanted to know, in a voice that squeaked like a defensively resistant hinge.

"No reason." The childish simplicity and ease with which this lie emerged amused him. He looked for a twinkle of mischief in her long green eyes, but the light in them was cool. Their past fled by him in a whir, like one of those little children's books whose pages are flipped to produce animation. He would like to have said, "Whoa," and settled in for a leisurely review, but her soft, unhappy voice was an antidote to nostalgia.

"I hate this house," she said, in a tone just plaintive enough to arouse in Anderson a dollop of sympathy. "The next time it's going to come right down on our heads."

"I doubt that," said Anderson, sincerely.

"I want to get away from here." Her tone sank into a lugubrious, wet morass. "I want to sleep at night. I hate everything about this place, Anderson. I'm going to go away."

"With or without me?" Anderson's articulation of this question which floated enormous and dirigiblelike across the blank sky of his mind managed to surprise him, it was so definite and conclusive. Even as his eyes took in the exaggerated flare of her nostrils above the pouty distension of her upper lip, the redwood bench upon which they sat lengthened and the space between them increased at a logarithmic rate. In the distance he could see a silver, snaillike trail from her eye to the curve of her lip. "Either," she said.

Despite a tedious interlude of silence interrupted only by the creaks and groans of the past, Anderson really knew at the moment she uttered the word "either" that she would crook a hurried arm about his neck, peck his cheek, and whisper, "I'm sorry," then vanish into the sunlight that exposed the crannies where all of his failures and shortcomings cringed. Their past turned into a ghost that dragged a chain across the floor in the middle of the night, and awake for hours in the dark he found himself walking across the campus of the university where they had met, making love to her in dewy grass, gazing at her with such concentrated wonder that the rest of the world receded into a distant and irrelevant blur, out of focus, out of sync, a whir of noise like the crackle of electrical lines, the rubbery hum of traffic, the buzz of silence in the ears when absolutely nothing is going on.

Alone for the first time in years, feeling no urgency to examine the particulars of his situation, loathe to imagine a future, Anderson instituted only the most minor alterations to his routine, which, he could see for the first time, was independent and self-sustaining. On weekday mornings he drank coffee while watching the news on TV, sitting in the chair he had always sat in, wearing the bathrobe she had gotten him for a birthday, sitting in a placid silence bereft only of the sounds of her movements—the steamy hiss of the shower, the clunking flood of the toilet, the grating slide of the closet door, other ambiguous noises whose absence didn't dismay him as much as he might have guessed. Solitude reminded him of moments from his childhood, old enough to remain at home without a baby-sitter, alone with a profligate sense of freedom that led him into such unnatural acts as playing the stereo at full volume while watching TV, making long distance calls to strangers, masturbating into the pot from which his mother's ficus grew. Absolute freedom, he thought, meant not having to discuss, to inform, to share. He went to work and came home, unlocking the door with a quiver of expectation, as if time inside had been suspended and he would hear her humming "Eleanor Rigby" while chopping vegetables at the sink. He switched on lights and opened the mail. With a queasy sense of her antipathy he put a Rolling Stones album on the stereo, turned up the volume to a level that precluded further reflection, and went into the kitchen and piled a dish full of chocolate ice cream to eat in lieu of dinner.

He began to ride the five or six miles to work on his bicycle, arriving early enough to skim the newspaper in the employee lounge, where with one ear casually cocked he listened to rumors of merger and argument over the imagined number of eliminated jobs. The fact that he was no longer part of a couple became general knowledge within a few weeks, but the solicitude of the people he worked most closely with was just a bright flash in the darkness of routine—there is nothing more stimulating than news of someone else's tragedy, Anderson decided, nor more boring than its lingering consequences. Thus he was treated with utter kindness for about a week and then abruptly ignored, even avoided, he thought, with possibly rampant imagination. However, a woman recently divorced suggested, without a trace of the juvenile embarrassment that caused him to stammer and equivocate, that they try sleeping together. "If we're compatible, then we can proceed," she said. "Of course, I'm trusting you to have been in a monogamous situation. I don't want to take any chances. I don't believe there's really such a thing as safe sex, do you?"

Complication, complexity, the possibility of a grand mistake, with all its attendant indignities, made Anderson wary. Solitude, celibacy was infinitely preferable to a situation from which he would have to extricate himself. The memory of his indulgence in verbal and physical whim that seemed at the time not only clever and appropriate but somehow necessary caused him, at an analytical distance, to grimace, and with the enhancement of inexpensive wine he listened to the Rolling Stones and Creedence Clearwater Revival, overdoing it twice and waking up with a hangover that transcended purely physical pain to become a strident voice in his ear, a finger wagging in his face, accusing and reproaching.

He lost his desire to go to the movies, to restaurants, to drive to the ocean, to leave home for other than pure necessity, and with weekends free and the masons he called only slightly more receptive he decided to rebuild the chimney himself, convincing himself not only that he could manage the job but that the work would furnish the vacant rooms of his mind with some elements spiritual and profound. His neighbor Pete, whose life appeared to revolve around various home-improvement projects, wrote up a list of materials and agreed to lend Anderson a wheelbarrow, a trowel, and a tool like a garden hoe with two round holes in the blade. Pete showed Anderson how to mix the sand and cement, how to place the mortar on the bricks with a trowel and tap them into place, gave him heart when it appeared that he was far too clumsy to succeed in anything other than creating a mess.

Although Anderson's relationship to the older man began to evolve into a mild sort of friendship, he didn't tell Pete that Coral had alighted in San Francisco after flitting like a moth around various portions of the Northwest and had written a jarringly impersonal letter setting forth her suggestion that the house be sold and equity divided, even though Anderson had put the money down and made all the mortgage payments, even though he and Coral had never gotten married, had only lived together in a kind of permanence that neither had ever articulated, an arrangement without the formal constrictions of duty stated or implied. Why? he wondered, his mind stumbling through the letter for the third or fourth time, coming to a cold rest at her conclusion that a lawyer might have to be consulted if he didn't agree. Blisters on his hands, his back a mosaic of aches and pains, his mind a slowly revolving cylinder of rote instruction—three shovels of sand, one shovel of cement, handful of lime, consistency of mashed potatoes, butter the ends, tap with handle of trowel, straighten, plumb, level—he once more pulled the limp, overhandled letter out of the envelope and stared at the familiar script as if some mitigating sentence or phrase that he had somehow missed might swim up out of the offensive prose. In heat, he recalled with a wince, he had acted the part of a dog, panting, yelping, snuffling through the bedsheet, growling with his nose in various redolent places. "Ibbly dibbly wibbly one," he had called her, or something to that effect. He felt a crimson bloom in his face.

With a rueful, inward smile he reflected upon the fact that the sight of the unopened letter in his hand had convinced him, just for a moment, that she had finally decided to enter a plea for forgiveness and beg to be taken back. At the bottom of the page, preceding the ungracious formality of "Sincerely, Coral," was a telephone number that Anderson finally dialed, hanging up in a panicky failure of nerve after the second ring—a failure engendered by the probability of groveling incoherence, speechlessness even, at the sound of her voice, which could only be cold and unfeeling in light of the sentiment posed in the letter. He got out a bottle of beer and oiled the congestive dryness of his throat. "Coral," he practiced, moving his lips but producing no sound. "I still love you. I want to work this out." No. "I am prepared to take every means necessary to defeat your preposterous demand." This turgid construction swelled within him along with the gaseous beer, and he liberated a belch that rang through the empty house and put her, just for a moment, in her place.

He was tempted to destroy the letter, but discretion got the better of his injured valor and he buried it deep in a desk drawer. He sat down once or twice with the idea of composing a reply, but was defeated at the start by the choice of paper—the pewter-colored stationery that she had left behind, with the hilly Italian town embossed in the upper corner; the plain white typing paper which in her absence had collected a sheen of dust and begun to curl, a sheet or sheets from a yellow legal pad that had languished on a shelf for years. Weeks went by and the only news to directly affect him arrived in the form of an interoffice memo stating, in plain, uncharacteristic language, that gossip about possible mergers and restructurings adversely affected morale and productivity, and that anyone deemed to be spreading such rumors would be dealt with in a harsh and summary manner. A week later he held in his hand a letter containing an entirely different voice, a voice predicting with a barrage of positive modifiers a brave new future for the company under its new board of directors, its new management team, its new financing, its new corporate logo— a voice concluding with abrupt regret that Anderson's position would cease to exist on a certain upcoming date, his absence constituting a vital part of the grand new scheme. This voice described the generous amount of severance pay he would receive, a voice that straddled a line between sympathy and menace as it alluded to the delay and complication that would ensue from a failure to sign an enclosed form accepting this check as payment in full, forever and hereafter, and in perpetuity.

In December, long after the work had lost its spiritual value and become simply tedious, Anderson finished the chimney. At Pete's insistence he bought a spark arrestor, a black affair of metal and wire mesh that mounted atop the flue, and with the deliberate care of one with far more time than things to do he bolted it down, put the ladder away, and embarked upon a search for kindling. He affirmed the magnitude of his accomplishment even as the blunt red shaft of the chimney appeared to be a sum of far less importance than its vanished parts, the stack of bricks, the mound of sand, the bags of cement, the frequent visits of Pete, his own labor that blistered his hands and strained the muscles of his back and neck and arms. He delivered the kindling to the hearth and noted with satisfaction that a chill had descended into the room. He arranged the kindling, wadded some newspaper, and struck a match, concentrating upon a snap of flame and smoke that threatened to drag him into reminiscence. He watched with a flutter of excitement and then dismay as smoke bloomed in the firebox and curled out under the lintel and climbed like ivy over the mantel and up the wall. With dull incomprehension he watched the smoke spread and thicken.

Finally aroused from a stupor of disappointment, he opened the door to the deck. The kindling quivered into ash as the smoke drifted out the door; he shivered from the cold as he reached into the fireplace and pulled the handle of the damper. He jerked and the damper moved perhaps a quarter of an inch. He pushed and pulled but it only seemed to wedge more tightly. With a glass of water he quenched the last bits of glowing tinder, creating a hiss that sounded like a final deflation of his self-esteem.

He sat on the sofa staring at the fireplace, but before the ragged shards of information could coalesce into an idea the telephone rang. He sat, letting it ring, and then he got up abruptly, almost in a panic, to answer.

"Anderson." Surprise delayed recognition, and after she uttered his name there was a silence in which he suddenly saw their situation as inextricably connected to the recalcitrance of the fireplace.

"Coral," he said, the smoke causing his nose to twitch, the prelude to a sneeze. He felt suddenly voluble. "I fixed the chimney myself—I mean, Pete showed me how to do it—and just now—before you called, I mean—I started a fire but the damper won't open and the smoke all comes out in the room." He stopped, the unfamiliar loquacious feeling a product of his solitude, the stored-up things he had to tell her if she proved to have a sympathetic ear. But the letter rushed like a bullet into his brain. "What do you want?" he added, coldly.

"I don't have any money, Anderson." Her plaintive tone took him all the way back to college, to the time she thought she had failed an exam and wouldn't have enough credits to graduate, or hadn't gotten her period on time, or had believed that Anderson had flirted with another girl at a party. "All they want an English major for is to type. I'm sick of typing, Anderson. I never want to type again."

"What about the book?" he asked, referring to the novel that Coral had been writing for years, a story based upon the life of an aunt who had been secretly married at the same time to two different men.

She snorted ungracefully. "Did you get my letter, Anderson? And if you did, why didn't you write back?"

"It was pretty snotty," he said, that adjective coming to mind for the very first time.

"I'm serious. If you don't come to your senses I'm going to get a lawyer. It's only fair, Anderson. It's really only right. You men are going to have to learn to give up your power, because you're not even a majority, you know."

Anderson let her go on and at a point he remembered later as the moment that she seemed about to utter the word "asshole" he hung up. He paced the room for half an hour, her invective gradually getting mixed up with the problem of the fireplace, which had assumed some symbolic proportions that overwhelmed him. He drank from a gallon jug of wine, listened to a Waylon Jennings album that had languished at the bottom of a pile for years, slept badly, and spent the next day wandering in and out of his shop, his mind unable to conceive of projects that didn't require the radial-arm saw that entered into a unity with the dysfunctional chimney and thus ganged up to taunt him. Just before the sun disappeared he called Pete, who arrived with his usual enthusiasm to climb to the roof, unbolt the new spark arrestor, and shine a powerful flashlight down the flue. Anderson watched Pete descend, head nodding vigorously, as if in full agreement with some elemental conclusion.

"You've got bricks down there. Can't see how many. They've jammed the damper shut."

"They fell in, I guess," said Anderson. "In the earthquake."

"Sure," said Pete, pleased to have unearthed this dilemma. "They fell both ways. Now you've got the problem of how to get them out, don't you?"

Anderson listened with imperfect attention to Pete's detailed analysis of the situation. He listened, even though he had concluded in a storm of thought during Pete's descent that he would simply leave things be, abandon the fireplace to the condition which fate had assigned it, put the house up for sale and give Coral half the money and go to Mexico, to a beach in Baja they had visited once, a warm, brown place where it seemed possible to live very cheaply, fishing, collecting fruit from trees that grew in the surrounding hills, sleeping in the sun, doing nothing.

"Thanks," he interrupted. "I really appreciate it." The older man shrugged, looked mildly puzzled, but was a man of action and not reflection, and therefore willingly abandoned Anderson with a few suggestions that swam through Anderson's brain like fish in murky water, unseen, unheard, of no concern to those who see a shimmery surface and cannot imagine what exists beneath. Despite her shrill, ungenerous manner Coral was right, Anderson decided: together they had been an entity, a state of being in which the details are less important than the whole, and cleaving this thing, this monster or whatever it was unfairly would surely offend some deity and cause him grief. He went into the house and opened the telephone book to the section headed "Real Estate" and began, with both dread and relief, to dial numbers.

On Christmas Eve Anderson hung a sock above the moribund fireplace, unsure of his own intentions—whether this was the joke it appeared on the surface to be or an act arising from any number of unfulfilled needs, none of which he cared to consider or enumerate. In the morning he awoke and listened to the sound of instruments created by a thick fall of rain—the muffled percussive beat on shingles overhead, the thinner, higher, cymbalic rattle on windowpanes, the metronomic drip on something metal, the hydraulic gurgle of pooling and drainage. He stood at the window staring at the solid black of the forest smeared and distorted as if by enormous sorrow. He pinched off the illogical disappointment that arose at the sight of the empty sock above the fireplace and, as a gesture to the occasion, abandoned his usual routine of eating Granola in front of the TV and put the only album of classical music he owned on the stereo and made an omelet, a fussy process involving the lengthy consideration of ingredients and consultation with the authors of several cookbooks.

When he was finished, when the dishes were washed and dried and put away, he realized with a pang of dismay that the day had only begun, that the implication of his scuttling of routine was a block of empty time stretching away into the hazy horizon, a slow tick of hardly perceptible advancement. He telephoned his parents, his sister, and his grandmother who lived in a nursing home and did not remember who he was. There was snow, they told him. Ice. The rain slackened and he decided to go for a walk, but by the time he dug his poncho out of the closet and chose the proper footwear the wind gusted like an imprecation and dragged a sudden torrent from a deceitful lightness of the sky.

After long deliberation in front of the bookcase he selected one of the mysteries that Coral had seemed to require like a drug, but the first page remained completely blank after having been read three times, and he returned it to the shelf. The grandfather clock that he had built from a kit one winter struck the hour, and he picked up the telephone and dialed her number. By the second ring he convinced himself that she wasn't there, that she had moved, that the line had been disconnected, and thus he was startled by the familiar, moderately drawn-out and sensual roundness of her "Hello" and with a juvenile lack of poise he stammered, cleared his throat, and lurched without preamble to the subject.

"I listed the house." This real estate agent's jargon made the information seem impersonal. But again he felt strangely garrulous. "They gave me this form where I'm supposed to list all defects that I know about. They call it disclosure. It's the law, I mean. I put down that the chimney is plugged up and she—the agent—said that this could be a problem because everyone wants a fireplace that works. She said I ought to get it fixed."

"Well, why not?" Coral seemed irritated. What was she doing? he wondered. She wouldn't have hung out a sock, he knew—she didn't have his sense of the ironic or absurd. He suspected—knew, actually, without any evidence—that she had taken a lover, and that perhaps this man was even at the moment in the room with her. Sudden anger clutched at him like a child demanding a parent's attention. He took a deep breath.

"I guess it's not so important. A couple from Palo Alto came down last week and made an offer." Instead of comment he received an ambiguous sigh. "By the way," he said, "Merry Christmas."

"Merry Christmas," she answered, mechanically, as if required to repeat whatever he said.

"I'm thinking about living in Mexico," he said.

"You don't speak Spanish." The statement, true in a practical if not absolute sense, implied a tiny flaw in her indifference. He began to wonder, with a mixture of illogical hope and distantly-remembered dread, what she was sitting or lying upon, how her limbs were arranged, whether or not she was wearing clothes. Wind rattled a window sash, loosening a tactile memory of the night that love suppressed the agony of elemental fear. The jiggle and texture of flesh produced a chill that slid from his neck to his toes. He opened his mouth and her name emerged, as if it had been sitting for hours on his tongue, awaiting liberation.

"Mmmm?"

"If you're so afraid of earthquakes, then what are you doing in San Francisco?"

"Anderson," she said, in a modestly scolding tone. Then her voice turned upward into a more affirmative, hopeful register. "I can see Mexico. Sure. But your Spanish is so grotesquely bad."

"You could come with me." He didn't exactly blurt this out, but it nevertheless violated the cautious quality of their connection and inflicted upon him, just for a moment, a paralysis that rendered him unable to speak, feel, or hear. Thus her reply, hardly louder than a murmur, was lost forever, since he could not conceive of repeating his proposition. His failures bulged into the swollen silence of their conversation. Rain slashed at him beyond the glass door to the deck, and wind sent a shiver through his feet. In unison they muttered good-bye.

Two days later a man arrived at Anderson's house with a clipboard and pen, a screwdriver, and a yellow device with prongs and colored lights. The man crawled under the floor and through the attic, turned on all the faucets, poked the yellow device into the electrical outlets, stuck the end of the screwdriver into wood, standing aside with the professional aplomb and caution of a doctor expecting something to spurt. "Nice place," he said, his gaze not on the house but the surroundings, the little meadow above the garage and the live oaks brightened by the recent rain, the redwoods erect and timeless above. "Too bad so many of the houses around here are substandard." The man described the sight of redwoods snapped like toothpicks, of houses that had slid from their foundations, of roads interrupted by cracks so deep that you couldn't see to the bottom. What did you find? Anderson thought to ask, but only after the man's car had descended the driveway and disappeared.

A week later the real estate agent arrived, bearing news that the couple from Palo Alto had decided, with regret, to exercise their legal right to withdraw their offer. "Structural problems," said the agent. "If you're willing to come down fifty we might be able to sell it as is." She was a woman of Anderson's age, attractive and stylish in a conventional way, but the masculine quality of her speech and bearing did not appeal to him even as a fantasy paraded with stiff formality across his mind. He realized that despite Coral's ability to put her desires into the form of a demand, she was essentially diffident and vulnerable, what he had always expected a woman to be. He articulated to himself for the very first time what he must have felt all along; that his relations with Coral, like the earth, were fluid, uncertain, subject to waves of motion arising like an enormous heave, a shrugging off of affliction—indifference, care, duty, malaise, annoyance with things infinitely huge and inscrutably minute. He listened to the hum of the real estate agent's car, fading into the redwoods that cast perpetual shadows on the road.

He went into his house. He looked at the dark, empty, irrelevant fireplace. Despite the chill in the air he did not turn on the gas heater that protruded from the wall between the living room and kitchen. "Sometimes these guys aren't vented," the man with the clipboard had said, removing the heater's metal cover and peering upward into the wall. "Very dangerous. Carbon monoxide, you know." He had paused, grinning, as if waiting for a look of horror to appear on Anderson's face. "But this one's okay." Anderson had seen, on television and in the newspaper, houses only a few miles from his own, twisted, askew, collapsed, crushed by the foot of a fairy tale ogre who had trod in psychotic fury or possibly just insensitive cloddishness through the hills. The man's report, the real estate agent said, had called attention to certain cracks. Somewhere in the months past Anderson had listened, his mind only partly engaged, to Pete's description of the measures he had taken on his own house prior to the earthquake, a monologue sprinkled with soporific terms like "uplift," "shear value," "lateral reinforcement." He decided that he would speak to Pete. Rebuilding the chimney had not awakened any desire or aptitude for such undertakings, but as long as he had time on his hands he might as well find out what he was capable of.

He sat outside on the deck in light from a hazy sun that now emerged for only an hour or so from the swamp of the oak and redwood forest. A neat little fantasy spun through his mind, born of the thought that he could thwart the malign intentions of the earth and thus win back the woman that he loved. He smiled. He would write her a letter on the pewter stationery, reminding her of the night on the rug in front of the fireplace, of the urgency with which they struggled out of their clothes and how she had clung to him, whispering, "Don't ever leave me," over and over until he said aloud, "I won't. I won't." He grinned. He laughed out loud, but the sound that echoed faintly from the trees was not of gaiety or ease, it was the laughter of irony, of absurdity; like the lovemaking that had suffused the hills that night, it was something meant only to dismiss, to eliminate, to banish the terror of what can never be known.

The Girl Detective

At the age of eighteen she confessed to her mother that she had always wanted to be a boy, and in a tone of pained surprise her mother disclosed that after the birth of her brother certain steps had been taken to abet the conception of a girl, steps involving a thermometer and chart, abstinence at prearranged times, the use of vinegar to deter the male sperm. "Justine Baum," she said, staring past her daughter to address an invisible third party, "was an absolute project." A pouty swell of her lower lip implied that she expected something more than ingratitude for these extraordinary efforts, but Justine was too overwhelmed by a sense of having been created, not by the biology of love but the hiss and crackle of mad experiment, to express the slightest remorse.

"Vinegar?" she said, feeling her nostrils twitch.

Her mother's lips pursed as if the taste had entered her mouth. She stared at Justine and then in the direction of the hallway and the door to Justine's brother's room.

"It's not so wonderful," she glumly declared. "Being a boy."

No, Justine said to herself, nothing is so terribly wonderful, unless you are rich or beautiful or the president of something, the United States or some huge corporation. But, vinegar? With a slightly queasy feeling she reviewed her recent virginal surrender to passion on the dewy grass of the municipal golf course beyond the autumn red and yellow of her college campus, a coupling that had resulted, not in the ecstasy she had persuaded herself to expect, but in the yelping of a dog from an adjacent house and the prowl of a police car with a spotlight that just missed grazing her disarrayed self as it shivered in a little hollow of sand below a green. Her mother's assertion about the ease with which the male sperm could be discouraged from an upward swim through the body somehow disappointed her, seemed without logic to be at odds with a lingering childish fantasy of becoming a private eye— not Nancy Drew but Philip Marlowe, Sam Spade, Lew Archer, even the virulent, violent Mike Hammer.

"I'll never get married or have any children," she said, avoiding her mother's eyes, which even at the best of times appeared to regard her daughter with a look of slight horror.

"Never is an awfully long time," her mother replied, with a real or imagined sniff.

Outside the windows of Justine's parents' apartment the day looked drab and even the Manhattan skyline in the distance appeared pinched and uninviting. Justine nodded, less in agreement with an irrefutable fact than in recognition of the way their conversation had sputtered along a familiar path that led, not to truth or even uneasy accommodation, but to the disenchantment of the dead end. On that next-to-last day of Christmas vacation her remaining hours at home appeared infinite and impossible. Her brother lurked somewhere in the apartment, but the thought of seeking his company and being forced to listen to yet another exposition upon the beauty of physics caused the germ of a headache to wriggle between her eyes. She stared at the black and silver skyscrapers poking into the solid gray of the horizon. She would take the subway to 77th Street, she decided, walk to a certain bookstore on Madison Avenue, and find a mystery to read on the plane that would whisk her, in less than twenty-four hours, to Chicago, to the bus that would sway through the utterly flat and featureless landscape and finally deliver her to the noisy, crowded, delectable freedom of her dormitory room. A stir of anticipation rose from her toes through her shins and her thighs and quickened the pulse of her heart. A mystery with a female protagonist, pretty and sly, virtuous though not to a fault, plucking apart the tightly raveled threads of a conundrum. Murder, preferably by poison or other arcane method, in an exotic setting—Italy, South America, the Far East—involving a man too clever by half, outfoxing himself in the startling denouement.

Without looking directly at her mother she murmured that she was going to see her friend Vanessa, who in reality was at her boyfriend's parents' house somewhere in Pennsylvania.

"And just when are you planning to pack?" her mother said, but in a tone that hinted at the possibility of conciliation. For a moment Justine was terrified that her mother might do something abrupt like kiss her, or burst into tears, but her eyes merely widened to an alarmed scrutiny. "And do you have a sweater on underneath that coat?"

She descended to the blustery chill of the courtyard and passed through a gap in the hedge that formed a barrier between her building and the noisy avenue. A pair of gargoyles leered from limestone columns, prompting an image of the boy she had huddled with on the golf course, a boy whose suave veneer of experience had dissolved into an eager, messy fumbling identical to her own, and had disappointed her in some conclusive manner. She walked quickly beside the hedge, taking note of scraps of paper, a rag, a soda can trapped in the branches to which a few brittle leaves still clung. Fully leafed in summer, this foliage was nearly impenetrable, and she remembered how, at the age of seven or eight, she had concealed herself within it, lying on her stomach to spy on passersby, taking note of faces with darting eyes, obviously phony limps, clothing bulky enough to hide any manner of contraband. She remembered the dry, cool smell of the earth and her mother's demand to know how she had managed to get so dirty. At the corner she waited to cross the street, standing far enough back from the curb to observe without detection a very old lady attached to a cart overfilled with bundles of such ambiguous shape that Justine saw in her mind dead cats, stolen silver, potions, and other items belonging to the repertoire of a witch.

She felt an urge both to hurry and to dawdle, a conflict between a love of motion and adventure and the memory of a desperate desire to put off arrival at school. When she was old enough to feel self-conscious lying in the hedge, she had taken to loitering around the subway stop, pretending to examine the breads stacked in the window of the Italian bakery while keeping an eye out for a person sufficiently suspicious to warrant being followed. This person might have been gaudily dressed, or might have walked in a herky-jerky gait, or might have simply gazed about as if checking the air for secrets. This person might have been completely ordinary—so unremarkable as to invite distrust. She would follow him—for reasons she hadn't reflected upon this person was almost always male—at a discreetly professional distance until he turned into an apartment house, at which time she would rush to the door before it closed and then pretend to dawdle in the lobby while watching the ascent of numbers above the elevator, thus learning the floor on which the person lived. She never considered what practical use she could make of this intelligence, allowing the activity to remain in the realm of the pure science of detection.

When at a lighter than normal moment she told her parents that she wanted to become a private eye her mother had laughed and said, "You'll look just lovely in a trench coat," but her father had taken her seriously and expounded at length on what he believed to be the true nature of such a profession, which was the gathering of evidence of male adultery in order to help avaricious wives fleece their husbands in divorce court. At the end of this discourse a sour look had spread over Justine's mother's face. Her mother believed that Justine's lack of aptitude for math and glib facility for speaking backwards to her friends—"Tomorrow school to going you are? Skirt yellow your borrow I can?"—meant that she ought to concentrate on French and Russian with an eye to becoming an interpreter at the UN. However, the idea of listening all day to diplomats droning on and on about nothing of possible interest made her so irritable that she failed her initial course of high school French, and just eked out a passing grade in Spanish, purported to be the simplest language, although it felt to her like someone banging on a pot right next to her ear.

Her father had known a man who specialized in locating missing heirs. "He makes himself a nice piece of change," her father had said. "But if you want the truth, it's just a lot of plain hard work. This cloak-and-dagger business—that's just TV. Movies." As she heard the rumble of an approaching train she recalled a distant afternoon in which she had fallen asleep beneath the leaves and branches of the hedge and then awakened suddenly to see through a greenish mist her father, his briefcase swinging against his leg and his coat slung over his back. Viewed from her secret observation post he had appeared to be a double agent, carrying secrets such as those that had done in spies like the Rosenbergs, and she had felt for some time deeply afraid and had finally gotten the nerve to sneak a look into the briefcase, which had proven to contain only notes and figures that seemed to pertain to the sale of cabbage. He was never anything other than an accountant, she told herself, arriving at a sudden decision to take the advice of her college roommate and move, after a distantly imagined graduation, to California.

She entered the car along with a man in a shiny coat who lurched and brushed his forearm across her chest, forcing her to mutter a furious "Excuse me!" and then glumly enumerate to herself the freedoms denied her simply because she had been born a girl, trapped in a web of expectation and duty that seemed to endure despite the appearance of enlightenment and change. If she had actually been born a boy—beyond adolescence this self-image blurred into a generality consisting of traits such as wit and gallantry and the prospect of being admired and feared just a bit. The train dived into the darkness beneath the river and instead of getting off where she had intended she rode all the way to Eighth Street and walked through a leaden chill to Soho, where she imagined herself an artist whose works were hung on the cool white walls of galleries into which she glanced but did not enter. She went into a bar and ordered a martini, but the bartender's query— "With an olive?"—so flustered her that she stammered and felt herself turn crimson, a signal for the bartender to ask to see her identification, and she fled back to the subway station and pushed through a thickening crowd into the uptown train.

Justine Baum. She had concocted other names for herself, some Anglo-Saxon, some Italian, some Slavic and even possibly Eurasian. After reading random paragraphs and a rare entire page of *Ulysses* she had wanted desperately to be named Molly, and had practiced an Irish brogue in the privacy of her room, under cover of Aretha Franklin on her tape player. She tried to read *A Portrait of the Artist as a Young Man* but got no further than resenting the fact that she couldn't stand up to pee. Being a girl, she had been forced to conclude, meant always wanting to be something different, someone else, unable to accept the facts that some of her friends seemed to consider, amazingly, a stroke of the utmost fortune.

She thought of Molly Bloom, then someone tragic named Catherine, as she sat between a woman with a child and a shopping bag containing a stuffed panda and a man who hummed a song that she associated with an ancient group like The Supremes. Will I ever be happy? she asked herself, at the same moment that a man in a tuxedo entered her field of vision and slowly displaced her nearly subliminal contemplation of an English composition she hadn't even started although it was due the following week. The man in the tuxedo stood beside a woman who possessed a self-confident air, and his eyes seemed to turn from time to time in brief, casual inspection of the woman's face, which wasn't the least bit pretty but had an angularity that Justine first admired and then envied. What was this man doing, at four o'clock in the afternoon, dressed in a tuxedo? He wasn't carrying anything. She could see a squarish ring on one hand, but the other was curled around a pole and the fingers hidden. She guessed that he was thirty, or possibly even forty, although she was aware of a deficiency in her ability to estimate age, which in men was complicated by things like baldness and facial features obscured by hair.

She concentrated on a fan of lines from the corner of the man's dark eye, as if these were the rings of a tree, but she was too far away to see them distinctly enough to count. The man's forehead was broad and high and his dark hair curled over the tops of his ears. His eyebrows were thick, level strokes of black. She guessed that he was Italian, a conclusion that she rejected almost immediately on the grounds that it was obvious, and therefore wrong. She studied the olive tint of his skin, blackened by the ghost of a beard that faded into the stiff, white collar of his shirt. She noted a subtle upward curve of the outside corners of his eyes. He was Greek, she decided. Or from one of those other countries. The word "Bulgaria" slipped into her mind as she tried to compose in her head a map, but she was almost as inept in geography as in language and all she could see was the brown and azure blur of continent and ocean, floating free of the restraint of latitude and boundary, an amoebic mess that made her feel just slightly dizzy.

As the train slowed to her stop the man gave the woman a final, possibly evaluative look and turned toward the door, filling Justine with a fever of mystery and expectation so acute that her teeth momentarily chattered. Where did he live? She had not tailed anyone since her final year of junior high school when—she closed her eyes to concentrate on this memory—a swarthy man had rushed from the subway platform down to the street with an expression of such intense distaste that she followed him for a block and a half, only to see him turn into a bar that was known in the neighborhood as the scene, many years before, of a murder.

She looked at the elegant back of the man in the tuxedo. She imagined an opulent apartment filled with mirrors and gilded furniture, and a beautiful woman wearing a gown and loads of jewelry, although she had never seen anything, anyone like that in her neighborhood. She followed the man out of the subway car and across the platform, acutely afraid of giving herself away, deciding that she would tail him to his apartment house and then, for the very first time in her career as an amateur detective, casually and indifferently enter the elevator with him, get off with him at his floor, try to steal a glimpse inside his apartment. Perhaps they would even speak! She wondered where the man could live. Not in her building, which despite the columns and gargoyles was ordinary, unornate, or the buildings of any of her friends, which were boring places that you tried, as much as possible, to escape from. The man descended the platform and stopped with his back to the bakery window, his dark chin lifted as if to test the air for a particular scent. Justine took the steps down in the cadence of the elderly or infirm, one foot then the other on successive treads, wondering why the man didn't wear a coat or appear to be in a hurry to get out of the weather, which was chilled enough that vapor like cigarette smoke puffed from the lips that crossed his face at a slightly ironic angle.

The woman with the panda strained in the opposite direction of her child at the foot of the stairway and within the general noise of whines and threats Justine heard the word "pizza." I'll never have children, she promised herself again. I'll never get married. She shivered, wishing that she had actually worn the sweater her mother had inquired so annoyingly about, the sweater that had forced her into a characteristic deceit. The bakery door swung open and a couple emerged, a woman with a face that appeared to be crumbling, followed by a man who whispered furiously into her tall, black pile of hair. When the couple reached the Five and Ten, the man abruptly stopped and threw up his hands but the woman continued on, and the man turned with his arms in the air as if to ask, "Just what am I supposed to do?" Justine thought she saw movement on the lips of the man in the tuxedo, the slight tug of a smile. She thought of the eager grin of the boy on the golf course, and the teeth and lips of the boys she had occasionally resisted in high school, desire written across their faces in bright, blocky letters like those that advertised a once-in-a-lifetime sale at the jeweler's next door to the bakery.

She saw the man in the tuxedo raise his coal-black arm, tug back a thick white cuff, and look at a watch that she guessed to be expensive even though from a distance all details other than the fact it was gold were indistinct. In an hour, she guessed, it would be dark, and as if taking her observation for a signal the man set off in a long, determined, expedient stride away from the bakery window, not in the direction of the apartment houses arranged on both sides of the avenue, but into the perpetual gloom below the subway tracks, into a part of the neighborhood where trucks backed up to loading docks and muscular men could be seen in the summer working without their shirts. A foreign country into which she had ventured once or twice, in the company of her father, on some forgotten errand. The wheels of another train squealed above her head as the mystery suddenly deepened. What could the man's destination be? She stood on the next-to-last step of the iron stairway listening to a stampede of feet across the platform. What would Marlowe do? What would Hercule Poirot do? When the man had gone half a block Justine overcame a fever of indecision and set herself into sudden, panicky pursuit.

She felt both reckless and cautious, wanting to stay close to the low, nondescript buildings so that she could duck into a doorway if necessary to avoid being observed, and at the same time maintain enough distance from those same doorways, where a person with suspicious or malevolent purpose might lurk. She heard the distant click and scrape of the man's shoes on the sidewalk. She recalled her father's polemic on the nature of a private eye's business, and it did seem possible that the man was a rich Manhattan businessman coming to initiate or promulgate an affair with a woman other than his wife. Details such as champagne glasses and schmaltzy music floated through Justine's mind. But where would a lovers' assignation take place in this neighborhood of grimy buildings and sidewalks so cracked and heaved that she had begun to feel slightly seasick?

She tried to picture herself as the man's mistress, awaiting his arrival with pent-up passion that she guessed would be manifest by a glow of intense heat given off by all parts of her body, something like having a fever without nausea or an overwhelming desire to sleep. She was disappointed, suddenly, acutely, by the fact that the man hadn't bought flowers at the shop next door to the Five and Ten, or gone into the jewelers to find a locket or pair of earrings. But perhaps there was already something in his pocket, a small package containing a mysterious, highly original surprise.

Having slipped into reverie about this imaginary gift, she stepped off the curb and was greeted by a blast of warning from a truck that groaned and rattled to a stop directly in front of her, blocking her view. The dreamy feeling faded into a flutter of nervousness. What if I lose him? she said to herself, at the moment she saw, at the edge of her vision, a man in layers of shabby clothing shuffling toward her. The possibility of defeat, of failure, attacked her like a sneeze, freezing for a brief moment all her senses.

A gravelly voice said, "You got something for a poor man, little Miss?" The man's face was slashed at an angle with a yellowish, whiskery grin. She shook her head. She considered circling around the back of the truck but suddenly there was a car and another truck from the opposite direction. The man persisted loudly.

"I don't have anything," Justine said. She had stuck her wallet into the pocket of her coat because she hated being burdened with a purse. The man's body listed in her direction and then he took a single, deliberate, heavy step toward her.

"I don't have any money," she lied, hearing in her voice a nervous flutter.

The man nodded, as if he believed her. She felt, in a vague and distant way, sympathetic; she had written an English composition on the plight of the homeless and her description of the encampments of people on the streets of New York had greatly impressed her roommate, who was from a small town in Minnesota. But she hardly ever thought about politics, or world events, or felt a desire to vote or even express an opinion beyond asserting that all elected officials were hopelessly stupid.

"Here," she said, reconsidering her earlier denial. She dug into her wallet and dropped some coins into the man's gritty palm. He stared as if in awe, then gave her a sly look and said, "God bless you, little Miss," and something got hold of her, something perverse and uncontrollable. As the man embarked upon a slow, cumbersome retreat she said, "I don't believe in God." She regretted this immediately, and the man's voice rose in a loud, predictable clamor of argument. The truck failed to move, and she skirted around it, the man's voice rising and falling behind her. In front of her, in the distance as far as she could see, the sidewalk was empty. A shower of bitter disappointment rained down upon her.

She walked a few steps without purpose, gazing into the wilderness of dull buildings and vacant, lumpy street. She stopped at a window darkened with grime and stared at a display containing three or four door locks of different types, a dusty chrome toaster, a rake that looked like a fan with long, narrow blades and a wooden handle. The window, she realized, was the window of a hardware store to which she had come with her father to buy some brackets to put up shelves in her room. A hint of odor caught in her nostrils, something along the lines of her father's cologne, only dryer, more leathery, more tinted with musk. She sniffed. She was prepared to turn away, to go back to the avenue, back to the impossible dissonance of voices in her parents' apartment, when she caught a glimpse of something familiar—the shiny black stripe of tuxedo trousers in a narrow space between circular tiers of bins containing, she knew from the earlier visit with her father, various kinds and sizes of nails. The sight stuck like something pasted into a dream, then slid into oblivion as a hand attached to the plaid arm of a workshirt reached out and revolved a section of bins.

She bit her lip and clenched her jaw and feigned intensive interest in the display of locks, which was propped against a mound of green confetti that flowed like grass over the hills and valleys of a diorama. She concentrated on taking deep, regular breaths. Her eyes turned along the green landscape and came to rest upon a set of screwdrivers. He will have to come out, she told herself, eventually. As an exercise she carefully deduced, from the different sizes and shapes of their tips, that the screwdrivers were designed to perform different functions, although she could not imagine what more than one or two might be. She felt that a private eye ought to know about tools. She tried to envision the items in the toolbox her father kept in the kitchen closet with the broom and vacuum cleaner, but then she heard the groan and scrape of a door and looked out of the corner of her eye to see the man in the tuxedo emerge, carrying a pair of scissors, and without so much as a glance or other indication that he was aware of her presence continue down the street in his long, unrushed but efficient stride.

Justine felt fingers of frigid air between her collar and neck, and she considered walking as quickly as possible in the opposite direction, getting a slice of pizza and then wandering back to the apartment and hoping that her mother wouldn't barge into her room and offer an opinion upon the order in which she was packing things into her suitcase. Turning from the hardware store the man had slid the scissors into the pocket of his jacket, points down, so that just the top half-circles of the silver handles were visible. Justine shivered. She heard screams and saw the points of the scissors dripping red as if dipped into a can of paint. She heard in a frozen moment of silence the click of the man's heels on the sidewalk. If she turned away from the hardware store window and hurried back to the avenue, she thought, she could allow this image of horror to fade, she could satisfy a sudden craving for pizza, but she would also be forced to think about the English composition, about the boy on the golf course who had written a letter that had aroused her mother's unsolicited interest, about literature and philosophy and the fact that her roommate was always borrowing her shoes, which were the exact, perfect size, and leaving them scuffed and dirty.

A block away, the man in the dimming daylight was a nearly solid form of black with marks of white like light caught at his neck and the tips of his sleeves. Justine watched him cross an intersection, then turn abruptly without stopping and disappear into a doorway, an act that set her heart off on a wild gallop. Did he intend to wait for her just inside this doorway? Having known all along that she was tailing him? Why had he bought the scissors? Why was he wearing a tuxedo? She felt exposed, standing outside the hardware store without any reason, and when she heard an ambiguous noise the fingers of cold stalked through the hair on the back of her head. She had never come alone into this neighborhood, no more than six or seven blocks from her apartment house but so remote from her understanding that it might as well have been China or Russia or the Antarctic.

When the beat of her pulse in her ears abated somewhat she thought once more of retreat, of giving up, of submitting to the ordinary and mundane, which was what had ganged up to afflict her so profoundly. In her mind she walked lightfooted across the damp golf course holding the stiff hand of the boy who went on and on about how he would build houses out of some kind of fiber when he became an architect, and with a feeling of impenetrable gloom she considered how nothing aside from being a private eye had ever even modestly seized her imagination. She thought of her parents' blithe interference with nature and how they had precluded any possibility that she would grow up contented, like her brother, almost giddy with optimism. If she had been a boy, she thought, she could have played with her brother's chemistry set and helped him fire off experimental rockets in the far reaches of the park, instead of poking herself with a needle as her mother tried to cajole her into learning to sew. She stood staring at the empty space in front of the invisible doorway which had swallowed the man, imagining her life as a long, downhill slide from the exhilarating solitude of the hedge, a reprise of which she had felt descending from the subway with the man in the tuxedo firmly in her sight. She sighed and a sudden gust of self-pity blew cinders into her eyes.

The promise of mystery, of the hidden and unspeakable, faded into a whisper so faint that all she could hear was a buzz like that of distant traffic, or an air conditioner, or mosquitos outside her window on a summer night. She decided that all the mysteries she had read and imagined were merely fantasies, that there was a perfectly logical explanation for the tuxedo and the scissors that would simply cause her to feel tricked and deceived. She walked rapidly and without incident back to the avenue, bought a slice of pizza, and ate it on the way to her apartment house. She didn't so much as glance into the hedge. With a feeling of vast though momentary gratitude she saw that her mother was on the telephone when she entered the apartment, and she was able to slip into her room and lock her door. She sat for a while on her bed with her mind blank, then got out her suitcase. She opened a drawer of her dresser and began to throw pieces of underwear into the suitcase, then sweaters, then pants, then a skirt and a pair of blouses from her closet, then shoes, without regard for order. There was a knock on the door and she stood perfectly rigid and silent until she heard her brother's voice.

"I'm never coming home for vacation again," she said, trying to decide what to remove from the suitcase so that it could be closed.

Her brother nodded, not in understanding, Justine guessed, but in recognition of her silly, impetuous nature.

"When I graduate I'm going to California," she said, trying not to pout.

He nodded again, threatening to irritate her so badly that she would have to throw something at him. The only time she had discussed with him a possible career as a detective he had said, "The department of agriculture. They hire people to go around and spy on farmers." The memory fitted a sense that everything had become absurd. "Why would anyone spy on farmers?" she had asked, giving her brother the opportunity to explain in a supercilious tone a kind of fraud involving terms so arcane that she gave in to a fit of irritability involving, as nearly as she could remember, the throwing of a shoe to chase him from her room. She raised her hand and nibbled a fingernail. Regardless of the reality of gender or situation, she suddenly thought, a real private eye would through sheer persistence have gotten to the bottom of the mystery—would have crossed to the opposite side of the street, passed the doorway or alcove or whatever the man in the tuxedo had stepped into, and observed from a circumspect distance until he came out, until something happened.

"I've decided to go to graduate school," Justine's brother said.

His deftness at turning attention to himself she thought another male attribute. Despite herself she said, "Why?"

"There's no use really getting into something unless you get into it really deeply. I mean, that's what's really interesting, when you find out everything there is to know about something."

She didn't want to analyze this statement, because the sound of it conflicted with her latest conclusion upon the subject of mystery, which was that at the core of the unknown existed something that could only disillusion and disappoint. Why had he been so fascinated, she wondered, by the fact that inside the atom are small things whirling or darting around when the very same knowledge caused her to yawn, nearly gave her a headache? The boy from the golf course was for some unfathomable reason fascinated by the mechanics of microscopic bodies as they related to what he had euphemistically called in his letter "the event." She hadn't been able to think of an egg without seeing a glossy yellow yolk surrounded by a crisp circle of white, or a sperm as anything other than a tadpole she had once seen just beneath the surface of the lake in Central Park. The ephemeral odor of vinegar caused her to scowl. She saw the tadpole wriggle in heroic pursuit of an objective, then suddenly become motionless, struck dead. She felt resentful and abused. The boy whose name and face she wanted to erase completely from her mind had kept whispering, "Shhh," even though she had been completely silent. She looked at her brother, who, to her knowledge, had never had a girlfriend, who had once confessed to going to Times Square to have sex with a prostitute, although she had never believed him.

"I'm going to be a stuntperson in the movies," she said, that idea occurring to her for the very first moment in her life.

"Yeah," said her brother, in a condescending tone. "Those women are all lesbians, you know. And they get killed at about the rate of one for every three or four movies."

"You're ridiculous," she said, jerking random items of clothing from the suitcase and flinging them in the general direction of her bureau. If she had been a boy, she wondered, would she have been a clone of this brother, whose vision and expectation seemed to lie within a narrow band of foolish self-absorption? She directed him to sit on her suitcase and was able to close the latches. They were all accidents, she thought: her brother and mother and father and the people on the avenue and in the subway, all of them created by a random collision of invisible forces, all of them except herself, who was the result of a specific intention and would as a result have to suffer, suffer through absolutely no fault of her own.

She flopped face down on the bed and groaned, and her brother said, "What's the matter?" but he didn't have the patience to wait for an answer, he was too engrossed with another subject in his head, and in a voice that clanged on the closed door to her mind he said, "Did you know that it might be possible, under certain really unusual circumstances, for a particle like a photon to exceed the speed of light?"

The Apocryphal Story

The river curled through Jason's dream like a snake, a tropical snake enormous enough to coil around him, squeeze the life out of him, and swallow him whole. He heard himself moan, and smitten with dread he awoke in a shudder and opened his eyes to patterns of light and dark that gradually evolved into forms familiar and reassuring. His wife Maddy snored very faintly beside him, the sound the repeated assertion "You think you know. You think you know." He tried to recapture the moment when they left for the party, when she had smiled at him with a mixture of eagerness and warning, saying, "You're going to have fun, aren't you, Jason?" He had replied, "Of course I am," with only a trace of doubt or sarcasm. But he hadn't counted on the river.

Now that he was awake the river became wide and torpid, a jungle river suggestive of heat and disease. His mind traveled up this river until it dwindled into a mist of gray and he found himself again at the party, talking to a man he didn't know, an agitated man whose face glistened with belief as he shared with Jason his analysis of geopolitics.

"And what's your field?" the man had asked, his emphasis on the word "field" producing in Jason's mind a child's rendering of a meadow—a smear of grass, cloudlike trees, perfectly conical mountains, the sun with vacuous grin in the sky.

"I'm an attorney," Jason had said. He was able now to shut his eyes without fear of tumbling back into the dream, where the river's current had parted around the bodies of wading figures so small and distant that he was unable to warn them of an invisible danger, a curse. His fingers glided through darkness to Maddy's lips, which were moist and warm, and with a sharp intake of breath her body shuddered and reconfigured itself into an unknown shape that he might have conformed his own to if he weren't so immobilized by the lingering dread of the dream.

The man he talked to at the party had received the news of Jason's occupation with a grimace that portended a polemic on ethics and social responsibility, and Jason had excused himself ungracefully to go in search of Maddy. Someone had put Aretha Franklin on the stereo and couples had begun to stir and Jason had wanted to dance with Maddy, to abandon himself to the pure physical thrill of loudness and motion. "Sweetheart," he had said, intruding into a circle that looked alert and expectant, "are you going to sit and talk all night?" He had bent with the idea of nuzzling her, but when he gathered her hair in his fingers she shook it free and said, "Shhh! I want to hear this."

They were crossing the river under the noses of the army. The father had the baby in his arms . . .

Sleep seemed an idea too arcane for Jason's intellect to grasp. He tried to let his mind drift, but instead of the oblivion he sought he saw his office, in what seemed excessive detail—the swirls in the plaster above the panel wainscot, the shape of the molding between the plaster and the paneling, the angle at which his desk sat in the room and its proximity to the table upon which he spread his various papers, the color of his telephone, the date on his calendar. From his office window he could see much of the city, and it was this view that Maddy had remarked upon in the car on the way home from the party, this view of the city that spread out from his feet. Because he could stand at his window and look out over the city, she had asserted, he believed that he knew what was going on inside the houses, in the buildings and the cars: what was being said, what was being thought. He had excused her incoherence on the fact that she had drunk at least three glasses of wine, but the umbrage she had taken was so disproportionate that he was forced, now, to stand at the window and look across the city bathed in a light that wasn't morning or midday or afternoon, but pale and ghostly like the light that exposed the wading figures in the dream, and consider the sense of what she said.

The baby began to cry and the father couldn't hush it.

There were six. Himself, Maddy, another lawyer he had met on a case involving a tenant's dispute with a landlord, the lawyer's wife, a man with short white hair who nodded his head in vigorous agreement with everything said, and a woman with whom Maddy was apparently friends, although Jason had never met her. The lawyer's wife was speaking. When Jason first saw her she had seemed sullen, her skin bloodless, as if she weren't entirely alive, but in the circle her voice and demeanor were so vivid that the attention of the others was a kind of awe. She leaned forward from the sofa where she sat between Maddy and the white-haired man, speaking softly, opening her hands as if the story had shape and weight, was both an offering and a danger that she would attempt to protect them from.

If the soldiers heard the baby, they would be discovered and probably killed.

"It takes guts to call yourself a liberal nowadays," the man he had been talking to had said, apropos of Jason's statement that people who believe world events are determined by multinational corporate conspiracies probably also believe in elves and Santa Claus. "What do you believe in, Jason?" Maddy had asked him on the way home in the car, her voice distant and strained, as if she had already reached a conclusion. "Is this a rhetorical question?" Jason had asked, on guard in an almost rote and professional way against being put on the defensive. He imagined briefly that each tasteless, moronic joke about lawyers that periodically made the rounds had become a truth, a part of her canon. He often told

Maddy these jokes when he heard them, even though she was never very amused, and it occurred to him that this self-deprecation might not have appeared to her as humility, but as arrogance, a self-righteousness in the face of a larger, public perception.

"This is a true story," the lawyer's wife had said, and Jason guessed that at that moment, his eyes drawn to the glass of wine in her hand, he had decided that the story would prove to be apocryphal. The tilt of her glass, which contained the red wine that he had tasted and judged to be inferior, made him suspect that she was slightly drunk and prone to histrionics. Feeling suddenly tense, he had watched the wine come dangerously near the slanted rim of her glass; he was about to warn her when she suddenly set the glass on the coffee table and opened her palms and stretched her arms as if to encompass something.

They couldn't take the chance of being discovered, so the father held the baby under the water . . .

Fully awake, dismayed by the solitude in which he found himself, Jason groped for Maddy. She slept on her side, back to him, and he pushed his fingers into the flesh alongside her spine, imagining that the tension in her body was flowing away, that she was softening, yielding. He kissed the hollow beneath her shoulder blade and tried to turn her toward him, but she resisted. His hand curled over her breast and she murmured, "No, Jason."

Jason stared at the ceiling, at the softly focused image of a ladder cast by the window blind. The third woman, Maddy's friend, had looked directly at him and said, "A woman could never drown her own child." He got out of bed, put on his robe, and moved through the silent house to the kitchen. He supposed that she was right. The father was a man, with a mind able to encompass larger questions, to process information critical to everyone's survival, while the woman's instinct is to preserve the life of her child, at all costs, at any cost. She had said it twice, in a flat, unemotional tone, a simple fact. "A woman could never drown her own child."

He heated a cup of milk and gazed at the newspaper which lay on the table where he had read it that morning, the headlines a litany of disasters, some of them natural, some man-made, a few enormous, others so personal that he wondered why he should care. To the man at the party, Jason had stated his belief that the majority of people in the world are satisfied, disinterested in change, in fomenting revolutions. He had eventually persuaded Maddy to dance, observing that she allowed herself to have fun despite the lugubrious presence of those like the man who had stared at Jason as if he were profoundly stupid, or insane, and the woman who related the story, and the others who with enthusiastic outrage believed it, all of them unable to analyze—people whose attention was seized by the unchallenged assertions of voices that admitted no doubt, that required only agreement.

"You think you know," she had said. Leaving, dispensing good-byes, she had seemed in a state of excitement, but in the car she was pensive. "Doesn't it disturb you, Jason?" she had said, her feet drawn up to the edge of the seat, her arms hugging her knees, her face concealed by her hair. "Aren't you bothered?" Her voice was thickened and ripe, the words like fruit on her lips, but in some contradictory way also brittle, as if charred by heat or fire.

Jason sipped the milk, recalling details of this scene, the red glow of the stoplight under which they sat, the catch in the idling motor, an imperfection that seemed irrationally personal, in the nature of an affront. "You already know that I agree with you," he said, impatient with a childish facet of her personality. He tried to view his superior ability to reason, to see all sides of an issue in a cool and logical manner, as merely a difference and not a dissonance, a divide. "We're making matters worse in those places. We're probably on the wrong side. But using apocryphal stories to support your position is just plain propaganda, the same thing you accuse the government of."

"Apocryphal stories?" Her voice was flat and low and yet imperfectly controlled, tinged with hysteria.

"The thing about the baby. The people crossing the river."

"You don't believe it?"

"No." Jason stopped himself from saying, Of course not. "Haven't you heard it before?"

"Before?" She would irritate him into saying something he would later regret, and perhaps have to apologize for. He was ready and willing to apologize for real failings, but resented any pressure to merely appease her. He was disappointed, he realized, in the naivete that had once amused and charmed him.

"There's the same sort of story about Jews who were hiding from the Nazis. These soldiers were searching right outside, so when a baby started to cry the father smothered it with his coat so they wouldn't be discovered. It's an apocryphal story."

"Why?"

"Maddy." The light had turned and he wanted to say, Shhh, so that he could listen for roughness, for a lag in the acceleration that would require him to take the car, which was nearly new, back to the dealer and demand that it be made perfect. Instead, he looked at her, seeing only the slash of hair across her face as if to deliberately conceal her expression. "An apocryphal story," he began, aware of some fragility in the situation, "is a story . . ."

"I know what apocryphal means, Jason."

"Well, when the same story keeps popping up in different situations, doesn't it tell you something?"

"What?"

"What? Do you really not understand, Maddy?"

"I understand that, for whatever reason, you don't believe it, Jason."

"I don't believe it because it's too easy, Maddy. I concede that it could have happened. There may have been an actual incident somewhere, sometime. The problem is that it's a perfect story for propaganda because it involves these powerful emotions, and therefore people can't resist the temptation to use it over and over, for their own reasons."

"You've got it figured out, haven't you?" she said, in a voice that led him to believe she had conceded, if not gracefully, then in fact.

"It's just that this story fits with your view of how things are, so you assume it really happened," he said. "You want it to be true."

"Jason, you're really a jerk," she said, with a sharp little intake of breath, as if she had shocked herself by use of this epithet. "Do you have any idea what it's like?"

"Emotion just leads to demagoguery," Jason said, hearing his voice curl toward inaudibility, burnt by her insult. "I just don't believe in using it that way."

What do you believe in, Jason? He turned the pages of the newspaper, looking for something he hadn't already read, and words swam before his eyes like the sounds of the night, too disembodied and distant to involve him. I believe in truth, he said to himself. In logic. In the rational part of the mind. What other defense is there against chaos, anarchy? He briefly closed his eyes and saw familiar faces—a judge, another attorney, a jury to which he would deliver a final argument in less than forty-eight hours. In the hush of the courtroom he saw the face of his client, the plaintiff, and then the face of the defendant, a man who had surely provoked suspicion, not because he was an immigrant who spoke with an accent but because of an obviously devious and insincere manner, a mixture of slyness and naivete so broad and obvious as to strain credulity. "Before you came to this country," the attorney had asked the defendant, "did you ever sign a contract? Did you ever see one?" This defendant, Jason realized, with a stab of unease, was from the same part of the world as the apocryphal band of guerillas, the river in his dream, the father and the baby, the soldiers.

He attempted to read an article in the entertainment section, but his mind wandered back to the jury, which, instead of faces he believed to be sympathetic, was for a moment composed of Maddy and her friends, the lawyer's wife, the gray-haired man, the man he had talked to, with his unequivocal analysis of the world situation. Of course, a lawyer's wife would never have been impaneled in the first place, but the others—what expression, what manner, what tone might have revealed their sympathies? What question that he had failed to ask?

He shut his eyes in an effort to erase the image of people with minds completely closed, stuffed with preconceived ideas. He listened to his own voice in patient explication of what appeared on the surface to be convoluted, unclear. The defendant, despite a pose as a man simply trying to move up the ladder as immigrants have always done, uncertain of customs, laws, regulations, was really a venal man who had accumulated a great deal of money and property through shrewd but ethically questionable dealings. Jason would emphasize this fact without seeming to be on a mission of persecution, or biased in any way, but he realized that Maddy and her friends might see all of these people as victims simply because of the place in which they were born.

The defendant's attorney had already attempted to exploit the fact that his client grew up in an impoverished country full of strife and hardship, and could be expected to dwell upon this irrelevancy in his final argument, but Jason could not imagine, given the preponderance of evidence in his client's favor, that the jury could find for the defendant. "Jurors allow themselves to be swayed by emotion only when the facts haven't been presented clearly enough," he had said a number of times. Some of his colleagues considered this belief naive, even humorous, but Jason told himself that he was right, that he had reached the correct conclusion, that he could forget about Maddy's friends and the story and the river, that he could return to bed and sleep and awake in the morning content and assured that truth and logic would prevail.

You don't understand, Jason.

He slept late, watched a football game on TV, and took a walk with Maddy, who seemed herself again, cheerful, her mind engaged by everyday matters. As he left the house on Monday morning he said, "I love you," and gave her a sincerely passionate kiss. He felt pleased and expectant. His speech to the jury seemed a gift that he would unwrap to the delight of everyone but the defendant and his attorney, but when he saw these two leaning casually against a rail in the courthouse rotunda, looking relaxed, almost jocular, the story told by the woman at the party returned to his mind with a pang of unsettling doubt. The defendant grinned and nodded at Jason, a breach of propriety that caused him to feel unreasonably annoyed. He saw another attorney he knew, a man he played racquetball with, and after a desultory exchange of greetings he asked the man if he had ever heard a story such as the one about the people crossing the river.

"I did, yeah. It was in Vietnam, I think, right after the Americans left and the Viet Cong were running amuck. These people were hiding in a tunnel . . ." The man offered to buy Jason coffee but Jason said no, he wanted to go over his argument a final time. He felt in some way vindicated, and he both began and concluded his appeal to the jury with a sincere expression of his confidence in their ability to put aside emotion and employ their minds in a rational analysis of the facts. He recalled for them the fact that the defendant, in a display of theatrical absurdity on the witness stand, had produced actual tears. "But how does this change the facts that you have heard?" he said. They appeared to listen attentively and when Jason sat down he felt immodestly gratified. He was absolutely certain, at that moment, that he had prevailed.

The opposing counsel's turn, predictably, was calculated to obscure the very facts that Jason had so carefully presented, and as the jury filed out of the courtroom the defendant again looked at him and smiled, causing him to wonder once more if he could have been mistaken, if the vast majority of people might be impervious to logical appeals, might believe no matter what in conspiracy theories, in the comic-book simplicity of televised ideas, in apocryphal stories. After all, Maddy could weep at the thought of the imaginary child held under the water by its father, even though Jason had tried to teach her how to think, to judge, to read between the lines, to analyze.

He had lunch with the attorney he had spoken to in the morning, and they talked of winter and skiing, of a strange decision handed down by the court of appeals, and of a sports car the man was thinking of buying, and when Jason returned to the courthouse he felt relaxed and assured once again. The jurors did not reenter the courtroom, however, until late in the afternoon, and when the foreman told the judge that they had not yet reached a decision, Jason's confidence sank like a stone through layers of apparent self-delusion—the length of their deliberation almost surely meant that they would find for the defendant. He felt adrift, askew. He thought he saw the defendant wink at him, and he felt a rush of turgid anger. In the rotunda he saw the defendant's attorney smoking and talking to a woman from the district attorney's office whom he recognized as one of several lawyers who had recently interviewed for a position with Jason's firm. The woman was young and intense in a way that Jason found appealing, although he didn't recall her name, didn't remember ever having spoken to her. He wanted to call Maddy and tell her that he would be late, solicit from her some sympathy, but instead he approached the man and the woman.

"Congratulations," he said, attempting to affect a tone of un-concern. "I figured an hour and I've got it nailed, two hours I've still got a chance, any more and I'm dead in the water."

"Who knows?" the defendant's attorney said, with throaty mirth. "They may have just wanted dinner on the county." He winked at the woman, who was one of those women who seemed ambitious, and in some manner of speech and bearing, dissatisfied. The thought that she might find him useful rose like a glimmer of light in Jason's mind, and even as he found the idea undignified he felt a small shiver of anticipation that led him to agree when the defendant's attorney invited them to the bar across the street for a drink, although he drank infrequently and found the loud and smoky atmosphere of such places to be somehow frozen in the past. The place was filled with a crowd of attorneys and others involved in the business of the courts, and Jason ordered a scotch on the rocks, despite the fact that he almost never drank anything other than wine or an occasional beer. The defendant's attorney, a florid man who looked at home in the noise and the dusky, grainy light, a drink in one hand and cigarette in the other, engaged in jocular conversation with a younger man and the woman from the district attorney's office while Jason allowed various vague and shapeless fantasies to drift through his mind. The passage of time seemed arrested. He asked the woman her name. At some point he noticed that her glass was empty and with an uncharacteristic lack of reflection he asked if he could get her another.

Jason, you're really a jerk. He suddenly felt tired—of logic, of analysis, of action reasoned, ethical, right. He sat, breathing the poisonous air, and heard himself laugh at a story told by the man who had been his adversary for the past two weeks, an adversary who had seemed in contrast to Jason poorly prepared, ignorant of many points of law, and if not unprofessional, at least careless and seemingly unconcerned in matters of conduct and appearance. The morning the trial was to begin the man had proposed a settlement, a practical if not legal admission of guilt that the jury would unfortunately not be allowed to consider, and Jason recalled how he had countered with what he knew to be an untenable deal, and how the man had squinted at him, saying nothing, making him feel, just for a second, the same twinge of fear he had felt when the dark-faced defendant had grinned at him in the courthouse.

Now he was almost giddy with laughter at the attorney's story, which had to do with the sexual indiscretions of a certain judge. He got himself another drink. The liquor, the atmosphere, the subject seemed to have charged the air, and when the man excused himself with a "See you later for the hanging," Jason laughed once more, feeling already intoxicated, incapable of knowing whether the remark had been directed at him or the others. The woman looked at him with a steady gaze, and a fantasy of startling detail rolled through his mind.

"He took me to the cleaners," Jason said, a clot of emotion just beneath the unfamiliar layer of intoxication. He gazed at the woman's thin-lipped mouth that was bent in a crooked, ironical smile.

"He's brilliant," she said. The young man with them, whose face had turned hazy, touched her arm and said something Jason didn't catch. He disappeared. Jason felt a pressure in his chest. "He beat me in this rape case," she went on. "He had the jury in the palm of his hand. It was amazing."

Her utterance of the word "rape" excited Jason in some way that he wasn't willing or able to reflect upon. All the logistics of adultery tumbled through his mind in a rush, and instead of trying to banish this idea or even organize the chaos of imagined detail he did nothing.

"We should have settled," Jason said, taking a drink of the scotch that had burned like acid in his throat but now turned suddenly smooth and entirely potable.

"So now there's this guy," she said matter-of-factly, "who has probably raped a dozen women, maybe more, out there on the streets somewhere."

"Looking for a victim," Jason agreed, suddenly wanting to change the subject but unable to select a topic from the feverish matter in his head.

"It's the system," she said, in a flat, deliberate voice. "The fact that he raped her and threatened to kill her carries less weight than the fact that she was doing drugs and had slept around with a lot of guys and got into the car with him voluntarily and therefore she asked for what she got even if all she wanted was to smoke some crack and get high and forget for a couple of minutes the awful, fucked-up life she's had."

"I'm sorry" was all that Jason could think of to say. He was both shocked and titillated by her use of the obscenity, although it was so commonplace he didn't know why he should be. He looked into her face for a sign of emotion, but her mouth and eyes remained impassive. Smoke burned in his own eyes and he turned his head to cough. He felt that he was in a foreign country, possibly lost. She lifted her glass and the bend of her long, painted fingers seemed in the nature of an invitation. She was one of those women languishing in the district attorney's office, Jason knew, waiting for an offer from one of the firms like his own that already had enough women. Hanging out in the bar, where she might meet someone useful. He wondered if she knew who he worked for. The thought made him feel a little sleazy, and at the same time emboldened. He asked her if she wanted another drink.

"What do you want?" she asked, in a toneless voice.

"What do you mean?" he said, his mind muddled by the liquor.

"Do you want to sleep with me?"

He hesitated, then said "Yes," unable to concoct a wittier, more circumspect alternative. An electric shock of anticipation ran up his spine.

"Why?" she said. Jason realized that he was inebriated, scarcely in command of his wits, while she was utterly sober.

He said, "Because you're attractive." On some primal level he recognized the insufficiency of this answer. "Because I'm lonely," he added, feeling a sudden alarming pressure behind his eyes, and a cold, invisible shower of dismay.

"Are you married?" She seemed prepared to keep up this interrogation indefinitely.

"Yes."

"Separated?"

"No."

"What's her name?"

Jason started to say Maddy but without knowing why he caught himself and said, "Maria."

"Maria?" She repeated the name as if it were a fact of doubtful authenticity uttered by a hostile witness. "Well, why don't you go home to Maria or whatever her name is and forget about sleeping with me? I would never sleep with a man I didn't know a whole lot better than I know you. I have my faults, Jack, or whatever your name is, but I'm not stupid enough to get it on with a stranger, not even a married one out looking for a thrill."

"Jason," said Jason, feeling entirely stupid.

"Good-bye, Jason," she said. "Good night. You're not a part of my life." As he watched with a combination of fascination and horror similar to that which he had felt the first time he examined a set of accident-scene photographs, she stubbed out her cigarette, delved into her purse and took out a stick of gum which she folded into her mouth, turned without a glance at Jason, and made her way out of the smoky, din-filled room.

The jury didn't find for the defendant, but reported that it was hopelessly deadlocked. The judge took under advisement a motion by the defendant's attorney to dismiss the action. The man clapped Jason on the back in the courthouse rotunda and invited him to cross the street for another drink. Jason declined, feeling hungry, still intoxicated, but in a dull, depressive way. The man gave Jason another of the insinuative winks. "Get anywhere?" he wanted to know. "She's a sharp little number, eh?"

"I'm happily married," Jason said glumly.

"Damn," said the man with a guffaw. "So am I. So am I. What is the relevance, counselor?"

Jason decided to call Maddy. He had gotten aspirin from the bailiff, but a headache persisted, a sharp blade of pain above and behind his eyes. In the men's room at the courthouse he had examined the eyes, which were red, watery advertisements of his foolish, ungallant behavior.

"Let's go out for dinner," he said. He named a place, an architecturally elegant restaurant that he had recently been to for lunch with an important client. "I'll call and see if we can get a table."

"It's late, Jason," she said. "Its a weeknight."

"Maddy," he said, a fetal idea beginning to squirm in his mind. "There's something I want to talk about." The unfulfilled encounter with the woman had now suffused him with a passionate desire for his wife. He began to feel better. He decided to ignore the fact that she sounded unhappy.

They were given a table that he normally might have refused, and the clamor of comings and goings banished the sense of intimacy he had imagined. He had decided, leaving the courthouse, to bring up with Maddy the subject of children. He had decided that it was time for her to get pregnant, to quit the job that she didn't find entirely fulfilling anyway, to get started on raising the family that both of them wanted. He looked at her with fond, possessive warmth.

"Darling," he said finally, as they waited for coffee. "There's something I want to tell you."

"I feel guilty," Maddy said. She had been quiet, but Jason had been too involved with his own agenda to infer anything specific about her mood.

"Guilty?"

"About spending all this money on food when people are going hungry. It's a little obscene."

"Maddy." He resisted saying the obvious. He had met her in college, and he thought with disappointment that she had never grown out of her youthful propensity to oversimplify, to see a situation in the terms of a slogan, to embrace clichés as if they were fresh and incisive.

"Our whole life-style, Jason," she went on, a fork poised in her hand above her dessert, as if it were a menace that she meant to stab and kill. "There's something wrong with it."

"What's wrong with it?" Jason controlled an anger that flared up at the realization that this occasion so haphazardly planned had predictably gone awry. She had managed, as she often did, he realized, to center herself in the picture, to hog the stage. He felt like getting up and walking out, not even saying good-bye, letting her figure out how to get home. With a start he saw a picture of himself, suitcase in hand, leaving the house that had moments before glowed with the promise of a future entirely sublime. He thought, with a mixture of fascination and disgust, of the woman from the district attorney's office. He looked at Maddy, feeling betrayed. The same emotion he had felt in one of the very first cases he had tried, when a witness had volunteered a fact that he had been cautioned over and over not to reveal, giving Jason the sense that everything so carefully planned and constructed, his life itself, had shaken and crumbled.

"You're talking like a child, Maddy," Jason said. "You want to feel noble, live on the street, eat out of dumpsters?"

"You know very well that's not what I want, Jason." She abruptly pushed her plate away, as if the sight repelled her. "Why can't you ever see my point? Why do you have to disparage everything I think?"

"I don't," he said, with absolute belief, "disparage everything you think." He took a breath, and a hint of judicious equanimity began to soften his anger. "I can understand feeling guilty. I just don't happen to want to go around flailing myself."

Without looking at him, in a voice almost too low to be heard above the clamor of enjoyment around them, she said, "You don't understand."

You think you know. You think you know.

They sat in silence, Jason feeling glum, not wanting to think any further about the subject of children, of women, of sex. He wanted only to sleep. Finally she said, "Jason?"

"What?" He realized that he didn't want to hear, he recognized the tone.

"I want to let Maria go." She gave him what he interpreted as a look of desire for approval.

"Why? I thought you liked her. I thought she was doing a good job."

"She's wonderful," Maddy said, in a sad, resigned tone. "She cleans things that don't even need cleaning. It's just that I feel funny . . ."

"No, Maddy. Not this again." The turgid desire to leave made Jason feel dangerously explosive. "Don't bring up this crap again. I don't want to hear it."

"It bothers me, Jason!" She almost shrieked, her face twisted.

Jason blinked and took a breath. "You're giving her a job," he said. "You're helping to support her family. If you look at everything the way you're looking at it, everybody is exploiting somebody else. What's got into you anyway?"

He thought it had been settled, when they first hired Maria; he thought that Maddy had gotten over feeling guilty about having what she called a servant and all that the situation implied about class and economics. "Be reasonable," he had said then, with considerably more patience than he felt now. "You're not going to improve things by refusing to give work to someone who wants it." He had suggested, of his own volition, that they pay her a little more than the going rate, not because they had to in order to keep her, but because they could afford it. "We shouldn't have what amounts to a little more luxury at somebody else's expense," he had said.

"Maddy," he said carefully, "I want you to stop taking your pills."

"What?" She looked startled.

"I want to start a family. There's no reason to wait any longer. And you'll need Maria."

"Jason," she said, her voice measuring the two syllables, as if the name were unfamiliar, as if she had uttered it for the very first time.

He reached out and squeezed her arm, then on impulse rose and leaned across the table and kissed her slightly parted lips. Her wide brown eyes looked watery, about to overflow.

Finally she said, "Where did you go?"

"What?" He suddenly tasted the scotch, the sourness in his throat.

"There's cigarette smoke. And something funny on your breath."

"Maddy," he sighed, wearily. He felt defensive, afraid, needing to take care. "I had a drink while the jury was out." As he gazed at her unhappy face he suddenly felt a reckless desire to tell the absolute truth, to shake her out of her lugubrious state into a rage of jealousy. "With a woman from the district attorney's office," he said. "She's looking for a job with the firm."

"How many women in the firm?" Maddy wanted to know, in a neutral voice that somehow disappointed him.

"There are seven women and twenty-one men," he said. "You already knew that."

"I didn't," she said, with a hint of a childish pout on her lips.

"You did," said Jason. "Or you forgot."

"The other day I read that almost 50 percent of the people entering law school now are women," said Maddy. "Where do they go?"

"Government," Jason said, feeling weary once more. She wanted to start an argument, an argument that he would be compelled to take up and pursue to a conclusion. "There are a lot of women in the district attorney's office. In the federal agencies."

"Why not in private firms?"

"What is this, Maddy?" Jason rubbed his eyes, which made them burn. "Some feminist issue you feel like you've got to pursue right now, when I'm tired, when I'm depressed because I've lost a case that everybody thinks I should have won, when I just want to go home and relax and read or watch TV or do anything other than argue the issues of the world? Maddy, there's something wrong."

"What's wrong?" Her eyes got bigger.

"With us." He was suddenly, overwhelmingly thirsty. He drank his coffee, swallowing with some difficulty. "You've gotten this political slant on everything. It's coming between us, Maddy."

"I can't help it, Jason." She looked so forlorn that he began to feel sorry for her. "All this stuff going on in the world. How can you ignore it?"

"It started with that damn story of the river," Jason said, with waning confidence in his own mental acuity.

"You don't believe it," she said, sullenly.

"No. Besides . . ."

"It doesn't matter if it happened or not," Maddy said. "Can't you understand? All you think is important is whether or not something can be proven. Then when you decide, you can't rest until everybody else agrees with you. It's like a case you've got to win, Jason. But don't you understand? What's important is that people are living under conditions that force them to do terrible, dreadful things. Whether one thing really happened in exactly a certain manner isn't the issue, Jason. Maybe for you in your lawsuits and trials it is, but not in the real world."

Jason was unable to answer; they fell silent. He stared at the numbers on the undoubtedly unconscionable check. He was transported in his mind to his office where he stood looking at the city below, feeling that he had failed, that he had lost, not only with the jury but with Maddy and his client and his colleagues and the woman from the district attorney's office, whose opinion of people like him, whatever it was exactly, had been confirmed. As he stared at the buildings that spread and gradually disappeared into a haze, he saw the river once more as it had been in the dream, languid and snakelike. He saw a band of people in the river—adults, old people, teenagers, children. He saw a woman who looked like

Maria among them. "The country I come from," said the defendant in the trial, "life is very hard and many members of my family have died." Jason had said to the jury, "This man may have been miserable, poor, starving. His wife or his mother or his son or daughter may have been killed. There have been no facts presented to us about this, and for good reason. Such facts, even if they exist, are not relevant. In this country we do not say to a murderer: you can go free because you had an unhappy childhood. We do not say to a rapist: we will forget your crime because you came from a broken home. We do not say to a thief: you don't have to worry about going to jail because we know that you lost one of your parents. Everyone, regardless of his or her background, regardless of what traumas he or she may have suffered, everyone has the same opportunity and obligation to know and obey the laws that were written to apply to everyone, equally, without distinction of race, of religion, of economic status, of the conditions under which they grew up." The words trailed off, becoming irrelevant.

The light on the river was gray as dusk, and at the head of the band of people around which thick, muddy water eddied was the man with the baby. Jason lifted his head slightly and saw, at the edge of the haze, men in fatigues and rifles. He shut his eyes and saw Maddy, just for a second; she was walking away from him, and just at the moment she disappeared he heard her say, *You think you understand, Jason, you think you know.*

Space and Light

On his way to the Livingston house to mediate a dispute between Mrs. Livingston and the masons laying brick for the garden patio, Paul Westerly made a detour to look at a house designed by a man whose career had begun, one summer fifteen years before, as a draftsman in Paul's office. The house, on the side of a hill with a view of the ocean through a cluster of eucalyptus trees, was under construction, and as Paul made his way past mounds of dirt and scraps of lumber and lengths of plumbing pipe, a strange sensation overtook him, a feeling of being exposed to some unstated danger, of needing to hurry, to get out of the light. He ducked beneath a scaffold upon which a pair of workmen stood, nailing a curved strip of siding with a pneumatic gun, and as he straightened in the deeply shadowed entry one of the workmen cried, "I quit!" and the other unloosed a torrent of loud and profane abuse that felt to Paul—for a brief, irrational moment—to be aimed directly at him.

He stood in a large, irregular room whose ceiling ascended to the peak of the roof. The walls were not yet covered and pink blankets of insulation imparted to the interior a rosy, slightly ethereal glow. He could not immediately grasp the function of the various planes into which the space was broken, but he could imagine the drama of light and shadow that would play out in the room. That would be Jack, who had once declared himself the enemy of understatement, who had pronounced exaggeration to be a valid principle of design. The sky, enervated by a leaden haze, constituted most of the view through a high wall of windows, and Paul overcame an urge to inspect the glazing, to uncover defects and mistakes. He listened to the rapid, successive reports of the gun and the sudden whir of an air compressor. So the man on the scaffold wasn't quitting after all. He felt relieved, as if a disaster in which he was somehow implicated had been averted.

"Paul! Good to see you. Come in, come in. What do you think?" Dressed entirely in beige, with the exception of a red scarf loosely knotted, Jack stood above a set of blueprints unfurled upon a makeshift table in a room that appeared to be the kitchen. His clothes looked rumpled in a deliberate way. The two shook hands.

"I'll take a quick look around, Jack. Don't let me interrupt."

"No, no, no. I'll show you everything." Jack grinned disarmingly. "How is everybody? Suzanne. Your daughter."

"Well. Busy."

"You look great, Paul." Jack patted his modestly ample stomach in a gesture that looked to Paul more affectionate than rueful. "Still jogging? Eating health food?"

"Yes," said Paul, feeling again the need to find a space that was dark, enclosed, something that in this house he guessed would not exist. He followed Jack's plump finger through a chaos of lines on the blueprint.

"The contractor says this can't be done." Somewhere above their heads a loud scraping commenced—Paul looked up but Jack ignored it. His finger impaled a detail dense with arrows and numbers. "You know how these guys think. If only the damned architect would stay out of the picture, let them change whatever's different. Whatever they haven't seen before."

"It goes with the territory," said Paul, trying to sound more affable than he felt. He could still recall the first piece of design he had entrusted to Jack, how sloppy and inattentive to matters of construction it had turned out to be. He put on his glasses and began to consider solutions to Jack's problem while in the background Jack's voice outlined in a spirited tone his troubles with the plumbers and electricians.

"Look," Paul said. "If you shift this window about six inches..."
He sketched his idea, wondering if this was the reason that Jack called him out of the blue and invited him to see the house. Jack, he imagined, believed in a world divided between those blessed with imagination and those unable to conceive of how to build what he had designed. He had seen Jack's face, sober and reflective, inside a recent issue of an important magazine. He wondered, momentarily, if this client had given Jack carte blanche.

They stood outside and the winter sunlight, diffused by the haze, made Paul think suddenly of death, his own, even though his health was fine and he'd just turned fifty. The house that shimmered deep within the fender of a Jaguar he assumed to be Jack's had startled Paul and, in some way he failed to understand, disoriented him. He conceded, without envy or enthusiasm, the possibility that Jack was a genius. He looked away from the Jaguar to his own car, a Peugeot, a car he had once admired but that suddenly seemed insipid, of no more consequence than a Toyota.

"I can't afford it," Jack was saying. "You wouldn't believe what it costs. Just the license and insurance. I don't know what I was doing."

Paul ignored the disingenuousness. He said, "I think you're doing important work, Jack."

"I'm getting a lot of commissions." Jack rummaged in a pocket and produced a ring of keys. "More than I can handle. I was wondering..."

As Jack's voice trailed off they both watched the progress of a boatlike leaf being prodded along the gutter by a breeze. Paul thought of Mrs. Livingston, her long, annoyed face.

"If I want clients that you've rejected?"

"No, no. That's not what I mean, Paul."

Mrs. Livingston would by now have discovered that instead of the running bond at the far edge of the patio she would prefer the brick to be laid in herringbone. The leaf skidded under the Jaguar and Paul said, "What makes you think I'm in need of charity?"

"For God's sake, Paul." Jack lifted his chin to give his scarf a second turn. "If it wasn't for you, where would I be? I'm serious. When I worked for you my head was going in twenty different directions. Remember when I wanted to hop a freighter for South America?"

Paul remembered no such thing, but instead of saying so he looked at his watch and saw that he would be late. He felt tension, a pressure to get into his car.

"Sorry," said Jack. "I didn't mean to offend you."

"Forget it."

"Let's get together." Jack unlocked the door of the Jaguar and eased his bulk into the seat. "The four of us. I mean it."

Paul nodded. They shook hands and then the Jaguar spurted away from the curb, turned the corner, and disappeared. Paul had read in the magazine an article written by Jack and had found it incomprehensible. He had fired Jack. Or if he had not fired Jack, he had at least urged him to seek some other sort of work, and with this recollection came a sensation of dread, like a column of insects, moving up his spine.

He let himself into his office through the rear, where he kept a small workshop and racks filled with various materials he intended someday to experiment with. It was eleven-thirty. His assistant, Barb, had not expected him until after lunch and now she attempted to busy herself by moving paper about the disorganized surface of her drafting table. She followed him to his desk and said without enthusiasm that Mrs. Livingston had called twice, wanting to know why he hadn't come.

"What did you tell her?"

He knew this to be unfair—she would assume that she had made a mistake, said the wrong thing. Her face wore its usual melancholy expression, a reflection, he knew, of something askew in her marriage, something depressingly common that he wanted to know as little as possible about.

"I didn't get to Mrs. Livingston's. I had other things to do."

"She sounded upset."

"Mrs. Livingston always sounds upset. It's her normal state."

Barb stared glumly at Paul. "What do I tell her if she calls again? I mean, I'm sure she's going to."

Paul gazed at his desktop, which was perfectly neat and organized. He raised his eyes to his drafting table, angled in a corner so that the window light would fall upon it in the most propitious manner. A single sheet containing the first lines of a drawing of the gazebo for Mrs. Livingston's garden was taped to the table. She had shown him the gazebo she wanted in a magazine, a magazine full of houses choked with decoration, rooms through which it would be difficult to move without bumping into furniture, antiques, objets d'art. He turned his gaze to Barb. Her expression was uncertain and defensive.

"I'm going home," he said, repressing the urge to lie and add that he was feeling ill. He picked up the single pen on his desktop and dropped it into a drawer. His mind seemed to stutter, then grip the root of an idea. "I'll write you a check." He retrieved the pen and brought from another drawer his checkbook. As he wrote her name he observed that his hand was highly legible, even florid. He felt briefly that herein might lie a clue, some sort of explication.

"I don't understand," said Barb. The quaver in her voice was so pronounced that he began to imagine an embarrassing scene. "I mean, am I fired?"

A shadow drifted into the plane of the translucent window, then moved slowly on. The street had never undergone the renaissance that realtors had predicted and promoted, and there was always the fear of someone bent upon burglary, or assault. He had moved to the office three years before, when a partnership with two other architects had dissolved. Without looking up he could see the exact contours of a water stain on the ceiling. He desperately hoped that Barb would not begin to cry.

"I'm closing the office." He clapped the checkbook shut as if to demonstrate the reality of this act. "I'm sorry. I know it's sudden. This is last week's pay plus another two. That's fair, I think. If you don't think so, I'll give you more."

He felt a little giddy. He wadded the check and reopened the checkbook. "I'll pay you for a month. That'll give you plenty of time to find something. Maybe you could take a trip, relax."

Her motion in accepting the check was wooden, uncomprehending.

The telephone rang. It was Mrs. Livingston. He listened, looking at Barb, who didn't examine the check but kept staring at Paul's desk, as if waiting for its surface to speak up with an explanation. Finally Paul said, "Mrs. Livingston, you're an idiot," and hung up the telephone. He said it for the benefit of Barb, with the foolish expectation that it would make her laugh, but of course it didn't. He turned off the lights and lowered the thermostat. He told her to get her things and waited while she silently and mechanically gathered her pencils, rulers, erasers, squares, a small framed picture of herself and her husband in happier times. He helped her with her coat and walked her to her car. He leaned over the open door and said, "Good-bye. Good luck."

She stared up at him with eyes that in the daylight looked bruised and vulnerable. "I don't understand," she said gravely. "I think you're acting crazy."

On his way home he stopped at a florist's and bought a half-dozen roses, flirting very casually with the woman who waited on him, then went into a liquor store and spent twenty minutes selecting a bottle of wine. Suzanne did not appear surprised when he gave her the roses, nor when he told her midway through dinner that he wanted to build a studio onto the rear of the house, on the corner opposite the lanai, where there would be plenty of morning light. He had been prepared to argue but she allowed him to go on without interruption, explaining that he would let the lease on his office expire and work out of the studio—he didn't need a secretary, draftspersons, the various trappings of the profession. He wouldn't be able to accept as many commissions, but on the other hand he wouldn't feel compelled to take on work that didn't interest him. The fact that her income exceeded his no longer caused him any anxiety. Their daughter, in college and, like her parents, practical and levelheaded, would soon be a burden no longer, financial or otherwise.

She's listening, Paul thought, the way she must listen to a witness in one of her trials, with utter patience, waiting for an inevitable slip, an incriminating word or phrase. He heard his voice trail off and then she spoke, in a cool and neutral tone. It was not in character, she thought, for him to act so impulsively, but she had no objection to his plan. He lifted his glass, deciding that the wine he bought for this occasion was inferior, despite its inflated price. Disappointed, he gazed at the wall beyond his wife's head and saw a faint crack between the ceiling and crown molding widen, then narrow. She seemed far away, across a landscape out of which a grainy mist arose. He watched her eat. Her fork dipped to her plate, ascended to her mouth. She's getting fat, he thought. Not really fat, but—what was the euphemism? Mature. He smiled, very slightly.

"Schmidt lied through his teeth today," she said. "He's the auditor who saw the ledgers before they conveniently disappeared." She sipped her wine and he carefully watched but couldn't detect on her face any expression of distaste. He began to feel relieved.

"I tried to catch him but he wouldn't take the bait. I only hope the jury gets the impression that he's not the paragon he pretends to be."

"I saw Jack Dow today," said Paul.

"You did?" Her tone did not convey the message that this information signified something. "How is Jack? Where did you see him?"

He hesitated. "At the office."

"We should have him for dinner. I wonder if he's still with that woman."

"Melissa."

"Yes." She smiled a smile that Paul reciprocated with relief and gratitude. "If I had your mind, darling, my life would be so much easier."

The mist had vanished and he reached across the table to touch her hand. He felt the simple, unqualified happiness that follows a narrow escape from danger. He could not remember ever having lied to her before.

At the conclusion of a chaotic dream he arose, put on shorts and sweat shirt and sneakers, and went out into the chilled pastel of dawn. He ran slowly, huffing clouds of nearly transparent vapor, up and down the low hills that in a mile culminated in a final crest and steep slant of houses built down to the edge of the ocean where only surfers would be awake, a blond-haired species of sea life bobbing in the swells. He slowly picked up speed and by the time he reached the top of the last hill he was running as if pursued, his breath coming in ragged gulps. He finally stopped and walked, looking out over a cumulus blanket of fog that entirely obscured the ocean, and suddenly, without warning, he saw the studio in his head, complete and detailed and appended to the house so cleverly that a shock of excitement tingled over his skin. He saw windows, skylights, soffits, parapets, eaves, and for a few minutes he walked with no sense of time or direction until the structure, like the final scene of an amateur movie, flickered away. He had never believed in inspiration and even distrusted those who claimed it, for his own experience had always meant hours of tedious experimentation and refinement preceding an arrival at what he could call an acceptable design. In the article Paul had attempted to read, Jack had claimed to have designed an entire public complex in a dream. He laughed aloud, for what seemed ludicrous yesterday now possessed an interesting mystique.

His usual run took him down to the sand of the beach, but now he turned at the first intersection and forced himself to run without another pause back to the house. He didn't shower but mopped his face with a towel and pulled a pair of trousers over his jogging shorts. He got the Peugeot out of the garage, trying not to draw attention, feeling a little like a thief. Suzanne had not awakened; he would call her later. He drove to his office through the first perfunctory stirrings of rush hour traffic and let himself in, half expecting to see Barb and hear her tell him that he had another call from Mrs. Livingston. He crushed the drawing of the gazebo and pitched the ball of paper toward the wastebasket. He taped a clean sheet of paper to the drafting table. At some point later the telephone rang but he didn't answer. When the ringing stopped he unplugged its cord from the wall.

Awake again at dawn, Paul was startled to realize that he could only vaguely remember what he had drawn. He got up, turned on the coffee maker, and opened the front door to see that the newspaper had not yet arrived. In the bathroom he stared at his razor and then at his face in the mirror, wondering how he would look with a beard. An exaggerated fear of waking Suzanne made him feel like an intruder, and he carried work shoes, Levis, and sweat shirt into the kitchen, where he dressed and poured himself a cup of overly strong and bitter coffee. With a burst of furious energy he had completed the drawing of the studio, down to the smallest detail, and had gotten the drawing to the printer's minutes before it closed, but the question of precisely how he had arranged the windows and placed the doors would have to wait until the copies were ready later in the afternoon. Inspiration, a college professor of his had said, does not proceed in linear fashion but consists of flashes like lightning in a black sky of ignorance. Paul wondered if those, indeed, were the professor's exact words. He heard a car in the street and the thump of the newspaper on the lawn. He had last seen lightning on a trip to the mountains, and the sky had not been black but a deep, glossy green. The power of the professor's metaphor seemed diminished by this memory, although the idea of a huge, enveloping darkness had a sudden and disconcerting appeal.

From the garage he got a sledgehammer, a crowbar, and pair of wire cutters. He propped a ladder against the back wall of the house and carefully climbed, tools in hand, to the eaves. Bracing himself with his left hand on the ladder, he swung the sledgehammer with his right against the stucco wall and was startled by the loudness of the blow that echoed in the trees behind him. He stared at a crack, an indentation in the stucco, a sort of bruise that seemed to speak the truth that he had crossed a line and would never be able to return. He swung once more, then again, then a fourth time before the head of the sledgehammer broke into the cavity between the inside and outside walls.

He knew from watching workmen that the trick was to hammer through the perimeter of a section two or three feet square and then cut through the wire mesh beneath and pry the stucco from the wood to which the mesh was nailed and let the whole thing crash to the ground, or in this case, the flower bed, below. He tried to discover a rhythm of hammering that he could sustain. Although the air was damp and cool he felt a prickling layer of sweat beneath his shirt, and the fine powder raised by each blow of the sledgehammer burned in his throat. He felt the lurking despair of defeat as he heard a different noise and turned his head to see Suzanne, dressed for work, watching him from the open door of the lanai. He lifted his hand from the ladder and waved, then, like an employee bent upon impressing his boss, slammed the sledgehammer again and again into the stonelike hardness of the wall. When he stopped, gasping for breath, she was gone.

His arm felt like a useless weight, but he was loathe to stop for more than a moment or two because a wholly illogical voice in his head told him that any hesitation would continue to infinity, become a kind of death. A throb of pain arose in his elbow and climbed through his shoulder and into his neck, but he persisted in a dogged rhythm of hammering, cutting, and prying, and by midafternoon the entire structure of the wall—the top and bottom plates, the studs, the diagonal braces, the fireblocking—was revealed. Exhausted, he collapsed on the lawn and lay on his back, staring at what he had destroyed.

He cleaned up and drove to the printer's and when he returned a brown pickup sat in the driveway. A thick man with lead-colored hair stood pondering the demolished stucco, which in its unruly pile seemed to bear no relationship to the other, undisturbed walls of the house.

"Art. I'm glad you could make it." Paul carried freshly printed drawings under his arm. "Let me get you a beer."

"You did this yourself?"

"Why not?" Art's incredulity made him feel slightly foolish. He went to the kitchen and brought two bottles of beer.

"I could have got you a couple of men," said Art. "Look at your hand there."

Paul looked and saw darkened crusts of blood from wounds inflicted by the sharp wire of the mesh. He was annoyed with Art for pointing out what he imagined to be a sign of incompetence, amateurishness, the failure to wear gloves. He unfurled the plans so new that the odor of ammonia suffused the air between them.

"This section will cantilever," he said, guiding Art around the perimeter of the imagined studio. "We'll probably have to go deeper with the foundation here."

Art grunted. The drawings apparently translated into nothing familiar and therefore he would take a dogged, resistant tack. He turned the page of elevations this way, then that, an act that set Paul's teeth on edge. Paul wasn't normally impatient, but then he could not remember a project that had felt to him so urgent. Art rubbed his chin as if prepared for hours of deliberation, and Paul's nerves felt like a dry surface over which the passing seconds slowly scratched.

"I'm going right now to order the lumber," he said. "So you can start as soon as you're ready."

Art's eyes moved slowly over the exposed frame of the wall. This deliberate and careful nature which Paul had always admired now struck him as lassitude, or at least an unnecessary stubbornness. He had once watched Art take what seemed like fifteen minutes to show a carpenter the proper way of supporting a board while making a certain type of cut. The memory nearly made him squirm.

"I don't know," Art said, finally.

"I'll pay the labor and furnish materials." Paul swallowed the last of his beer and began to crave another, although he was not in the habit of drinking at all in the middle of the day. He looked up at the gray, ambiguous sky. "But I've got to get it done before the rains." He felt a small nudge of panic. "You need to get started right away."

"I don't know," said Art again, holding a sheet of details away from his body as if it might be infectious. "I'll have to look this over. Don't know if it can be done the way you want."

Paul turned and paced the length of the yard. Undefined emotion expanded dangerously in his chest, robbing him of breath. He picked up the sledgehammer, raised it without purpose, then let it fall to the ground. All of Art's virtues, he saw, would simply infuriate him, and Art in turn would withdraw so deeply into his stolid nature that nothing would happen. Crisis, disaster, chaos would be preferable to such a state. He saw a palm-sized scab of stucco in the grass and his fastidious nature caused him to bend to pick it up.

"Thanks for coming," he said. He took the plans from Art and stuck them under his arm. "I think it might be better if I do it my-self. I can hire a couple of carpenters. I'll probably need to make changes as I go." He wanted Art to hurry, to get into his pickup and drive away so that he could turn his mind to lumber, carpen-ters, nails. They walked together toward the driveway. Paul waved his hand, vaguely. "I may have something coming up for you to bid on. A remodel. I'll give you a call."

Art nodded. He didn't look disappointed, or annoyed, or even puzzled. He said, "What about that gazebo? At the Livingston house."

"I don't know," said Paul, rapidly discarding several fabrica-tions. "I don't think I'll be doing it. I told the old girl where to shove it."

"Is that right?" said Art, in a flat, observational tone. He got into his pickup and rolled down the window. As Paul turned toward the house he heard him say, "You're asking for it, my friend. What you've got here is a whole lot of trouble. A whole lot. You can take my word on that."

At the lumberyard Paul was given the name of a carpenter who showed up the following morning, half an hour late, in a truck with rock music blaring from the open windows. He looked like a surfer, with bleached hair and a uniform of shorts and T-shirt with the sleeves and lower part of the body ripped away. His eyes shifted rapidly about and his agreement with everything said was so immediate that Paul distrusted him completely. He had arrived prepared to work, however, and Paul had managed to convince himself that even a single day, a single hour of delay would trans-form his nervousness into unbearable anxiety. All of his natural patience and restraint had expired, he realized, somewhere inside the house that Jack had designed, and with a sense of foreboding he remembered a little speech—a lecture, actually—that he had delivered long ago to Jack on the subject of the architect's ego and how it must not be allowed to dominate a design. Jack had listened, he remembered, like the carpenter listened, nodding his head, saying yes, certainly, but all the while thinking he would find a way to do whatever he wanted. For just a moment, a very brief moment, Paul felt an intense fear, a loathing, a hatred even, of Jack.

The carpenter laid out the lines of the studio while a laborer Paul picked up on the street corner dug a trench for the foundation. The carpenter built the forms and put in the various bolts and reinforcing bars. The work took three days—longer, Paul thought, than it should have. An earnest, unsmiling man from the building department inspected the formwork, and the next morning a concrete truck rumbled up the street, followed in the afternoon by another truck carrying a blonde stack of lumber. Paul inspected the sky for signs of rain, unable to shake off an illogical sense of having been singled out by the threat contained in low, smoky clouds. Distracted by her mendacious witnesses, Suzanne paid scant attention to what transpired in the back of the house, a fact for which Paul felt grateful, because he had begun to dread the moment that she would come out to look at the completed project and feel required to utter some words of approbation. He went to bed and slept—fitfully as usual—and dreamed that a terrific wind had risen and scattered the stack of lumber all up and down the street. He then dreamed that Jack had come to see the finished studio and kept walking around and around, pointing out an infinite number of defects in both the construction and the design.

The carpenter brought a friend and as Paul stood with the blueprint they bolted the sills to the foundation and laid out the floor joists while the laborer brought plywood from the stack of lumber in the driveway, one sheet at a time, for the subfloor. Paul envied the ease and banter of the two young men, bent double as they rolled nails to their fingertips and set them with two or three blows of their oversized hammers. When he was in architecture school he had worked one summer on a crew building houses in a tract, and while his memories of the work and the people had blurred with time, a feeling of exhilaration connected to the smell of sawn lumber and the echo of hammers was undiminished. As a cold drop of rain struck the back of his neck he decided, with a shiver of regret, that his life had attained some pinnacle at the moment he stood astraddle the rafters of a house he knew, even then, to be substandard, mediocre, a creation not of the mind but of economics. He wanted to pick up a hammer and dip his fingers into the box of nails, but something closed and fraternal in the way the two men worked deterred him.

A radio played, too loud, but Paul decided to ignore it. He wanted to hear a weather forecast, but the loud and jarring music was interrupted only by equally loud commercials and disc jockey repartee that was apparently supposed to amuse but struck him as inane. He decided to wait until the end of the day before speaking to the carpenters about the need to work a little faster. They dropped so many nails that Paul told the laborer to pick them up, but the man understood no English and Paul could not convey what he wanted. He bent and gathered three or four nails from the grass that was now trodden and dusty. He was gripped by a fear that the carpenters would run completely out of the nails, that the work would come to a halt, that they would get into their truck and drive away and never return. Feeling short of breath although he hadn't been exerting himself, Paul decided that he would have to drive to the lumberyard and buy another box.

The traffic flowed with a maddening lack of speed and when he returned with the nails an hour had passed. The carpenters had finished the subfloor, had raised and braced a post, and had carried a beam from the stack of lumber in the driveway to the back of the house. Now they sat. Paul wondered why they were taking a break—it was only a few minutes past two o'clock.

"I don't know," said the carpenter with the torn T-shirt. He pointed to a detail on the plans. "I can't figure it out. Where is this going to go?" There was a defensive tone in his voice, as if he felt accused of something. A very light mist had dampened the sheets of paper, making them limp. The carpenter's friend hovered nearby, shuffling his feet, acting bored.

"I'll have to change it," Paul said, after staring for a minute or two.

"I don't know," said the carpenter again. "It's starting to rain. Maybe its going to rain all afternoon."

Paul breathed slowly and deliberately, in opposition to a swell of anger. The post, jutting up, uncut, seemed to jeer at him. He shut his eyes and in darkness the rage thinned and began to feel like fatigue. He had simply made a mistake, missed a point so elementary that hardly anyone could miss it, a detail lost in the torrent of creativity, the very kind of thing for which he had faulted Jack. So he had been right all along to distrust inspiration. He smiled and opened his eyes. The gray sky cracked like an egg and rays of sunlight slanted down.

"Forget the post." The carpenter's eyes followed Paul's finger uncertainly. "We'll just straighten out this wall and then the beam can sit over here. We don't need the post. You can take it out."

"Straighten the wall?" The carpenter followed Paul's route across the paper with his own finger, the nail blackened, misshapen, apparently from a hammer blow. "The whole thing?"

"That's not a big problem, is it?"

"No." He traced the line again, as if this path led to some insight, or hidden treasure. "Well," he said, as if revealing what he knew to be a truth, but with reluctance. "That changes the whole thing, then."

"Yes," said Paul. He felt compelled against his will to answer, as if he were a witness, as if the carpenter had become Suzanne, patiently but inexorably digging after a fact. He took another deep breath. "We've got the same problem here. On the other side. We'll have to move this wall, too."

The carpenter nodded, beginning to irritate Paul by the dragging of his finger across the already smudged and marked-up surface of the drawing.

Nothing matters, Paul said to himself, nothing but getting on with the work. But he didn't want to be given time to reflect upon this conclusion. "Sun's out," he said, feeling like a sergeant. "Let's get to work."

The carpenter dipped his fingers into the leather pouch at his waist and withdrew a dozen or so nails which he began to arrange heads-up in his palm. "What you had was pretty far-out," he said. "Now it's just going to be like . . ." He shrugged his muscular shoulders.

Paul smiled what he intended to be a benevolent smile. "It's fine," he said, wanting to give the carpenter a shove, to get him moving. "It doesn't really matter. It doesn't really matter at all."

At the end of two weeks the studio was framed and the electrician had come to put in conduit and boxes for switches and lights and outlets. By the end of another week the roof was shingled, the window frames were in place, and the wire mesh that would hold the stucco was nailed to the outside walls. In Paul's first drawing there had been five separate windows, but now there were only two. The French doors leading to a deck outside had disappeared, because Paul had suddenly felt that these doors would cause him to feel exposed. A stroke of his pencil had eliminated both of the skylights, an act he explained to himself on the grounds that the studio would have gotten too hot when the sun was overhead. The carpenters finished nailing the sheetrock to the inside walls and Paul gave them checks and the three of them stood for a while drinking beer, with nothing to say to each other.

He had shown Suzanne the original drawing, but she had never been adept at inferring a finished piece of work from a maze of lines and other details. Now, when she glanced at the studio through the windows of the lanai, her silence told him that she must have expected something much different, not this append-age so purely ordinary and uninspired. At dinner she was moody and complained about the dust that the work had brought into the house.

"We'll be going to jury next week," she said. "I'd like us to get away after that. For a few days. A weekend, at least."

Paul felt unreasonably pressured by this idea. "I've got to finish the studio," he said.

"You don't have to work on it every minute."

"I'll see," said Paul, although in reality the idea of leaving before the work was completely done seemed intolerable. He waited like a fidgety child as she dawdled with her food, and when she was done he rose and went directly into the studio through the opening that the carpenters had cut into the wall between his daughter's bedroom and the lanai. Street light cast a dim glow through the pair of windows, which after a few moments came to stare at him like the overdeveloped eyes of a science fiction creature. He saw a hammer on the floor and he picked it up and struck the window frame, the sound and the shock in his arm both magnified, out of proportion to the force of the blow. He heard Suzanne's voice but he didn't answer and presently a door slammed in a distant part of the house. He struck the frame again. He stood perfectly still until the light had completely faded and the eyes had disappeared.

The crew that would put the stucco on the outside walls arrived at seven o'clock, parked their scabrous mixer in the driveway, and proceeded to unload sacks of cement from their truck. Paul walked with the foreman around the outside of the studio.

"What happened to the windows?" the foreman wanted to know.

"There aren't any windows," said Paul, eager to discourage any desire on the man's part for an explanation.

"There were windows," said the man, calmly stubborn in his belief. "I saw windows when I was here to measure."

"It's going to be a laboratory," said Paul, feeling stupid.

"Yeah?" said the man, in a tone that divulged nothing of how he felt about this statement.

"It has to be perfectly dark," Paul went on, irked by this need to fabricate. "I hadn't realized that before."

"Yeah?" The foreman gestured to one of the men lounging about the truck. "You're the boss. You don't want windows, you don't have to have windows."

"That's right," said Paul. Why can't they hurry up? he said to himself, watching a man who stood leaning upon the handle of a shovel and another squatting beside the mixer, smoking, waiting for an order to begin whatever they were supposed to be doing. He felt so nervous that he went into the kitchen and opened a bottle of beer. He had never drunk beer this early in the day, and the freedom implied by such an act exhilarated him, even while the familiar, rational part of his mind sent out a warning of danger.

He entered the studio. The light was gloomy and the exposed nails in the sheetrock looked so much like rivets that he imagined himself deep inside a ship, or an industrial tank of unknown purpose. He was planning to build a wall of shelves and his own tools were neatly arranged in a corner—his power saw, a hammer, an electric drill, a level. He stood in the center of the room and shut his eyes. He was beginning to feel relaxed when the sudden scratch of a trowel and mutter of voices disrupted his solitude, and he finished the beer and went outside. The haze had finally dissipated and the sun shone powerfully from a vault of chalky blue sky. The men were on a plank below the eaves, steadily working, and Paul felt the pulse of his blood like the driving compulsive rhythm of the carpenters' music in his head.

By noon the walls were covered with gray cement, mottled and scored; the driveway had been washed down and the mixer and truck had disappeared. Paul thought about making a sandwich, but his hunger wasn't as urgent as the idea that licked like a flame at the edge of his consciousness. He found three warped and discarded two-by-fours on the pile of debris awaiting removal to the dump, and he carried these into the house and dropped them in the center of the studio floor. He felt an odd sense of detachment, as if he were observing another person undertake these labors. He found his tape measure with the other tools and he measured the height of the opening cut through the wall for the door. He felt as he had the day he went to his office to draw the studio, as if intuition had wholly superseded the normal, known mechanics of his mind. He cut the three two-by-fours to length and nailed them into the opening, breaking out in a sweat from the exertion, feeling an almost palpable rush of time, like wind on his face. From a stack of sheetrock scraps he found two pieces that would cover the opening, and these he measured and cut to fit and nailed onto the two-by-fours.

He didn't know whether he had been asleep or just deep in reverie when he became aware of sound. He was sitting on the floor, back against a wall. Light entered the room only through the joint between the two pieces of sheetrock that covered the opening, but he sat beyond this crack of slight illumination, safely in the dark. "Paul?" He now connected a clicking sound to an image of Suzanne's heels crossing the tiled foyer floor, and a dull thump to their progress over the hallway carpet. "Paul? Are you here?" She was close now, on the other side of the wall. She sounded bewildered, a tone he could not remember ever hearing before. He felt trapped. He decided to stand up, and the hammer that had for some reason been lying in his lap bounced with a thud on the floor.

"Paul!" He heard fright in her voice and then, on the far side of the sheetrock, a scraping noise that he guessed was made by her hands. "What are you doing?" The noise like fingernails on a hard surface caused him to shudder. "Where is the door? Paul!"

"I'm here." Even to himself his voice sounded distant and muffled.

"Paul." Her tone descended to a level of deliberate calm, carefully measured. "Paul, I want you to come out."

"I can't" he murmured.

"What? Paul? I can't hear you."

"I can't come out," he said.

"Paul!" He heard sounds that he could not define. Finally she went away, he heard in the distance the thump and again the click of her heels, and then the sound of a door pulled open and slammed shut. He felt relieved. She didn't interest him any longer, he realized. She was something permanently in the house, a piece of furniture whose style had once attracted him but now was out of date, a presence so familiar that it might as well be invisible. His daughter's face flickered in his mind, but the features were generalities. He allowed himself to sink slowly back to the floor. The compulsive energy of the past few weeks had run its course, leaving him with a feeling of relief, of peace. He felt very tired. His eyes closed and he drifted into sleep.

"Paul!" Something crashed against the sheetrock, causing it to bulge, raising a fine shower of dust. Another crash, then another, and the dark iron head of his sledgehammer appeared like a vision in a shaft of sudden yellow light. In a panic he scrambled to his feet, looking frantically about for a place to hide that the rational part of his mind told him did not exist. In a rain of dust and noise the remaining sheetrock shattered and he saw his wife, an apparition, her hair wild and white with bits of plaster, coming out of the light into the dusk toward him. He shut his eyes and moaned.

The psychiatrist, Dr. Nathan, short and bearded and profoundly relaxed, had asked Paul, at one of their earliest meetings, "What exactly do you believe in?" Paul had been at a loss to answer and the doctor had glimpsed something in this failure that compelled the writing of a few lines on a pad. Paul thought, in retrospect, that the question had been too large and unwieldy to answer, although he could have offered homilies such as "I believe in life" or "I believe in love" or even something clever like "I believe in clients who pay on time."

He took the medication that Dr. Nathan prescribed, faithfully, although he wondered if the pills could be responsible for the deep malaise that encumbered him through his waking hours. The doctor had not immediately asked him what he thought he was doing when he sealed himself up in the room, and when the question arrived after a dozen weekly sessions Paul was startled and could only mumble that he didn't know. It seemed unfair, after hours of exploring his feelings about matters apparently unrelated, to suddenly spring this question. It seemed like a trick. He wondered if the doctor was a charlatan, or worse, a fool.

He spent long, sluggish days inside the house, and the divisions of time—hours, days, weeks—were blurred and unimportant. For a few weeks Suzanne stayed home from her office, her legal papers spread over the dining room table, the telephone in more or less constant use as she gave directions to her various associates. Some afternoons, if he was able to overcome apathy, they walked for fifteen or twenty minutes in the neighborhood. They walked very slowly, like an elderly couple—his jogging apparel hung unused in a corner of the closet and he couldn't imagine ever having had the desire or energy to actually run through the surrounding hills.

The doctor advised against a longer trip, so they flew one weekend to San Francisco. The city for which Paul had long felt an almost evangelistic affection was on this trip so cold and gray that its beauty became yet another trick, a mirage, its inclines so cruelly exaggerated that he collapsed, exhausted, on the bed in their hotel at the end of the day. Long silences marked their time together, like ropes strung between posts to keep back a curious crowd. He thought of asking her "Do you think I'm sane?" but decided that she must, for when they spoke—of the weather, of places to eat, of the possibility of leaving on an earlier flight—they did so in

a lucid, rational manner. He decided that he was neither introspective nor keenly interested in the workings of another person's
mind. He decided that within this observation must reside some
significance that he would share with Dr. Nathan.

He grew tired of watching rain drip onto the ledge of the hotel
window, so he asked Suzanne for a sheet of paper. She looked at
him, he thought, in the same attentive, judicial manner that she
had always looked at their daughter when weighing even the most
trivial request. She must be bored, he thought suddenly, tired of
this sort of faithfulness.

"Are you all right?" He half expected her to touch his forehead,
test for fever.

"Fine. I want to sketch a little. See how it feels."

"Should you discuss it?" He tried to remember, with a feeling of
vague regret, when they had last made love. "With Dr. Nathan?"

"I guess so," he said. "But what am I supposed to do?"

"What do you mean?"

"About earning a living."

She let this roll around like something spicy on her tongue, and
he knew that when she responded whatever she said would be in
some way definitive. With effort he decided to speak first. "He
said, 'Some parents never come to terms with a child's success.' "

She frowned, making herself look worn, he thought. "What's
that supposed to mean?"

Paul shrugged. Had their conversations always had a quality of
disconnectedness, like freeways running on different levels, in the
same direction but never joining?

"I had an idea," he said.

"You don't have to rush anything," she said. "We've got enough
money right now."

"It's all right," he said. "If I ask Dr. Nathan he'll just turn it
into a question for me. That's how it works, you know. You ask a
question and get a question in return."

And that of course is what had happened. He had said to the

doctor, "How do you keep from resenting somebody else's success?" and the ensuing questions had drawn out the business of Jack and the house, which was what the studio had started out to be, before it all went haywire. And the session had ended with the statement "Some parents never come to terms with a child's success," a statement that had caused him to think, Even if it's true, what does it explain?

He got up, bent to kiss her forehead in a habitual way, then found stationery in a drawer. "How do I understand what has happened?" he had asked the doctor. He sat at the desk in the room for a long time, staring at the paper, which was something foreign in shape and texture that would take getting used to. The idea that had prompted him to ask for the paper in the first place had completely vanished. He did not possess a single idea. But he couldn't simply sit and stare at the paper after it had been the subject of so much attention. So he drew a window. The window was ordinary and in appearance opaque. He drew two more windows, identical to the first. He realized without any particular emotion that he was good at this sort of drawing. The windows lay in the flat plane of the paper. He wanted, somehow, to open them. Finally he drew some lines around the windows. Each line existed as itself and did not suggest another, but he kept drawing. It took him an hour to finish, and he had a sort of soaring structure composed of lines and angles such that individual planes could hardly be discerned. The effort had made him tired, but it was the fatigue of exertion, not the ennui that had descended like an aberrant blessing the day he had closed up the doorway to the room.

Suzanne did not comment when he placed the drawing on the bed for her to see. It probably resembled nothing to her. She did not seem to want to spend time looking at it. That evening after dinner he noticed that she was staring at him. He smiled but her expression didn't change.

"I was thinking that we should move," she said.

"Move?" Paul was startled.

"Yes. Get a different house, in a different neighborhood."

"Why?" said Paul.

"The studio. I mean, what are we going to do with it?" She grimaced. "I didn't want to bring this up, Paul."

Paul smiled again. He didn't feel agitated or depressed, whatever it was she feared. "I could put in the windows. They're still in the garage. I looked at them the other day."

"I don't mean you should do anything, Paul. We could call Art. I could speak to him."

"It's all right." He felt undisturbed, relaxed really. They were having wine again. They had been having wine more frequently. "It'll give me something to do."

"Whatever you think," she said, a little glumly, he thought. She drank more than she used to, he noticed. She had been having a cocktail after work, he could taste the alcohol on her breath when he kissed her. She had always showered and changed before dinner, but recently she had been arriving at the table in the clothes she had worn all day, looking rumpled. Paul wondered what these changes meant, but when he asked himself a question he was presented, as with the doctor, a question in return.

The morning after they returned from San Francisco he got the sledgehammer from the garage, set up the ladder, and began to break the freshly hardened stucco from the section of wall that had contained the windows. He had to frequently pause to rest and catch his breath, and when he finished it was late in the afternoon. In the dying sunlight he stared at the openings where the windows had been, awaiting the arrival of some emotion from the distant past. He waited but nothing came to dispel an odd feeling of indifference to what he had done.

In the morning he got up earlier than usual, went outside, and carried the windows from the garage to the back of the house.

He poured himself a cup of coffee but instead of sitting to drink it he got out the ladder and propped it against the wall. He finished the coffee, standing beside the ladder, and finally he heard Suzanne leave for work. He climbed the ladder and nailed the window frames into the openings. He carefully leveled and shimmed the frames, but when he stood back to look he could immediately see that the placement of the windows was too symmetrical—he would have to move one of them, possibly both. All his energy had turned to fatigue, but he forced himself to pick up the hammer and strike the wall between the windows, breaking through the stucco once again. He continued to doggedly hammer. He moved slowly along the wall, getting down every few minutes to move the ladder, until the stucco was broken in a solid line from corner to corner. His damp shirt clung to his skin. He stood still for a few moments, staring, but what he had done did not seem similar or even related to his earlier act of destruction.

"Do you feel a sense of loss?" the doctor had asked. "Do you feel that something dear to you is missing?"

The next morning Paul got up even earlier, and drank three cups of coffee while waiting impatiently for Suzanne to leave. In a furious burst of exertion he continued breaking and stripping away the freshly hardened stucco, and by midafternoon all three walls of the studio were exposed, and without taking a break for food or rest he shut off the electrical breaker and began yanking the new wiring from the conduit. At five o'clock he climbed a ladder to the roof and pried off shingles with a bar. It was dusk and Suzanne was not yet home. She had been getting home later and later, he observed. With leaden arms he started to pry a rafter from the ridge board. When Suzanne's car turned into the driveway, the streetlight had begun to glow.

"I'm going," she said, after Paul had beaten dust from his pants and shirt and followed her into the kitchen, where she was drinking beer from the bottle, something he had never seen her do before. "I can't take it, Paul. I'm sorry."

"What do you mean?" said Paul, although the scene had for him an air of inevitability, of predictability even.

"I can't take it," she repeated. "I'm leaving. All this . . ." Her arm rose and fell in a gesture that seemed encompassing and final. "I'm sorry, Paul."

He felt that she was probably right, justified. He felt prepared to defend the propriety of her decision, because the rational part of his mind observed that the facts were all in her favor. She looked disheveled, slightly deranged, with her puffy face and reddish eyes, and briefly he felt pity for her.

"We'll have to tell Jennifer."

For a moment he was adrift, and then with a shock he realized who she was talking about. He realized, with a start, that what he had done was to destroy what he had invested so much of himself into designing and building. But that was all right, it wouldn't have enhanced the value of the house, not even the original design, which would have put too many people off, made them fearful. Perhaps they would sell the house and he would buy a condominium. Their daughter would come to visit father and mother, each in turn. In a moment the idea of their separation, something that had never occurred to him, appeared to be accomplished with hardly any fuss.

He decided to have a glass of wine. He asked if she wanted a glass for her beer and she shook her head abruptly, an act that drew his attention to the fact that her eyes had filled with tears which spread in tracks down over her plump, reddened cheeks. He poured wine into a glass and suddenly thought of Jack, with a little regret—they wouldn't be able to get together now, the four of them. He thought he might have an idea that would interest Jack. He thought he might sound out Jack about doing something together, a joint venture, and he began to think about how he would state this proposition. Jack could handle the design, and he would arrange the practical matters of construction, deal with the contractor, the plumbers, the electricians. He heard his wife sniffle, but he didn't look at her. He looked through the window, just catching a glimpse of the jumbled wood and debris in the nearly faded light, and he didn't feel afraid, or even nervous; he felt that the past was complete, a book he hadn't been able to put down but which, once finished, had rapidly leaked from his memory.

"Well," he said, with an ethereal, fleeting sense that the light on the ceiling was about to blink off and leave him again enclosed in darkness. "Where do we go from here?"

And in the manner of the psychiatrist, she answered his question with a question. "Why did you tell me that you saw Jack in your office?"

The light appeared to flicker, a stutter of disorientation.

"You talked to Jack?" he said.

"It was just coincidence." She sat slumped ungracefully at the table. "We're representing a developer he's involved with. When we went to look at this building he happened to be there. He said he had seen you. At a house he had designed."

Paul felt cold and naked, his life turned inside out, all of his forgotten secrets and deceptions exposed to public view. He felt a squirm of panic, and the old dormant urge to run. To run until he found another space that he could enter and then close up behind him. He opened his mouth to speak in his own defense, but his voice did not seem able to penetrate the thickness of silence between himself and his wife, who in any case appeared to have abandoned her interest in him, who sat staring like a drunk at the bottle of beer encircled by her hands.

In a voice just slightly louder than a murmur she said, "It doesn't really matter, Paul."

She had receded to the end of a long tunnel, and Paul had to blink to restore the proportions of the room, to bring her back to the place where she sat, not more than five or six feet away, close enough that he had a sudden urge to touch her, to caress her, to tug her to her feet and lead her to their bed. He was frightened momentarily, as by a loud noise or the jolt of an earthquake, but this fear was rapidly displaced by the knowledge that the space in which he stood was circumscribed and constant, that the light that banished the nearly solid darkness outside the windows was as reliable as anything in the world can be. Suzanne, Jack, Barb, Mrs. Livingston, Dr. Nathan, his daughter—they would all move in and out of the space, back and forth through light and darkness, but he would remain, alone perhaps, or with his wife, or even with someone yet to be imagined, where he had always been.

The Consequences of Desire

He stood in the shadow of an awning, watching a woman in a green dress waiting to cross the street, and in a characteristic way he calmly considered opposing courses of action—stepping into the sunlight and calling her name, remaining in the shadow until she crossed the street and faded from sight. Although he hadn't seen her for years he was certain that she was the girl he had marched with down this very street, the girl whose hand he had held while singing an anthem whose words he didn't care to recall, the girl he had lived with briefly in a commune deep in the woods. She was heavier, he thought, and softer than the girl whose image was that of a fairy dancing in firelight, dark and lithe and uninhibited. He observed that her face looked slightly drawn, as if by permanent tension or anxiety, and finally he abandoned the shadow, reached out to touch her arm and say, "You remember me, don't you?"

She stared at him. The street corner, the parallelogram of sunlight that formed an enclosure in which they stood, the blue metal rectangle bearing the words TELEGRAPH and AVE, the handful of strangers waiting for the green permission of "Walk" all receded beyond the memory of an intimacy that took sudden and insistent possession of her senses, like a loud noise or a peculiar odor. She stared at smooth cheeks rounded by the breadth of a smile. The face was unfamiliar but the voice tapped on the door to a room full of embarrassing secrets. She felt a sudden pressure behind her eyes.

"Boyd Carroll," she heard him say, allowing her hand to be

squeezed with fingers that had touched, she suspected as a tingle of ambiguous energy flowed up her arm, other parts of her body. When he spoke he exposed teeth and a glimpse of tongue, possibly insidious things. "I remember a few times you wrote your name and people assumed you'd put your last name first. Thought you were Carol Boyd."

"I'm sorry," she said. He appeared professionally calm, unrattled by that which startled and made her feel the breathlessness of lurking panic.

"David," he said, and an image rushed into her head, the cleft chin invisible within a dense aureola of beard, the brown eyes slightly distanced by circles of glass. "David Remington." He laughed as at a joke told to himself, a characteristic so deeply interred in her subconscious that its appearance shook loose a torrent of memories that caused her vision to blur. Their bodies drifted together and as he felt her contour and mass he saw in brief, photographic detail the faces of his wife and children. She sniffled. She found a tissue in her purse and blew her nose. Once more she said, "I'm sorry."

"No need to be."

"It's something about that time." She felt resistant to conferring upon him any power, because this appearance of a man she had never expected to see again, a man she hadn't thought about in years, made her feel unfree. "The other day I saw these boys and girls with long hair and beads and I got all choked up. Isn't that silly?"

"Not at all."

She continued to stare, as if he were in some way deformed, a freak. "It's incredible. I mean, after all this time . . . do you live here?"

"No." He observed her with a directness that was both a matter of professional reflex and a reiteration of a way he remembered that they had been. "Business. I had some time to kill so I thought

I'd do this nostalgia thing." He recognized her uncertainty and diffidence of manner, and like a curl of smoke from embers the memory of a distant event arose; he saw himself read a letter, place the letter in a drawer, then later, months perhaps, a year, clean out the drawer and reread the letter and let it drop into a stack of things consigned to the trash. He could not remember anything specific in the letter, nor could he remember how it made him feel, and yet he could see himself as clearly as if it were yesterday, taking the letter out of a drawer and reading it and then dropping it with other discarded things into the trash. He noticed a sifting of gray through her hair at the same time an idea entered his mind, a concept both as palpable and as ethereal as the fog that he could see clinging to the hills beyond the dark sections of bridge that crossed the bay.

"Come have a drink," he said. "Do you have a minute?"

"I don't," she answered, feeling nudged toward a particular destination without having made up her mind about where she wanted to be. "Drink, I mean . . . I go to AA." Their time together, she began to remember in bits of detail floating up from a deep recess of her mind, had often been spent in confession. "I've been sober now for a year." This urge to explain made her feel defensive. His smile and the frankness of his gaze made her feel that she was being evaluated, considered for some possible use. But she felt curious, too, a child's curiosity about the unknown, unmarred by knowledge and cynicism.

There was a place, just down the block, where they could get coffee, espresso. His teeth seemed to have brightened with age. "You look great, Boyd," he said, in a male tone of approbation that thrilled her even as it burdened her with the requirement to behave in a certain way, to avoid doing anything that would disappoint or disillusion.

They sat on opposite sides of a small, round marble table. "You look good, too," she said, with a feeling of imperfect enthusiasm.

His appearance—skin tanned, polished, hair perfectly trimmed, shirt and jacket stylish and fitted—caused a sudden ache of resentment. She decided without additional evidence that his life had been a glide of contentment and satisfaction, while her own—she wanted to concentrate on the more distant past, to escape into nostalgia—had consisted of bumps and ruts. She glanced out on the street, the avenue down which they had marched when they were students, and she remembered a long, dreamy trip north to the commune in a redwood forest. "David." The name lived in a deep corner of her mind, along with a boy in sandals and ragged jeans and beard that made him look neither older nor wiser but charmed her nonetheless.

A small stream of detail threatened to swell to a flood. The day a friend drove them to the airport in San Francisco in a rattling pickup truck, a day that was a drug-impelled collage of color and noise within which David's fever touched her own head, and his thin body shivered in her arms as images of deathly beauty flowed before her eyes, "I'm going to die," he had said, and she had not demurred, and the three of them had cried like children and then gotten into increasingly hilarious ideas of how his funeral might be conducted. In the airport she had hugged him, feeling his sickness, saying, "I love you, David," and it was only after the plane had lumbered into the sky that she considered the fact that he might not return even if he didn't die, might simply blink off like a light, leave a dark spot in her life.

David. The name felt sweet but heavy, like a chunk of pure chocolate, in her mouth. When she last heard from him he had nearly recovered and was dabbling with the idea of going to law school. Looking at his hand on the marble surface of the table, his manicured nails and a gold ring with an arrangement of stones, she remembered an assumption that if he became a lawyer he would work in legal aid, in some anti-poverty program, or consumer advocacy. Her last letters had gone unanswered, but by then she had escaped the commune and hitchhiked back to Berkeley, where her misery and resentment were displaced by the intense beginnings of an affair with a medical student whose dream was to establish a free clinic on an Indian reservation. She stared at David Remington's face, with the illogical feeling that he had sought her out, that this meeting was the result of calculation, and would proceed to a prearranged conclusion about which she would have nothing at all to say.

"I have to go down to Monterey." He leaned forward, the space between them slight enough that she felt a stir of apprehension. "I want to go to the aquarium there. Have you been?"

"No." The subject pushed forth another memory, of their fanciful pursuit of the idea of getting a boat and sailing off in escape from the inevitable chaos of war between the rich and the poor, black and white, young and old. She imagined a wall of glass beyond which fantastically shaped and colored things swam in a lurid glow that was neither day nor night. "I've heard it's quite nice," she said.

He smiled and nodded, as if she had uttered something profound. He gazed at a shadow that hovered on her upper lip. He realized that he had always been stimulated by women with olive skin and a judicious amount of hair on their faces, although the woman he married was blonde and had a perfectly smooth body with hair in small amounts where it was required. He thought of his wife, this attractive woman alone with their well-adjusted children in their lovely house, and he told himself that if he and Boyd had stayed together they would have run out of things to say. The confessional sprees in which they indulged would have quickly become dull instead of exciting; their rigid ideals would have clanged against reality, creating a din that would have been impossible to endure.

Without being obvious about it, he looked at his watch. In an hour he would be in his rented car on the freeway, heading south, to Monterey. So she was in AA, so her life had turned messy, at least in that respect. With a feeling of distaste he imagined her sloppily drunk and maudlin. Despite her shyness there had always been something loose and unrestrained about her. He thought he could recall an argument over the subject of self-control. She looked unhappy. He could not abide unhappy people and yet the force of an idea kept him from getting up, giving her a peck on the cheek, saying something of questionable sincerity like "Call me if you ever get down to L.A."

"Why don't we have dinner?" he said, at the very moment that the memory of anger over his failure to answer her last letters seized her like a chill and caused her, for a second or two, to hate him. She had once believed, lying against him in the cold darkness of night in the commune, that they would be together the rest of their lives. Despite the chills and fever his illness had not seemed really ominous until she reread his final letter and observed that his plans were his alone and did not include her. It wasn't that she would have wanted any part of Southern California, or law school, or what she suspected that he had become. She had just wanted to be important enough to be considered, to be allowed to say no, to try to change his mind.

She looked at his face in contrived or genuine composure, wondering with a slight shock of queasiness how it had felt to kiss him, to put her tongue in his mouth. His patient gaze seemed to say that he would wait indefinitely for an answer, and against her will she thought of the man she lived with, of how patiently he awaited expressions of the love that she felt for him in a smaller degree than either of them desired. The immediate future appeared to her like the untidy corner of the place in which they lived, a chaos of messy detail impossible to organize. David Remington, she decided, had already planned everything—where they would eat, what they would say, what they would do afterwards, what lie he would tell his wife if that became necessary. She was shocked by the fact that even as this affair was beginning to take shape she knew nothing about him beyond his final letter—whether he had indeed gone to law school, whether he even had a wife. His appearance implied that he had money. But then, the few times she had been to Los Angeles an improbably large number of people looked like they had money. She remembered how they had related to each other their fantasies, no matter how personal, how mortifying. But this intimacy had an antic, theatrical quality that seemed frozen in that past.

"I was married for seven years," she said, aware of a pretense that nothing had really changed. "To a doctor. I have a son. He was nineteen just this month. He's a freshman at Santa Cruz." She caught her breath, realizing that she was rushing, filling up some sort of void. "What about you?"

He smiled at her, even as he felt the question to be unwelcome, possibly even hostile. The fact that we are sitting here, he wanted to say, is a matter of pure chance, an accident. What reason is there to go beyond that? He didn't want to know anything about her husband, about her son; he didn't want to say anything at all about his wife, his children, his career.

"I'm happily married," he said, and as soon as he heard his voice he suspected that she would hear it as sarcasm and take offense. "I'm a partner in a law firm. I own a very nice house. I have two beautiful daughters. I drive a Mercedes." He felt the unfamiliar tension of self-consciousness. "Should I apologize?"

He had hoped that she would laugh, but of course she didn't— what he remembered as her naive and affable self-absorption had turned into a deadly seriousness not only about herself but the world in which she had apparently suffered pain and unhappiness. That she would cry over the sight of kids affecting the style of the hippies they had once been struck him as ludicrous. The immediate future presented itself in the form of an impersonal kiss, a hurried good-bye, but he was restrained by the uncalculated desire—he didn't move, he said nothing, he felt that he might wait as long as necessary for her to either come closer or withdraw.

"You don't need to apologize," she said. The last thing she wanted was to be confused with doubts about his sincerity. She disliked the few lawyers she had met, socially and otherwise. She distrusted them, perhaps unfairly. She felt that they would evaluate, categorize, and store away whatever they were told in even the most casual conversations. She wanted to tell him how she had become an artist when she was married to the doctor, how she had made sculptures from discarded objects, how she had given this up after her divorce and begun to make things of glass and metal that could be sold, how the man she now lived with had admired her work and then her self with such extravagance that she had tumbled, literally, into his bed. How her son had survived a bout of delinquency and begun to turn into the man that she had an almost desperate need to admire. She couldn't allow the idea of intimacy with this man from her past to take shape in her head without a preamble of confession and revelation. She wanted to tell him so, but suddenly felt a girlish inhibition, a gawky state in which she feared that if she opened her mouth something foolish and inappropriate would pop out.

Both thought then about sex, although in different ways—she recalled with a nostalgic warmth that eased her nervousness the weight of his body and texture of his breath, while he tried to remember as if it was vital whether or not she had expressed any pleasure the first time they made love. He immediately discarded the idea of asking her. In his mind, all was suddenly, neatly accomplished.

"There's a great place for seafood, right on the ocean," he said. She lifted her hands and pushed them through her hair, exposing a construction of glass and metal that looked homemade, and he remembered a bauble hanging from this ear, but only its color and not its shape. "I'm staying in a bed and breakfast. It was written up in a magazine. Some kind of historic house."

"In Monterey?"

"We could go to the aquarium. If we leave soon, we'd have time."

"You'd bring me back?"

"Of course." He smiled a smile intended to reassure her, but in fact the contamination of the pragmatic began to make him feel indifferent. She didn't promise anything so sublime as to require a great deal of effort, emotional or otherwise. He looked at her objectively, as at a potential client, noting that her hair was somewhat messy, that there wasn't any makeup on her face, that the dress she wore, a dress of grassy green with large white buttons down the front, suggested an inexpensive copy of a past year's style. If she had been married to a doctor, then she ought to have gotten some money, he thought. But he didn't really care.

"I live with someone," she said, feeling girlishly nervous again. "He's a sculptor." She wanted him to know that this artist was a decent, even admirable man, not someone to be looked upon as a fool, a cuckold.

"Call him," he said. He felt in his element, dealing with process, motion, deception, if that was necessary. "Tell him you ran into an old friend and are going out to dinner. If you want, you can call him after dinner and say that you decided to drive down and see another friend in Monterey or Carmel or wherever and because it's so far you're going to stay the night, talk about old times." He could have added any number of other details for the sake of verisimilitude but he paused, taking note of a look of fear that crossed her face. He wondered if she was afraid of him. He decided that she was merely afraid of offending some idea of how the present and future ought to be. He disliked fearful, tentative people, and when he spoke he was aware of a brusque tone in his voice.

"It's simple enough." He looked again at his watch, openly. "If we're going, we have to leave in an hour."

"David," she said. It was the first time she had spoken his name to his face since the long trip in the pickup truck to San Francisco.

Time had passed, she thought, but some things hadn't changed—
he was still ready to rush into any enterprise he deemed to be desirable, without committing it to discussion, to notice how she felt.
That was it. Her ragged emotions that floated on the surface for
anyone at all to see were invisible to him. He would put forth a
proposal and she would say yes or no. Perhaps he had always calculated everything, that once he was on the plane, feeling he really
wouldn't die, he had decided to change his life, to abandon the
past and all that it included and implied. His shallowness flooded
over her like harsh, penetrating light. A cloud of anger floated out
of her and she saw him frown. She swallowed, then said, "Why
didn't you answer my letters?"

"Boyd." He winced ungracefully. He wouldn't be able to escape,
not unless he rudely called for their check and stood and said,
"Good-bye, it was nice to see you, take care," and walked out on
the street and let her face drift back into the distant, invisible past.

"We're talking about twenty years ago."

"Twenty-one."

"I didn't keep track. Are you resenting something that happened
twenty-one years ago? If you are, I'd say you have a problem."

"I do have problems!" She heard her voice edge upward toward
a shout, a scream. "I suppose you don't. Well, aren't you lucky?"
She was gripped by a familiar, desperate desire. "I hadn't thought
about you for years and suddenly, out of the blue, there you are.
For me, this brings back a lot of things that I probably wouldn't
even care to think about if I had a choice."

He said, "You have a choice."

"Yes." She pressed both hands to the sides of her face and
breathed deeply, seeking to calm herself. "You're right. I have a
choice." In her mind she stood up and said, "Good-bye, David.
It was nice to see you again. I wouldn't mind having dinner with
you. The idea of sex has its appeal, too, but not with a stranger.
And right now you're a stranger."

"Boyd." She heard in his voice a surprising, almost plaintive tone. "The past is the past. What's the point of dragging it up?"

"It's interesting," she said, although that wasn't precisely what she felt. She felt awkward and exposed. "It's what I have of you, for instance. The you of the present is just a stranger, really. I'm sorry but I can't get interested in a stranger just like that."

"Yeah," he said quietly. "There isn't time."

"For what?"

"To get to know each other. Maybe there's something but we'll never know, I suppose."

She wasn't prepared for this conclusion. It felt like acquiescence to a concept that had to do with alienation. Maybe, she thought, they could have dinner with the understanding that he would bring her back, that nothing further would happen. The idea appealed to her. All at once a large scene flowered in which she met his wife, his daughters, in which all of them, her son and the artist and David's family got together for some occasion and ate and talked and laughed. The picture suddenly seemed silly. Maybe, she thought, he reminds me too deeply of what I was and what I wanted to be and what I have become.

"All right," she said, without knowing precisely what she was agreeing to. Why, she asked herself, couldn't she just say good-bye and walk away? Did this encounter promise to outweigh the possibilities of complication? Did she believe he might arouse something in her that the artist, with his earnest displays of affection, could never quite reach? She scowled, to stop the questions in her head, and a look of concern appeared on David's face.

He thought that she looked slightly tortured. He remembered that when they took LSD she had always been the first to dissolve into the spasms of glee that eventually evolved into contortions of pain, and frightened him just a little. She had been too serious about everything—about having fun and laughing as well as coming to terms with the basic elements of life. He observed that what he wanted was simply sex without the facet of danger that would exist if he pursued this fantasy with one of his wife's friends, with a colleague, with a secretary in his office. He would never need to see Boyd again. Or perhaps he would fly up once or twice a year and they would get together like the characters in a play that he had seen. He felt momentarily pleased. Once more he smiled at her, reached out and covered her hand with his, and gazed with calm assurance into her wary eyes.

They drove in sluggish traffic along a street of boxy wooden buildings that had once been canneries but now were transformed into restaurants, shops, other businesses designed to arouse the temporary cravings of tourists. The glass and concrete mass of the aquarium rose at the end of the street, and as David parked the car he remembered diving into a river and swimming beneath the surface, gliding up to Boyd's naked, out-of-focus form and reaching to touch and startle her. For just a second he was engulfed by a wave of desire—hot, impatient, adolescent—that began to corrode to a sense of unease, which he told himself was simply a predictable nervousness about the fact that he had decided, after sixteen years of marriage, to betray his wife.

As soon as the word "betray" entered his mind he felt an intense distaste for it and told himself that it wasn't the right word at all; to call an encounter such as he envisioned betrayal was wholly excessive, it was more of a small deceit, a tiny lie, a piece of business that really meant nothing about the domestic arrangements into which he had long been settled. He was startled, though, to feel as nervous as he might have felt in a courtroom, facing a particularly irascible judge, dealing with some matter whose outcome could profoundly affect his reputation. And perhaps he didn't trust her. He had never trusted her, not because of anything particular that she had done but because she tended, he remembered, to blurt things out, to reveal too much, to lack a sense of what was appropriate and what was not. He couldn't rely upon her to be discreet.

He considered, for a second or two, the possibility of going back, of telling her that the idea was a mistake, that he would take her back to Berkeley. But the thought of driving another two hours with silence as thick and unpleasant as fog in the car led him to conclude that he was being foolish; she couldn't make trouble even if she wanted. She didn't have his address. His home number was unlisted. She wouldn't come to Los Angeles, and even if she did she wouldn't be able to find him. He felt silly. She was angry about the letters he had failed to answer, but she didn't seem distraught or on the verge of doing anything ridiculous. She wasn't the calculating type—whatever she did would be impulsive, he decided. But she wouldn't have an opportunity, even if she wanted, to cause him any trouble.

They entered a tall, cool, softly lighted space crowded with a mixture of slightly echoing sounds—gurgling water and murmuring voices and the occasional screech of a child. He decided that a prim look on Boyd's face meant that she had acquiesced, if not yet in body then in mind, and he wondered if she had decided to limit their encounter to a reprise of pure sensation and not allow any further relapse into the emotional geography of the distant past. He hoped so. He felt both able and willing to peel back protective layers of resistance, as long as he wasn't expected to plead forgiveness or indulge in any self-loathing over failings he felt should be subject to an implied statute of limitations. He put his hand briefly on the small of her back to guide her, and a current of anticipation entered his fingers and spread through his body, turning into a flare of heat that threatened to incinerate his normal caution and restraint.

They walked together—like teenagers on a date, she thought, making conversation, contriving to touch now and then—along a two-story wall of glass. "Look," she said. She had moved a few steps ahead of him and was staring at a large brown shark that slowly swam through a conglomeration of much smaller fish, rays, crabs, eels. The shark swam past them, a foot or so from the glass, an animal that looked plump and contented although the knowledge of what it was made it menacing. As they watched, the shark turned smoothly about the circumference of a wide circle and within a couple of minutes glided by them once again.

"Isn't it dangerous?" she said. "I mean, for the other things. Doesn't it eat them?"

"I imagine they feed it," he said. "Keep it satisfied."

She nodded. She perceived the shark to be swimming on this endless circuit while patiently awaiting some opportunity that might not occur for a hundred years. She looked at the other fish, of various shapes and colors, a few familiar but many fantastic. One of these fish might simply disappear one day. A draft of chilled air like an unfamiliar hand brushed her legs and caused her to shiver. David had wandered off, and although she could see him standing with his hands in his pockets and gazing into a tall, rippling forest of luminescent kelp, she felt alone and vulnerable. She felt that once again he was on the verge of disappearing, and that she would be left to wonder what had become of him, whether he was alive or dead, whether he was happy or depressed, whether he had found someone to make love to and what this other looked and sounded like. The shark turned along the same circular path and once again approached her. David was clearly visible, casually gazing into the kelp, but she felt utterly certain that he would at some point disappear, like one of the fish in the tank with the shark, be swallowed up by a way of life that excluded her, that turned her into the object of a transitory need.

"David," she said, catching up as he crossed a space toward another tank in which a glistening otter dived in a stream of silver bubbles. She wanted to tell him about her husband, the man who had never gotten to the Indian reservation, the man who had seemed disappointed with everything, including her, and who had grown more and more angry as his practice thrived and had finally lost his temper and struck her, like a clumsy boxer, on the ear with his fist. She wanted to say that she had loved this man differently than she had loved David, who had abandoned her to a life so inferior to the one she had once imagined for themselves. David looked at her and smiled—a noncommittal smile that nevertheless dispelled a swarming dismay that had seized her like a fever. She wanted to believe that he had loved her differently than he loved his wife—not more profoundly, just differently. In some inexplicable way, more intensely. But she couldn't state this. She reached out to touch his hand and their fingers for a moment entangled. Then, as on the street corner, their bodies drifted together and she felt, for just a moment, that despite the intervention of time and circumstance nothing had changed, that they were together and nothing else mattered, that the world around them would recede and leave them in the perpetual solitude of this embrace.

They pulled into a parking space at the back of a large Victorian house that sat on a corner of a quiet street affording a hazy view of the bay. The flare of the sunken sun had faded from a metallic cream-colored sheen to the dull gray of impending dark and David said, "I'll find the owner and tell him that my wife decided to come up at the last minute. It'll be okay. I'll give you the key and you can go on up to the room." He thought he detected a frown, a shadow briefly darkening her face at his utterance of the word "wife," and he saw, for the first time clearly, that her conception of what had brought them to this point was very different from his own. Perhaps she was still in love with him. And jealous of his wife. He decided, on impulse, to kiss her, but at the moment he leaned toward her she turned to gaze out the window and he thought, It's better, it's better that she doesn't get ideas, it's better that she feels used, taken advantage of, if that's what she ends up thinking. Better, he thought, with a curious feeling of wonder, that she despise me rather than believe we're still in some kind of love.

He watched her ascend the staircase that led up from a large room populated with comfortable chairs, a long dining table, a fireplace surmounted with a mirror and flanked with shelves of books. He watched with modest approval the relative harmony of her movement, and the immediate future unfolded before his eyes with perfect clarity—the act of undressing and getting into the bed, the eating of dinner in the afterglow of passion, a walk in the dark on the beach and then a slow arousal of desire and indulgence in the morning. He found the owner and made the necessary arrangements. He felt a childish anticipation that was difficult to contain. He felt a sudden urge to hurry, and when he heard his name, just as he reached the staircase, he stopped but didn't immediately turn around—he wanted to ignore this dissonant sound, he wanted to believe that he hadn't heard anything more than the slamming of a door, the scraping of a chair, a cough, a sigh.

"Remington." He turned deliberately enough that when he faced the direction from which his name had come his expression did not betray his sudden fear. A chill gripped him momentarily as he approached the man who had spoken his name, an attorney he knew from Los Angeles, a man who David might have described as a friend. They shook hands. David smiled warmly as the man patted his shoulder, an act that David illogically perceived as sly, insinuative.

"Deposition," David said, in response to the man's question. "One more session and then back to L.A. tomorrow night. What brings you up here?" The coincidence seemed hardly possible, in a mathematical sense, running into Boyd, then this man, on the very same day. David listened to the man's description of the business that had brought him north and nodded at the proper moments while his mind constructed boxes into which to put the details that would add up to a coherent plan. The man asked David if his wife had come with him, and without hesitation David said no, because even though he was certain that his wife and the man had never met, he felt that to add a charade to his infidelity would cross a line and offend some power ready to rain trouble and misery down upon him. Even if they pretended to be man and wife he would have to worry that Boyd would make a mistake, reveal the truth through carelessness, or at the very least introduce suspicion, and he would have to worry that at some later time he would meet the man in the company of his wife and be perceived not only as an adulterer but a liar. He could simply allow the truth to be known and rely upon the man's discretion, but the idea of any-one possessing such intimate knowledge about him produced a queasy sensation in his gut. Perhaps he and Boyd could come and go separately, maintain a pretense of being strangers. No, there was too much danger of something going haywire, given the in-credible coincidences of the day. They would eat dinner and then he would take her back to Berkeley. They would eat somewhere on the way. They wouldn't go to the restaurant he had told her about, because the events of the day suggested to him that despite the astronomical odds against it he would run into someone else who knew him.

A slender woman materialized at the lawyer's side and was introduced to David as the lawyer's wife. With a sense of his irra-tionality David wondered if this were true. They had gotten onto the subject of the aquarium, which the lawyer and his wife had visited that very afternoon. The lawyer's wife had found the sea otters charming and the kelp forest fascinating. David nodded. He conferred upon the woman a calm, unhurried smile. In a mo-ment he would escape. He saw in the mirror above the fireplace the reflected curve of the woman's neck, the graceful ascent of which brought him to an old-fashioned but stylish bun of hair, and disappointment gripped him like a fever. Instead of the inelegant Boyd, he realized, he wanted this man's wife, this utter stranger.

He nodded again and said, yes, he thought that what had been done to the old canneries was indeed tacky. His eyes grazed the tan landscape of a shoulder at the spot where it disappeared into the silk of a blouse and at the same moment detected movement on the reflected staircase—he smiled and said, no, he'd love to have dinner but he had to meet a client.

In the mirror that he imagined momentarily to be the glass of the aquarium tank he saw Boyd descend with a fluid, watery absence of speed to the landing and stop there and stare out over the room with an expression of uncertainty, as if unable to decide whether or not to proceed. Although he looked at her and she looked at him, their separate visions did not seem to intersect. David turned without alacrity to the lawyer and in a calm, apologetic tone interrupted a description of a condominium that the man and his wife were thinking of buying and said he had to make a call to L.A. before everyone left his office. He turned and walked to the foot of the stairs and went up in an unhurried but deliberate pace, passing Boyd without so much as a glance at her, bearing close to the wall in the manner of a stranger politely avoiding contact. He heard her begin to speak, nothing coherent but just a truncated question or remark, a sound in her throat that he believed, that he hoped, had not attracted the attention of the lawyer and his wife. He went along the hallway, passing pieces of antique furniture and portraits and photographs of a bygone era hung on the walls in polished wooden frames. When he reached the room he remembered that he had given Boyd the key. He tried the door and it was locked, and he walked to the end of the hall where above the roofs of nearby houses and a dark canopy of cypress trees a window framed the faint glow of the dead sun on the horizon at the far side of the bay. He waited, listening carefully, but heard no more than a murmur of conversation, the click of a shutting door, the hum of a vehicle on the street outside.

Boyd stood for what felt like hours on the landing, staring at the man and woman with whom David had been talking, but the gradual realization that his failure to acknowledge her possessed a definite logic did not diminish her sense of having been the victim of abuse. After the initial moments of confusion the situation plainly stated itself in her mind, and she felt like a prostitute, a stranger he had picked up off the street, to comply with some momentary imperative. She wasn't normally a vindictive person, but the brilliant image of his profile as he passed her on the stairs led her to consider the possibility of further descent, of walking up to the couple who looked smart and well-to-do and introducing herself as David's mistress. She was capable of doing this, she decided. She wanted to do it, but then she thought that they would compare her unfavorably to David's wife, a woman she imagined to be as stylish and poised as the woman by the fireplace, a woman who appeared to be at least as old as Boyd although Boyd felt much older. She felt dowdy and exposed, waiting without any evident purpose on the landing, someone unable to decide what to do next, a pathetic figure.

The couple did not appear to have noticed her. They looked like a pair of things expertly tended. She envisioned in the most general detail an enormous house, a garage full of expensive cars, some beautiful children, and this picture shifted to a specific site and led her to the conclusion that she never wanted to see David again. She would walk out the door, find a telephone, call a taxi, go home to her artist, who was neither rich nor poor but satisfied, in himself and, to a lesser extent, in her. She wondered if she had enough money for a taxi, and where she would find one. She realized that she held the key to the room in her hand, the room in which she had left her purse, which held her money, her toothbrush, photographs of her son, of the artist she had so casually decided to deceive. The man with whom David had been talking said something to the woman and the woman threw back her head in a self-confident, almost arrogant manner and laughed. Boyd felt hatred like fog in front of her face, making her feel isolated, alone, unable to see or touch anything. She turned, gripping the key so tightly that it cut into her palm, and went back up the stairs. She saw him at the window, his head bent, his shoulders rounded as if by fatigue. He looked sad, and this caused her to feel less rigid, more willing to forgive if that was what he wanted. In her ascent of the stairs her anger had run down to the slowly dying tick of an unwound clock. She unlocked the door to his room. She saw her purse on the bed like a piece of incriminating evidence, and she opened it and stared inside as David pushed his hands into his pockets like a nervous adolescent, pulled them out, and sat on the edge of a chair.

"I'm sorry," he said. "I guess it's dumb, trying to bring back the past."

"Is that what we were going to do?" She took a mirror from her purse and looked at a section of her face containing her nose, eyes, and mouth. It looked like an arty photograph. She took out a tube and puckered her lips. She felt slightly reckless, unconcerned now with how anything would turn out. "We're here," said Boyd, stirring in the purse for eye shadow and something to put color into her pallid cheeks, so that she might look more like the woman downstairs. "We might as well fuck, hadn't we?"

"Boyd." This proposition, in those terms, sounded to David repellent. He thought of the lawyer's wife at the fireplace, a woman carefully refined, possibly to the quality of glass, cold and hard and dangerous if carelessly handled. The red imperfect shininess of Boyd's lips made him think of passion insincere and manufactured. He watched with a feeling of foreboding and distaste as she casually undid the topmost button of her dress, bringing the slightly bumpy depression between the initial swellings of her breasts into view. He hoped that she would not continue, but her fingers undid more buttons, exposing more of the olive and lightly speckled topography of her chest and the cream-colored lace of her bra. He knew that she was angry because he had ignored her on the stairs, although his actions were perfectly defensible, and that she was determined to punish him, although he didn't quite see in a rational way how her use of the word "fuck" and painting her lips and unbuttoning her dress constituted punishment. He only knew that she wasn't, at that moment, despite her lascivious manner, desirable.

"We ought to go," he said. He suddenly thought of how little he knew of her. With a brief feeling of terror so keen that he shuddered, he saw himself, wasted to skin and bones by disease, waiting to die. For just a moment he was appalled by his own recklessness. "I'll drive you back," he heard himself say.

"Crap," she said. She unbuttoned the last button at her waist and began to shrug the dress from her shoulders. Her shoulders were more freckled than he remembered, the flesh of her upper arms pendulous in a way he thought of as peculiar to females of a certain age. I'm going to see her body, he thought, her breasts which have stretched and sagged, her pubic hair which may have begun to gray along with the hair on her head, and it won't invoke any passion from the past, it will simply be a body with its own self-contained set of attractions, however mild or powerful they might prove to be. The dress collapsed into a messy pile of green at her feet and he said, "We're not a couple of horny kids anymore, Boyd."

"I know what we are," said Boyd.

"What do you want?" David imagined a smirk on the face of the lawyer downstairs, and an expression of profound boredom on the face of the lawyer's wife. He looked at what he could see of himself, his wrists emerging from the sleeves of his jacket, the pleated material of his trousers folding at his lap and traveling in a crease to his knees and descending toward the soft brown leather of his shoes. Despite the obvious sight and weight of this clothing he felt naked. When they were together they had often done without clothing, alone and in groups, and this had stimulated him, like the exciting dynamics of tag or some other childish game. For just a moment he imagined the four of them, he and Boyd, the lawyer and the lawyer's wife, all of them naked together in the bed, and he thought of the long elegant arms and legs of the lawyer's wife in contrast to the somewhat puffy, dark-veined limbs of Boyd.

"What do I want?" she asked. Facing him, her dress a puddle at her feet, she felt an unfamiliar sense of power. She thought that he might be afraid, and without real calculation she wanted to use this against him. She considered his question carefully, thoughtfully. I want to humiliate you, she might have said. I want to see what kind of lover you have become. I want to experience, just once, what we experienced long ago, before we became what we are now, which is possibly something so different from what we were that there is nothing to recognize.

She suddenly felt weary, and pushed the purse aside and sat on the edge of the bed. She leaned over, gathered her dress in her hands, and held it in her lap, then spread it across her knees because she felt a draft. She would put the dress back on, button the half dozen buttons, go down ahead of him, go outside, walk around the corner and wait. He would come down a few minutes later, get into his car, back out of the parking space, and pull up to the curb and lean across the seat and unlock the door for her. They would drive back to Berkeley, stopping on the way to eat at some coffee shop or other nondescript place. They would say good-bye, exchange a peck on the cheek, possibly allow, for historical reasons, an instant's conjunction of the lips. She would get into her car and drive to the studio and explain to the artist why she was so late, even though it wasn't in his nature to demand an explanation, and if he was hurt or disappointed he wouldn't say anything, he would simply be quieter than usual for an hour or two.

She lifted the dress by the shoulders so that it hung between them, blocking her view of him. He stared at the dress, which said something vague about lost opportunities, but he was already thinking ahead, what he would do tomorrow, what he would do when he got back to Los Angeles. She stared at the dress, wondering why she had bought it, thinking that it was probably unattractive, nothing that the woman who was with the man who had been talking to David would be caught dead in. She shook the dress, trying to animate it, to see herself as she was seen, but it remained without form, empty, suggestive neither of the past nor future, of nothing at all.

Bésame, Bésame

Richie's mother flew out to California for Christmas, just a simple, quiet two weeks with Richie and Consuelo and the kids, but it wasn't to be—on the very first day Richie came home from work to find her in her room, sitting on the edge of the bed, hands twisted and bloodless in her lap and a sour look of endurance on her face. It wasn't an entirely unfamiliar look, but neither were her swollen eyes what Richie wanted to see, not when he had gone to the expense of her ticket and taken time off to pick her up at the airport and allowed himself to imagine scenes of filial warmth just vague enough that he didn't have to consider their plausibility. He marched into the living room where Consuelo and her friend Margarita had the stereo turned up and were drinking wine in water glasses, and he spun the volume knob way down and said, "Can't you once, just once in your life, consider somebody other than yourself? Just once. Just one goddamn time?"

"I don't know what's the matter with her," Consuelo said, in a childish tone of injury. She turned and said something in Spanish to Margarita, and Margarita nodded, irritating Richie to the point where he began to feel loose and unconstrained. As if he might pick up something and throw it, not at Consuelo but against the wall, or the sliding glass door through which he could see the kids rolling across the patio in mortal combat, emitting a chorus of shrieks and yelps. Let them kill each other, he said to himself. He crossed the room and sat down carefully next to Consuelo on the sofa and stared into her bright black eyes.

"Her nerves are bad," he said slowly and emphatically, as if explaining something simple but at the same time complicated to one of the kids, why they couldn't stay up, or have ice cream right before dinner. "She can't stand loud noise. She's going to be here two weeks. Just two weeks. Fourteen days." He pushed his palm into the space between them and began to count aloud on his fingers. "One, two, three . . ."

She made a noise of suffering in her throat. "She doesn't like me."

"Huh?" Richie dropped the hand to his knee. He gazed at arcs of black at the tips of the fingers and a vein of dried blood running crookedly from one of the knuckles. A dull pain spread from his upper arm to his shoulder and throbbed at the base of his neck, threatening to enter his head and beat there like a drum. What had she been doing? Running around with Margarita? While he was busting his can, making enough to pay for the new bikes they had already bought for the kids, and whatever they would decide to get for themselves—a TV for their bedroom maybe, or a microwave oven. And then there was the cost of his mother's ticket.

"She thinks the house is dirty."

"She said that?" He had spent the past ten hours on his knees, setting tile on the floor of a large and opulent bathroom in a house being built for a doctor and his wife, and his Levi's were caked and stiff with mortar and his shirt was stained with sweat. Consuelo had reproached him in the past for sitting on the furniture before getting out of his work clothes and it made no sense whatever for his mother to criticize her housekeeping. He looked around. He saw nothing out of place. He couldn't see a single speck of dirt. The carpet looked as smooth as freshly combed hair.

"What did she say?" he asked, suspicion diluting his anger, turning it into the fatigue that he would mitigate by getting into the shower and then afterwards opening a beer and reading the paper or maybe watching the news on TV.

"She said, 'Do you vacuum every day?' "

"Yeah?"

"She thinks the house is dirty."

Richie heard his mother's voice in his head, threatening him with some forgotten punishment if he didn't straighten up the mess in his room. "She said she thought it was dirty?"

"She didn't say that."

"She just asked if you vacuumed every day?"

"Yes."

"Jesus." Richie stood up. He wanted to escape into the shower and stay there thinking about nothing until the steam and heat drove him out. Did everything planned, everything expected, always go haywire? "It's just a question," he said, his body feeling dense and heavy, filled with the sand and cement he had mixed all day for his mortar. "She wasn't saying anything about the condition of the house. She was just asking a question."

"You know she doesn't like me," Consuelo said softly, looking not at him but at Margarita, whose expression of utter sympathy sprung a pang of annoyance that leaked out of Richie's mind in the form of a scowl.

"She likes you," Richie asserted, this reprise of an old argument making him feel so tired that he wanted to shut his eyes and slide into a fantasy involving another person: a blonde, blue-eyed woman and himself in a place where everything was simple and you could have exactly what you wanted without any consequences. "There's no reason to think she doesn't."

"You know why," said Consuelo, her voice falling to just above a whisper. A tear hung for a moment at the pink rim of her eyelid and then slid halfway down her cheek. His mother, Richie imagined, had entered into a tortured empathy and had also begun to weep behind the closed door of her room. Margarita looked as if her glossy lips would crumble at any moment; all that was needed to complete the scene was one of the kids to come pushing and bawling into the room with a scrape or bruise or complaint about who had started the fight that appeared to rage unabated beyond the sliding glass door. These women could weep while he had to maintain a pretense of neutrality and self-control. To Richie this suddenly appeared unfair—grossly, hugely unfair.

"Consuelo," he said in a low voice that caused her eyes to widen, that caused Margarita to cock her head and stare. "If you make any more trouble I'll have to get even." A sense of power did nothing to lighten his fatigue; he wasn't even sure that they were afraid, that they wouldn't break into giggles after he left the room. Goddamn actresses, he thought. "I'll have to get revenge. Understand?"

"Yes," Consuelo said, in a whisper.

"What else?"

"What?" Her thin mouth opened like a shell to reveal small pearls of teeth.

"Dinner. Make something she will like. Don't make any damn Mexican food. She doesn't like it."

"Yes," she said, not looking at him but at Margarita, or perhaps beyond, where the kids were shoving to be the first to open the door and get inside, making a racket that prompted him to stand and head for the bathroom, which he imagined to be a piece of space and time imbued with quiet, where he could wash off not only the dirt and sweat but the whole idea of vengeance that had arrived, unpredictably, suddenly, like a brilliant conclusion, in his weary mind.

Consuelo fixed a casserole so bland that Richie got up to get the jalapeño sauce from the refrigerator, but then he sat down, because he wasn't ready to give her the slightest satisfaction, to admit that he might have been wrong. After eating for a while in silence interrupted only by the kids his mother said, "Do you remember Jerry Ropek?" It was the name of a boy in Richie's high school class, and he said, "Yeah," dreading what was coming next, a catalog of who had married whom, who was doing what—a testimony, it seemed to Richie, to the virtue of caution and predict-ability. She mentioned the name of a girl that Richie had briefly fallen in desperate love with, and he was forced to interrupt and say, "Mom, I really don't care about any of these people. I'm here and they're there. I doubt if I'll ever see them again."

"If you came back."

"What do you mean, came back?" The kids were apparently kicking or pinching each other beneath the table because there had risen a whining repetition of "Stop it!" Consuelo was studiously ignoring this disruption, and everything else, staring at her plate, moving things around with her fork and now and then taking a microscopic bite. "Why would I come back?"

"There's your class reunion," Richie's mother said, in a tone that seemed a glimmer of light in a dark void of resignation.

"You mean for a visit?"

"I guess it's too expensive."

"We could come for a visit sometime. I thought you were talking about coming back, like, permanently."

"I don't expect that," she said. Her eyes seemed to turn in wist-ful longing past Richie, Consuelo, the unruly children, then fell to her plate and remained there, as if staring into the future, where expectation had already been crushed by some arbitrary, cruel act of fate. Richie looked at the kids, then Consuelo. In their re-spective clamor and silence they seemed oblivious, and Richie felt alone, completely alone and abandoned.

On the day before Christmas Eve he finished grouting the bath-room tile and loaded his trowels and buckets and leftover bags of cement into his van. The warm, cloudless sky led to visions of midwestern winters that seemed to go on forever, and suddenly he felt lucky, almost blessed by the God and the Virgin and the vari-ous saints that Consuelo believed in with a fervor that caused him to chuckle when he remembered how worried she looked when he told her, not long after the priest had pronounced them man and wife, that he was an atheist. This wasn't precisely true, he had tried to explain in an effort to erase the anxiety from her face, he believed in God as nature and only found all these trappings—her Virgin, her saints, her prayers and confessions—to be ridiculous. He wouldn't have said anything at all if he hadn't been drinking the tequila that her uncle had pressed upon him with an urgency he couldn't deflect, it appeared, without giving enormous offense. Like a ribbon of film the memory ran past his eyes. Why had he deceived her? On his knees, literally, in a room below which a mariachi played and noises of gaiety continued unabated, he had begged to be allowed to consummate their union. He didn't remember the exact words that he used, only that he spoke in such a garbled mixture of Spanish and English that she could understand nothing. He might have wept. The only thing he clearly recalled was vowing with a spiritual ardor to never, never again be lured into drinking tequila with her uncle.

But he didn't go to church with her, and she no longer seemed to care what he did or didn't believe. She was a good mother and a more or less dutiful wife, so why was he dissatisfied? In some deep, distant, hazy manner, angry with her? Was it her apparent dislike of his mother? That mutual antipathy that was like the odor of something rotted or unwashed in the house?

He drove home with a coral sunset in his windshield, feeling a desire to come to Consuelo's defense, putting to himself the argument that she had never been, to his knowledge, unfaithful; that she didn't neglect the kids; that she didn't nag him excessively, or spend *all* her time watching Spanish-language soap operas on TV. This argument, however, appeared to consist entirely of negatives and thus failed to win him completely to her side. She was still pretty, he told himself, although she had let herself gain too much weight since the second baby was born. Her mother was fat. Her aunts were fat. Her sisters, even the youngest, still pubescent, had bodies that strained at their clothing, like ripening fruit. They all lined up in his head and gazed at him, plump, dark-haired, black-eyed women waiting to see how this *hombre palido* would treat their Consuelo. She and her children would be citizens of the United States and live, in comparison to her mother and aunts and sisters, a lavish style of life, but would she remember the Virgin and all the saints? Her *padres*, her *hermanos*?

The luminous sunset, Richie knew, was a phenomenon of a Santa Ana wind that had risen in the morning to carry the pollutants west, all the way to the horizon. It seemed a miracle and also a practical joke, this beauty consisting of fumes and chemicals that nobody would breathe if they had the choice. In the place where Consuelo's mother and other members of her family lived, the sky was almost always blue and clear, but there was also dust on everything, and pools of standing water and mud in the season of rain, and Richie could not help thinking of them as deprived although they all appeared remarkably at ease with their own destinies. The uncle with the tequila was a plumber—he and Richie had talked about the vicissitudes of construction before the man disclosed that because of a lack of work he had been forced to sell his most prized possession, an American-made drill. And yet the man had seemed intoxicated—not simply by the tequila but by the blessing of circumstance that allowed him such joys as celebrating the marriage of a niece that he loved like a daughter, an unconditional joy that Richie could witness but not quite share, not completely.

Richie's mother sat watching cartoons with the kids, stiff and upright on the sofa with her hands gripped tightly in her lap. He wondered if she had looked like this when his father was still alive, but his memories were of an egocentric nature, himself the center of a focus that softened into a periphery through which his mother and father moved with indefinite purpose, their voices murmuring beyond their bedroom door. He looked at the kids, lying on the floor too close to the screen. The volume was turned up high and a particularly loud explosion of noise appeared to make his mother cringe.

He told her that he was going in the morning to collect his final payment, and invited her to come to see his work. He was aware of a childish need for praise, approval. She nodded, looking alone and forlorn, and Richie thought of Consuelo's mother, a placid woman who seemed a vessel into which her children poured everything—anger, hope, fear, love. Consuelo was also placid—to a point. Now she was positively withdrawn—he had looked into the bedroom and the kitchen but hadn't seen her—and Richie felt abused by a need to divide up his loyalty. He turned down the TV and said to his mother, "Where's Consuelo?"

"She went out," said one of the kids, his voice distorted by hands propping up his chin.

"Did I ask you?" He gave the boy a nudge with his foot. "Didn't I tell you not to play the TV so goddamn loud? Huh?"

"She went with Margarita," said Richie's mother.

"Margarita." Richie had a momentary glimpse of this woman whose face was darker than Consuelo's, blood of the unlucky Aztecs in her veins. Together they looked like the young Latinas he seemed to see everywhere, poured into their jeans, lips and cheeks painted red, glass and metal dancing and flashing at their ears. Waiting to be noticed by boys in lowered minitrucks, much too sexy for their own good. Margarita had a husband but no children, which was a mystery he had never discussed with Consuelo. About a month ago, in a neighborhood bar he went to now and then to shoot a few games of pool, he had seen this man sitting very close to a woman who was not Margarita, and the memory caused a finger of apprehension to scratch in his chest. Richie suspected without any evidence that this man was in the United States illegally, that he possessed counterfeit papers. He went into the kitchen to see if Consuelo had laid out anything to thaw for dinner, but she hadn't, and as he opened the refrigerator to get himself a beer the thought of her in that bar, nestled against a strange man, went through his head like a cloud ready to burst with cold midwestern rain or sleet or snow, freezing, unescapable.

His mother appeared in the doorway. Her nature seemed to place her in doorways, never quite daring enough to enter a room without invitation. Richie said nothing. He sat down at the kitchen table with his beer.

"Does she always speak Spanish to the children?" his mother asked, just when the silence had thickened to the point where he felt compelled to say something, anything.

"No," said Richie. Goddamn it, he said to himself, making my mother feel left out, like a stranger. "I don't know. I mean, I'm not here every minute."

"They seem to be having trouble with their English."

"They're dumb," said Richie, feeling dumb himself, for this clumsy attempt at humor that couldn't possibly amuse her. "Like their old man. They'll probably grow up to be tile setters. If they don't kill each other first."

His mother gazed at him, as if pondering what she and Richie's father had wrought, a child they had once believed to possess the brains and motivation to get good grades and be the first in the family to go to college. To become an engineer, lawyer, doctor, anything. Not a machinist, like his father. Not a tile setter.

"Are you thinking of having more children?"

"I don't know," said Richie. Despite her devotion to the Virgin, Consuelo took birth-control pills. Richie had once committed the grave error of joking about what the pope would do if he found out, and he didn't want to get into this subject with his mother, who was a good Protestant and had already remarked upon the various images Consuelo put up on the walls, the fireplace mantel, the top of the TV. He wondered what she would think if she knew what he had been forced to memorize, to repeat and promise in order to be married by the priest.

He took a sip of beer. Light beer that he told Consuelo to buy because he was getting paunchy. But the beer was insipid, tasteless.

"I thought that the boys could come and stay for part of the summer."

He looked up, a little startled, both by this unexpected desire on his mother's part and by the thud of the front door against the jamb. From where he sat he could see Consuelo in a shadow, and he imagined getting up, meeting her just about at the living room sofa, and giving her a hug and a long, moist kiss, but his mother's presence inhibited him and the whole thing turned into a fantasy too silly to believe in.

"Consuelo's taking them to Mexico." At the sound of her name Consuelo turned her head and gave Richie a tight little smile. She disappeared into the family room and he heard the kids' voices rise in grievance or demand, he couldn't tell which. What had she and Margarita been doing? Vast suspicion welled up like a sneeze, taking over all his senses, then faded into a vague unease.

"They're going for two months. To her mother's."

Richie was aware of what this implied, and he either saw or imagined that he saw his mother wince. Why, he wondered, did she want these noisy, obstreperous boys, other than to comply with some ideal notion of family? He thought of the neat, quiet house full of noise and disarray, the boys whooping and breaking his mother's collection of bric-a-brac while she sat wringing her hands in a corner. He resisted an urge to laugh.

"Maybe next year."

His mother abruptly sat down at the opposite end of the table. "You didn't tell me." Her injured tone took him as far back as he could remember. He had intended to tell her, at the right time, but now he wondered when this time would have come. "Two months?" he heard his mother say. "Isn't that a long time?"

"Not long," he said.

She sighed, seeming to ponder this answer as she had pondered, when he was a child, his obvious lies. Then she said, "Where will they live?"

He wondered why she used the word "live" instead of "stay." Did she believe that once they were out of the country they would be gone forever? "They'll stay with Consuelo's mother."

"She has a house?"

"Yeah. She has a house." He knew what his mother imagined, illiterate savages in huts and caves, and he felt turgid and defensive. "It has electricity, even. Plumbing, too, if you can imagine that. Her mother even has a car. Amazing, huh?"

"You haven't been to your father's grave," she said in a low, injured voice. "Not since the funeral. Not a single time."

"Mom . . ." He wanted to say, you're not going to make me feel guilty. He thought of the death which seemed almost an act of will—his father growing up in the city where he was born, marrying the girl he had dated in high school, raising three children, retiring on a pension not to travel or putter with a hobby but to sit in his lounger as if awaiting the heart attack that killed him. Richie suddenly wondered if this picture was really a window through which his own fate might be glimpsed. Consuelo's father had died before Richie met her; driving home from the *cantina* one night he had skidded off the side of a bridge into a river. The uncle who plied Richie with the tequila had described the scene—the twisted, broken guardrail, the sight of the pickup's taillight poking from the water, in almost lyrical terms. In contrast to Richie's father's prosaic death, this demise of Consuelo's father seemed almost heroic.

Richie parked his van and led his mother through a chainlink gate and across a dirt yard littered with construction materials—lengths of pipe, partial bags of cement, bricks, broken tiles, odds and ends of lumber. The house was surrounded by junipers and shaded by a pair of enormous sycamore trees. Near the arched and deeply shadowed entry a mixer sputtered and rocked, its paddles churning stucco that in a semiliquid state was a bright apricot color. Richie's mother hesitated, as if in fear of this machine or of the dark, wiry man who stopped the motion of the paddles, pulled heavily on a lever, and disgorged the heavy soup of stucco into a wheelbarrow. On tiers of scaffolding above, plasterers dressed in white were troweling the stucco onto the walls, and as Richie took his mother's hand to draw her into the shadow of the entry he heard from a distance the rising whine of a saw and then, closer, what sounded like an insult, and finally good-natured laughter. The words of a familiar song floated through the air just as the man straining behind the wheelbarrow disappeared around a corner of the house. Richie knew the name of this song—"*Bésame*"— and was startled to hear it. A group of men with guitars and a violin had sung it somewhere in the tequila-blurred hours that followed Richie and Consuelo's wedding, and the romantic strains had made Consuelo cry. That was all that Richie remembered. The song, the phrase "*Bésame, bésame mucho*," and the transparent trail of a tear, shiny and luminous, on the plump and enticing curve of Consuelo's cheek.

The house contained five bathrooms, a fact that appeared to impress Richie's mother more than the sight of his work, the tile in complex and difficult patterns that had kept him on the job so late some days that Consuelo, usually agreeable, had complained. He pointed out this and that feature while his mother hung back near the doorways, as if afraid to intrude into a world in which she felt inferior. He was momentarily afraid that the owners of the house, the doctor and his wife, would appear and cause his mother to embarrass him with an exaggeration of deference.

He found the general contractor with the architect in the kitchen, watching a painter brush samples of color onto a wall.

The architect said, "Too much white," in an impatient tone. He did not look at Richie, who nodded to the general contractor.

"How's it going?"

"Getting there," said the man, who looked at Richie's mother in the doorway and politely smiled.

"Did you check the bathroom?" Richie didn't want to linger; he wanted to get his check to the bank, where he suspected a line had already begun to form. "Is everything okay?"

"It's fine," the man said. "It looks good. There's just one problem."

A heavy stone of dismay rolled into Richie's chest. "What problem?"

"They don't like the pattern. They want it changed."

"What's wrong with it?" Richie felt the presence of his mother in the doorway behind him, silent but watchful, forming some judgment that she would divulge to him later, a judgment that would reflect her sorrow over his having moved so far from home and produced a wife and children with whom she felt nothing in common. Although he felt a sudden, dangerous pressure that would cause him to blurt out something he would later regret, he aimed for a neutral tone.

"He gave me the pattern." Richie gestured toward the architect. "I followed it exactly."

"I know that."

"But if they don't like it I'll take it out. I'll do the whole thing over. No problem. Whatever they want. But they'll have to pay for it."

The man shrugged, as if the matter was out of his hands. He turned his eyes back to the fresh bands of paint that glowed on the wall.

"They'll have to pay for it," Richie said again, aware of fatigue brought on not only by the work but the fact that he hadn't slept well since his mother arrived. "If I have to do it over."

The architect, a small man of Richie's age, perhaps even younger, glanced away from the wall and said, "The point is not who's going to pay for it. The point is that it has to be done."

The man was dressed, to Richie's mind, in a foppish manner—loose white shirt, thin purple tie, baggy pants, and shoes with pointed toes. Richie had never felt from this man any recognition of equality and he wanted, right then, to cause everything to stop—the painting, the plastering, whatever else was going on—and to demand some declaration of respect. He wanted almost desperately to do this, but the presence of his mother deterred him, because she would make assumptions broad enough to include everything about his life she disapproved of and he would get angry and say something he would later regret. He needed, however, to get to the bank and make a deposit to cover checks he had already written. Because of Christmas the bank would be closed until the following Monday and then it might be too late. He momentarily considered telling his mother to go into the living room and look at the marble around the fireplace—some rare imported marble—but he didn't; he stared at the painter, who stirred in his can, then dipped his brush, tapped it on the side of the can, and placed a level stroke of color on the wall.

"What about my payment?" Richie said.

"I can't submit a bill until they're satisfied." The general contractor's voice seemed to come from a distance, and Richie felt suddenly and acutely abused by the system of which the man was a part, the system of power and authority that flowed upward from him to the architect and on to the doctor and his wife who felt it their prerogative to withhold someone's money until their whims were satisfied.

Richie said, "If they want it changed, I'll take it out. I'll start next week. But I need my payment."

"I understand," said the contractor, his eyes on the painter, who was silently enduring the architect's irritation over his failure to add enough blue to the sample. "But there's nothing I can do. I can't bill them until they're satisfied."

"That's shit," said Richie, feeling the rational part of his brain detach from the impulsive side with an audible click.

"Possibly," said the contractor, so cooly that Richie felt a chill. "But that's the way things are—there's nothing I can do about it."

Without looking at Richie the architect said, "Just the tile around the tub. It's not that big a deal." He was squatting, peering at the paint. "Too damn much white still." He turned his head to look, not at Richie, but at Richie's mother, who lingered in the doorway, staring. "Would you please move back?" He made what Richie interpreted as a dismissive gesture with his hand. "You're blocking some of our light."

Driving away between walls of foliage so nearly solid that only a piece of terra-cotta roof or a bit of a mullioned second-story window or the bricks of a chimney could be seen, Richie was silent, but his mother turned garrulous, pointing out the height of palm trees or some other interesting, even amazing feature of the landscape, trying to make it seem, Richie thought, as if nothing unpleasant or unseemly had happened. He remembered that when he was little and fell or bumped his head or got a particularly bad scare she would chatter on and on, as if silence had the capacity, by itself, to cause fright and pain.

"Mom," he said. "It's okay. Don't worry about anything."

"It was a beautiful house," she said, as if compelled to utter this approbation.

"It's all right," Richie said. Don't be unfair, he added to himself. Don't judge.

"You could have been an architect," she said.

Richie sighed. He hadn't stayed close to his roots, he hadn't gone to college, he hadn't married the girl he went steady with in high school, he hadn't given his mother a daughter-in-law and grandchildren that she could feel connected to in some primal way.

"I make more money than a lot of architects," he said. "It's just that sometimes there are these people . . ." He didn't wish to confirm her view of society as organized, and rightly so, for the pleasure of the rich and powerful. Nevertheless, he added, "These people can't relate to the fact that if I don't get paid on time I don't pay the mortgage. Don't eat."

"That's why your father never went into business for himself, even though he often talked about it," she said, predictably.

"I could never work for somebody else. Not now," said Richie, thinking of bosses, even the benevolent ones, their demands to get the job done faster because they were in danger of losing money. He hadn't taken them seriously, not until halfway through the first job he had taken after getting his tile contractor's license and discovering that when he subtracted the cost of his wire, his paper, his sand and cement, he would be lucky to make two or three dollars an hour. And then there were always the general contractors who badgered him into lowering his bid, and the homeowners who appeared to be stunned when he showed them his estimate. I live in a house, he sometimes wanted to say. I'm married. I've got kids. They eat. They wear clothes. Don't I deserve to make a decent living? These people who were usually doctors, lawyers, someone in the financial business, with houses being built or remodeled so lavish in contrast to the house that Richie grew up in and the houses of his friends and the houses in his neighborhood as to be of a different nature entirely. He did not resent this fact exactly, and discovered that by working faster, by organizing things more carefully, by getting to the job earlier and leaving later, he could make enough to pay the bills and now and then have a little left over for some very modest luxury.

He wanted to see himself as different from his father, who stood at the same machine in the same shop all his life and then retired and died, but the only real difference he sometimes perceived was that he wanted these small luxuries that his father had never been interested in. New car? His father would repair the old one until it literally could not go another mile. Vacation? They went, for two weeks each year, to the Black Hills, a drive across Nebraska and into South Dakota on the same route, year after year, a trip that was mostly so flat and boring that in high school Richie had manufactured excuses not to go. Everything in the house had to be old, the paint worn through, shiny spots covered with doilies and throw rugs, before being replaced, and then only after interminable searches for the best price, for sales.

He swung onto the freeway. The traffic was sluggish, and the fact of its being Christmas Eve didn't fill his heart with anything resembling cheer. One of his checks would bounce. He would eventually get paid, but not before jumping through hoops of flame to prove that he was deserving. A car cut too close in front, causing him to hit the brakes, and he cursed and blew the horn, an act he immediately regretted on the grounds that his mother would see this aggression and hostility as a product of a life he had chosen to lead so far removed from his real home. But she just kept chattering on and he turned up the radio so that he would have something else to listen to.

The house was empty—in a note left on the kitchen table Consuelo said that she was taking the kids to the church. For a pageant that he had forgotten. His mother, her garrulousness swallowed by the silent house, told Richie in a tone of slight reproach that she was tired and going to lie down in her room. Richie turned on the radio, low, so that it wouldn't bother her, but the murmuring quality of the voices annoyed him and he turned it off. He looked into the refrigerator but there wasn't any beer, just a single can of soda. He opened this and sat in the ambiguous light of midday considering his beliefs—he supposed there was a God, somebody or something in possession of power less self-centered and reckless than the power unequally distributed to human beings. But the Virgin? The saints? It seemed that an intelligent person with a certain degree of education would naturally view this as folklore, as superstition. He had gone—he couldn't remember if it was two or three times—to church with Consuelo. He had always been bored by ceremony, by the need to sit and listen to any sort of speech or lecture, and the incomprehensible drone of the priest had caused him to fall asleep and snore, acutely embarrassing Consuelo. He had been performing a duty that turned out to be unnecessary, that's all.

He looked through the window at the sky and imagined a distant white, scrimlike descent of snow. Suddenly he was bothered, acutely, by a picture of his kids getting down on their knees, sticking out their tongues to receive a thing of no more significance than the crackers he could see in a box on the counter, a box they had apparently opened even though they had been forbidden to do so. Consuelo indulged them, he thought, beginning against his will to resent her family—her affable brothers and sisters and uncles, her mother who never wrung her hands or chewed her lip, who appeared to have endured her children's noise, their complaints, their egotism, with utter, absolute equanimity.

The soda tasted metallic and he poured it down the sink. He turned the note from Consuelo over and wrote that he was going to take his van to the car wash. He knocked on his mother's door and when she answered in a voice that sounded just slightly frightened he told her he was going to run an errand and would be back in an hour. Richie hoped that she would not get up and open the door and gaze upon him, her eyes filled with the pain of abandonment. He went quickly through the kitchen and garage and got into his van and backed into the street. As he accelerated, then braked for the stop sign at the corner, he felt like a burglar who has just made the narrowest of escapes from the scene of his crime.

All three bays of the car wash were filled and a half dozen cars waited in line. He drove two blocks, turned onto the freeway frontage road, passed a gas station, a used-car lot, a place that sold campers and travel trailers, and approached a long, low building in the style of a western ranch house with a neon sign on the roof and an asphalt parking lot filled with cars, trucks, and, up near a rustic veranda, a trio of shiny customized motorcycles. He slowed, hesitated, then pulled into the parking lot, which was so full that he had to drive off the asphalt onto yellow gravelly earth and clumps of weeds that crunched beneath his tires.

He worked his way to the bar, found a stool at the very end, and sat half-turned, waiting to catch the bartender's attention. The place was a chamber filled with a din of voices and smoke that hung like a fog, making everything seem unreal. Before going to Mexico, before meeting Consuelo and deciding to settle down, he had spent many hours in such places, but now he kept beer in the refrigerator and although he missed certain things—shooting pool, jiving with the regulars, getting just high enough to forget how a certain boss had abused him—an atmosphere of lost time and hopelessness had even then begun to depress him. Now he dropped into this bar once a month or so to shoot a few games of pool and have, at the most, two beers. The bartender finally approached and drew him a glass of beer but did not appear to remember his name or recognize his face.

He turned completely on his stool to face the clamor of the long, low room. Christmas Eve, everyone taking off work, getting a head start on celebration. The pool tables all were busy and players appeared to be waiting. He saw a few familiar faces but none he wanted to speak to. He decided to drink the beer and leave and try the car wash again and then go home and face whatever music Consuelo or his mother or the kids had composed to wreck his peace of mind.

He heard his name before he saw a face. He turned his head in the wrong direction, then back to see, emerging from a cone of yellow light around a pool table, Margarita's husband. He carried a cue stick in his hand. He smoothly slid around obstacles as he approached, a white smile glowing beneath the double black wings of his mustache. Richie nodded, feeling the necessity of being alert, on guard, because he suspected the man of wanting something. The man always seemed to want something, but in an indirect, insinuating manner. To sell Richie something. In the past this had been both tangible—a car, a boat, a shotgun, a possibly valuable lottery ticket—and in the realm of idea—some money to be made, some pleasure to be had, some places to go and things to do there. The man's lips parted over a sea of glossy teeth and he said, "*Hola. Cómo estás?*"

Richie didn't want to speak Spanish, because that would seem to imply an intimacy he neither felt nor desired, so he said, in English, "I'm okay. Yourself?"

"*Muy bien.* Let me buy you a beer." Without waiting for Richie's assent he loudly called to the bartender. Richie had heard, a few days before, one of the kids call the other a *pendejo,* an epithet that precipitated a noisy clamor of demands and further insults. He didn't know what prompted this memory. He only knew that he did not want this man to buy him a beer because, by rules not of his own making, his failure to buy the man a drink in return would constitute an insult almost as bad as calling him a *pendejo.* He felt trapped by obligation—to this man, to Consuelo, to his mother, to the contractor and architect and the dissatisfied owners of the house. A second glass of beer materialized in front of him. What he really wanted to do was abandon both this beer and the half-finished glass in his hand, leave, stop at the liquor store and buy a six-pack for the refrigerator and then take another turn past the car wash on the chance that there was an empty bay. He did not want Consuelo to come home while he was gone and say and do something that—while unmalicious, inadvertent even—would further disrupt his mother's fragile nerves.

"This is my cousin," Margarita's husband was saying, pushing forward a stocky man who had appeared as if by sleight of hand. This cousin wore a faint smile on his face and his handshake, in the curious manner of so many of his countrymen, was limp. "Mauricio," said Margarita's husband. "You need some help, he'll work very good for you."

"Have you got papers?" Richie asked, regretting that he hadn't just said, no, I've got all the help I need. The man said nothing; apparently he didn't understand English. I want to embarrass these men, Richie thought, but then he knew that he was at the disadvantage, because Margarita's husband was quick as a snake; there would always be a card in his sleeve, or something hidden in the palm of his hand.

"Papers? Has he got papers?" The incredulity of Margarita's husband was so transparent that Richie wanted to laugh, although he wasn't in the mood to laugh, but only to escape. "What do you want? Driver's license. Social Security. *Tarjeta verde?*"

"I don't need anybody," Richie said.

"You don't need nobody? Things are slow, huh? Bad."

"I've got work." He could hear Margarita saying to Consuelo, "It's really bad your husband doesn't have any work," and Consuelo worrying, worrying about everything as she was prone to do—the kids, the mortgage, the credit card payments. "I just don't need any help right now."

"When you do you tell me, okay?" Margarita's husband took his wallet from his pocket and extracted a business card. On the card was a name, a printed telephone number crossed out with another written in pencil above it, and in three long lines of printing across the top of the card a list of trades so extensive and unlikely that Richie was forced to chuckle. Margarita's husband grinned, as if sharing a joke. Richie considered the fact that the man's face appeared to glow, probably from a quantity of alcohol.

"I forget your name," the man said, suddenly grave.

"Richie." He hadn't wanted to answer, but couldn't figure out how his silence wouldn't be taken as an insult.

"Reechee." From the man's mouth the name sounded effeminate, a joke.

"Richard." Richie said, irritated.

"*Sí.*" The man stroked the pool cue with silky movements of his fingers. "*Ricardo.*" He smiled expansively, and Richie decided that if the man wasn't drunk he soon would be. He spoke directly to Richie but his eyes drifted around in his head as if on the lookout for some opportunity elsewhere amidst the smoke and noise. Richie looked at the limp card in his hand. He didn't want to put it in his pocket, he wanted to leave it on the bar, or let it drop to the floor.

"Who is this?"

"My other cousin. *Tomás.*" He leaned toward Richie and placed a slender finger on the name printed on the card, which was not *Tomás* but Thomas. "Maybe you got some job you don't want to do, you give it to him."

"He's a tile setter? Among all these other things."

"For sure. He does a very good job."

"How much does he charge?"

"Oh, he is very reasonable."

"He has his license?"

"*Sí.* For certain. He has everything he needs."

Richie didn't believe this, but let it go. "He has insurance?"

"*Cómo?*" The man's affability seemed to be slowly leaking out of him, his lips sliding over his teeth so that his grin turned into something ambiguous.

"Insurance," Richie persisted, not out of interest but a perverse desire to agitate or at least discomfit the man, if only slightly. "If he's smoking a cigarette and sets a house on fire."

The man's circling eyes settled on Richie, causing him to feel, for just a moment, that he and not Margarita's husband was the foreigner, the alien, the man with roots in a different part of the world, making his presence open to question and inspection. The man laughed, deeply, as if this picture of a cigarette and a burning house were utterly hilarious, and Richie felt a deepening sense of estrangement. He knew that if he listened carefully to the cacophony he would be able to pick up the lilt and cadence of Spanish or accented English; he could not remember when he had last been in the place and not seen men and women with black eyes and burnished skin. He had felt this strangeness in Mexico, before falling in love with Consuelo and entering the warmth of her family, a sense of being unable to walk down a street unnoticed or engage in a conversation in which language, instead of disclosing or clarifying, obscured and concealed. Perhaps his mother felt this same sense of estrangement listening to Consuelo speak to Margarita or the kids. Perhaps it is true, he thought, that you can only be truly at peace in the place where you were born, among those who look and sound and act like you. For Richie, this meant the gray chill of a midwestern winter day; the blonde, blue-eyed girl he had longed so passionately for; the perpetual clatter and whine of his father's machine shop; a street of white clapboard houses occupied by people who not only know each other's names but much of their intimate business. He had tried deliberately, he suddenly thought, to escape into strangeness—he had fallen in love with the sound of Consuelo's voice long before she had stated her affection for him or allowed him to touch her. Now he heard Margarita's husband, speaking in Spanish to his cousin, and the words and accent that he had grown familiar with sounded like a taunt.

He got the bartender's attention, handed him a bill, and told him to take out whatever Margarita's husband and the cousin were drinking and keep the change. He was left with a couple of dollar bills to last until he got his payment. He turned and slid off the stool.

"*Qué pasa?*" The brown hand of Margarita's husband flashed

like a reptile's tongue in the space between Richie and the open door to sunlight and fresh air, and Richie felt himself go rigid, his fingers dig into his palms. I'll pop the son of a bitch, he said to himself, but there wasn't any threat—an exaggerated expression of injury crossed the man's face as they both contemplated the untouched glass of beer on the bar.

"Gotta do some last-minute Christmas shopping," Richie said, resenting this need to fabricate. "Before the stores close." Leaving the beer, he knew, constituted an insult for which there could be repercussions, although he was unable to imagine exactly what they might be. "See you around." The man nodded with such a mournful expression that Richie was momentarily sorry that he couldn't stay, clap the man on the back, get drunk with him, and sing a romantic song. Outside, feeling light-headed in the sun, he heard a snatch of carol in the air before it faded into the normal hum of traffic on the freeway. He suddenly wanted to see Consuelo, and the kids; he wanted it to be dark so that he could get the bikes down from the rafters in the garage, where they had waited, concealed by a tarp, for the past three weeks. Margarita's husband did not possess the means to cause him trouble, Richie concluded, then began to wonder almost immediately about the things Consuelo told Margarita, the things he knew women liked to talk about, personal things about family and husbands. He wondered how much Margarita told her husband about Richie and Consuelo and the kids and the strange, nervous Grandmama. The more he imagined Margarita pouring forth such information the more tense and defensive he felt, and when he turned onto his street and saw the car in the driveway a wind of anger blew through his mind.

"Consuelo." She was in the kitchen, alone; the TV blared from the family room and he imagined his mother, either in her room or on the sofa, grimly enduring for the sake of maintaining this tenuous familial connection. "How many times do I have to talk about turning the goddamn TV down? Huh?"

"I didn't turn it on," she said, scowling at the contents of a bowl into which she inserted a spoon and began to stir, raising a clatter. "That's not the point." He had forgotten to stop at the liquor store and now he wanted a beer. He shouted the oldest kid's name and after a long moment the noise of the TV diminished slightly. He sat down, wishing fervently that he had stayed in the bar and drunk the beer that Margarita's husband had bought him.

"How was the pageant?"

"It was fine."

"What about the kids?"

"Fine." She was miffed that he had forgotten, and he wasn't yet able to get up and put his arms around her and tell her he loved her and work his way back into her grace.

"I didn't get my payment. They want some of the tile done over."

"Oh."

"Yeah."

He had a perverse desire to tell her about the checks that would probably bounce, but the telephone rang and she picked it up and after listening a moment began to speak in Spanish. Margarita. Richie stood up. His knee banged a corner of the table and he kicked the leg and swore aloud. He saw Consuelo turn her head and stare.

"Hang up the phone," he said.

"What?"

"I said hang up the goddamn phone." He felt that some inner, unearthed self was speaking. He saw Margarita's husband, plotting an elaborate revenge, and he sensed the darkness of blood in his own face. This look apparently convinced Consuelo that he was serious and he heard her say that she would call back later. She dropped the receiver onto the hook, staring at Richie with wide black eyes.

"I don't want you to see Margarita."

Her chin trembled. Perhaps she was really frightened, and he began to feel his anger deflate into regret.

"I don't like her husband," he said, abruptly aware of the child-ishness of this conception, of the whole scene he had created out of thin air.

"She is my best friend," said Consuelo, her eyes glittering, a sign of imminent tears.

"I don't care," said Richie, aware of the sullen, poutish nature of his tone. "I don't give a shit."

Consuelo went back to her bowl. She stirred, then floured a cutting board and upended the bowl. She briefly kneaded the lump of dough, then flattened it with a rolling pin and formed it with her hands into a long yellow log. She took a knife from a drawer and Richie's mind conjured up a scene in which she sneaked up while he was looking out the window and plunged the knife into his back. He snickered, and her eyebrows lifted as she cut the dough into segments. He thought: Would I have had such a fantasy if she was blonde and blue-eyed, like the girl in high school? To himself he said this girl's name—Theresa. *Teresa. Consuelo.* The first time he uttered this name to his mother she had wanted to know what it was in English. "What do you mean?" he had asked, and she had said, "Like Maria and Mary, or José and Joseph," and he had said, "There isn't anything," and his mother had seemed reluctant to believe this. She still seemed reluctant to speak the name *Consuelo,* as if she found it difficult and abnormal, like some name in Russian, or Arabic. If she couldn't turn it into something else—Connie, perhaps—she could not believe it to be real.

"I stopped for a beer," he said, feeling that his ear was close to the grid of the church confessional, a slightly ominous thing into which he had glanced but never entered. "I saw her husband. What the hell is his name?"

"*Fidencio.*"

"*Fidencio.*" A malicious turn of Richie's mind anglicized the name to Fido. He laughed out loud. Consuelo turned her head and glared, briefly.

"He's an alcoholic," Richie said.

Consuelo shrugged as if to say that in her mind there were far worse things—like an unkind, unforgiving, unaccepting nature perhaps.

"He tried to sell me some cocaine."

"When? Today?"

"Not today." The single unfinished beer had been enough to make Richie's mind sluggish. "A while ago."

"He's going to a program."

"Yeah?"

"She told him she would leave him if he didn't go."

"I saw him messing around with another woman," Richie said stubbornly, defeat lurking like a ghost around the vision of his wife, who oiled a pan and arranged the logs of dough and placed upon the top of each an almond, a little crown.

"You saw him? Today?"

"A couple of months ago."

"What was he doing?"

"He was messing around with this woman."

"*Por favor.* What was he exactly doing?"

"Talking to this woman in the bar." Defeat in his nostrils displaced the smell of the dough. He watched her open the oven door and slide the tray inside. He admired, very briefly, the sight of her bottom stretched tightly against the pockets of her jeans. He was possessed, also briefly, by a desire to pull her to their bedroom and push her down onto the bed. If she resisted or struggled he would—he didn't know what he would do, probably nothing, give up, go watch cartoons on TV with the kids, or talk to his mother about people and places that he had forgotten, that he had deliberately ceased to care about. He finally arose, feeling stiff from the weeks of work on the bathrooms of the doctor's house, and went to where she stood at the sink, her back turned, her black hair rimmed with an aura of light from the sky in the window.

He put his arms around her and kissed the back of her neck and she neither resisted nor yielded, but just stood still, unmoving. He decided to continue to love her, because in another week his mother would be gone, and Margarita's husband had, after all, not done anything he hadn't done himself, which was to fall for a moment into a fantasy involving a different self and all the possible pleasures that would imply. In not so many years his mother would die and he would be sorry but also freed from any kind of choice her existence implied. He wondered if Consuelo loved him, at that very moment, or if his sand-colored hair and eyes and skin that grew red in the sun had ceased with familiarity to be exotic and only bored her. He drew her hair aside and nibbled the rim of her ear, and she said, "Stop it," but the tone was not entirely vigorous, and then he heard from the TV the same carol he had heard outside the bar, and he thought of the chorus of the other song—"*Bésame, bésame mucho*"—and his heart was filled with a romantic warmth that would fade, fade away, although he didn't, for just a moment, believe it.

Sawtelle

Charles lay awake in the pale light of dawn thinking of his partner, Ben, and of the predicament—Ben's wife messing around with the neighbor kid, a nineteen-year-old who went to junior college and lifted weights and rode a Ninja. What, exactly, did Ben need? Advice? Sympathy? Charles shut his eyes and saw the yellow frame of the house that he and Ben had begun that week to wire, a big two-story house whose unfinished state seemed to mock his faith in the certainty of domestic arrangements. He listened to the slow rise and fall of his own wife's breath and its very regularity made him nervous. She had never given him reason to suspect that she could be unfaithful, and yet as he lay in the fading darkness, listening to the unchanging rhythm of her breath, he felt somehow distrustful, betrayed.

Driving his truck into a spreading flare of sunlight, Charles thought of how the news about Ben's wife had come as such a surprise, and what this meant about his own perception of reality. "You remember that night we went to the Aztec?" Ben had said to him, interjecting the question into the middle of an argument started for no reason that Charles could see, other than sheer contrariness, over the proper place to drive the ground rod for the electrical panel. Ben had managed to squeeze a lifetime's worth of portents into an hour that Charles could not recall as remarkable in any way, with the possible exception of the fact that Ben's wife had ordered a hamburger from the American part of the menu, claiming that Mexican food gave her indigestion. "It's coming right at you," Ben had said to Charles, his eyes glittering as if with fever. "Right at you in plain goddamn sight, but you can't see it, then smackeroo!"

Charles guided his truck through traffic beginning to clot into the morning rush, trying to review in his mind a list containing the conduit, connectors, the other things he needed to pick up at the supply house. He felt apprehensive. He wished almost desperately for the Ben of old instead of the Ben who showed up late and made dumb mistakes and lost his temper three times in a single day— once with the general contractor, once with the architect, and once with Charles, who surely took it more personally than the other two. He pulled into a parking lot crowded with vans and trucks. Against his will, he began to imagine how his wife would spend her day—drive their daughter to school with the baby strapped in the back, drop the baby at the sitter's and go to her exercise class, come home and eat lunch and put the baby down for a nap, spend a couple of hours doing company bookwork. Irritated by sudden unfounded suspicion and the clogged parking lot, he blew his horn at the driver of a van who was taking too much time to back out of a space.

At the counter inside he saw the faces of strangers, heard the unfamiliar voices of men he suspected of bidding low just to get some work, men who made it hard for those like Charles and Ben who had long since paid their dues. By the time he gave his order to the man at the counter he was unreasonably angry. The man was young, blonde, his hair pulled back into a ponytail. Charles wondered why a woman the age of Ben's wife would be attracted to such a man, hardly more than a boy. The young man didn't know what he meant by a servicehead coupler and Charles said, loudly enough for everyone to hear, that whoever worked the counter ought to at least know the names of the things they had in stock. "Let me talk to Leo," he said, but Leo, the manager, was on the phone, and Charles said, "Fuck it. I'll get it later," and walked out feeling at least as stupid as the kid, or Ben, for having lost his temper.

The house was going up on a leveled-off ridge above a canyon dense with chaparral, and on a clear day the view encompassed newly whitened mountains, the crowded-together buildings of downtown, and the long tan curve of the beach. This wasn't such a day, however; as Charles backed his truck inside the chain-link fence surrounding the house he could see nothing but a bluish haze beyond the tops of the eucalyptus trees that grew at the foot of the canyon. Ben was already there, his truck backed up to the pile of lumber scrap that the general contractor had promised to have hauled away, a high, messy pile that forced them to circle around, to waste a dozen steps to get inside the house. Through the space where a window would be Charles saw Ben bent over and small beneath the high, vaulted ceiling, nailing boxes to the studs. The face of Ben's wife passed vividly through his mind and he felt a chill of unease, wondering what he would say or do if he ran into her.

He skirted the pile of trash and entered the house. Just inside the doorway he saw a box nailed to a stud on the wrong side of the lay-out mark that he had made, but he decided not to say anything, not yet, anyway. Ben had shown up on time and was working instead of moping around or complaining or trying to start an argument, and for the moment at least Charles felt relieved, almost happy. He looked up at Kevin, the apprentice, who was on the ten-foot ladder drilling holes in the joists. He hadn't braced the drill the way that Charles and Ben had taught him; if the bit grabbed in the wood the handle could snap around and skin his knuckles, or sprain his wrist, or if he was really unlucky, break something. Charles thought, why isn't Ben on the drill and Kevin nailing up the boxes, which is an easier job, less conducive to the chance of injury? He decided not to say anything, though. Who knew what might set Ben off? It must be tough, he thought. He imagined his wife, in the bed still warm where he had slept, in carnal embrace with the blonde young man at the supply house. Jesus, he thought.

"Hey," said Ben.

"Hey." Charles dropped the coil of conduit that he had carried in from his truck. Looking at Ben, whose mouth was a thin, hard line, he recalled for no obvious reason the moment, working as a journeyman in the union, that he had witnessed the aftermath of an electrocution. Christ, he said to himself, feeling a reprise of dormant emotion—fear, sadness, a queasy sickness in his gut. Get off it, he told himself, stop feeling so damn morbid. Again he thought of his wife, alone in the house, and again a feeling of betrayal seized him. But he was certain of her fidelity. Their marriage, like most, had gone through a rocky period or two, but in the year since the baby had come she had seemed content, less likely to complain about the hours he worked or other things that were out of his control. As for himself, he had never thought about adultery in any realistic way, had never considered acting out the fantasies that arose from urges temporary enough to suppress, to ignore.

He watched Kevin lean too far with the drill instead of getting down to move the ladder. Kevin wasn't a bad kid, he showed up on time, he didn't jerk off instead of working, he wasn't really dumb, but did have trouble absorbing the things that Ben and Charles tried to teach him. He was always nodding, humming, his body twitching to what Charles imagined was the music that they had forbidden him to play on the job site, heavy metal that was like a drill going right through Charles's head. When Charles gave Kevin instructions he sometimes had the urge to shout in order to cut through the noise inside the head that never seemed to stop nodding, swaying, rocking with a beat. He decided to bring Kevin down off the ladder before he got himself into a really dangerous position.

"Shultz was here," said Ben, arranging eight-penny nails heads-

up in his palm. He was staring past Charles, through a wide opening that would become a doorway in the wall, out to where a
mound of yellow earth rose beside the bowl-shaped excavation for
the pool. Shultz was the general contractor, a man no older than
Charles and Ben who drove a brand-new Bronco with a cellular
phone and wore a beeper on his belt. "He wants us to get the feed
in for the pool equipment. Today."

"Tell him to give us a trench." Charles felt in a hurry to get
Kevin down off the ladder.

"He says it's in our contract." Ben picked up a box and held
it in his other palm, staring as if it were something he had never
seen before. Maybe he had gotten over losing his temper, Charles
thought, and would now be in a state suggested by this oddly flat,
unemotional tone.

"Shit," said Charles.

"Says we provide our own trench."

"Christ," said Charles. He had written the contract, and surely
had excluded any trenching, because it took a jackhammer to get
through the earth here, decomposed granite, hard, yellow, flaky
stuff the hills all around were made of. A copy of the contract was
in his briefcase in the truck. He wanted to get Kevin off the ladder,
but instead he went to the truck and got out the contract and saw
the line that his wife had typed stating that "others shall be responsible for trenching" and how someone had x'd out the word
"others" and typed "subcontractor" above it. He shut his briefcase, breathing consciously, slowly. He went back inside, averting
his eyes from the pile of scrap that made him go out of his way.
He ordered Kevin off the ladder. He told Ben that Kevin should be
nailing up boxes, that Ben should be on the ladder with the drill.
He stared at Ben until Ben opened his hand and let the eight-penny
nails rain to the floor. Ben was normally neat, almost to a fault,
but Charles decided not to say anything about the nails. It was a
bad example for Kevin, who stood watching, waiting to be shown

what to do, but Charles felt the situation was somehow fraught with danger. He was afraid that Ben might explode, and that he might explode in return, and something might happen that both of them would regret, that would in some way be irrevocable.

"I'll go down and rent a jackhammer," he said. "I'll pick up a couple of laborers on Sawtelle." He took a deep breath and his chest felt tight. "How deep do we have to go?"

"Foot." Ben looked away again, staring at something, or nothing, an unpleasant picture in his head, his wife with the neighbor kid maybe.

"Foot-and-a-half," Charles said. "We'd better check the code."

"Twelve inches," Ben said. He said it with an obvious smirk and smutty tinge to his voice, as if describing a fabulous male member. The neighbor kid, thought Charles, feeling irrational. What did Ben's wife see in him, if it wasn't something like that? Sex. She was a year older than Charles, and to Charles's point of view Ben had always treated her at least as well as she deserved.

He got in his truck and drove a little too fast down the cool, shaded canyon toward the invisible mass of the city. Ben had two kids, both in school, and Charles wondered if they knew or understood what their mother was up to. He thought of his own daughter, a pretty, outgoing girl, and the thought of her carrying around the knowledge of her mother screwing a teenage boy made him feel turgid, almost ill.

At the bottom of the canyon he stopped at a minimarket and bought an orange juice and a newspaper to read at lunch and a six-pack of Cokes for everybody. The girl who took his money looked about eighteen, a little plump, a Latina with black eyes that glistened. Her fingers brushed his palm as she gave him his change and he felt a flutter in his chest. Back in the truck, in the slow, clotted traffic, he thought, yeah, it's easy enough to imagine. Getting it on with a girl like that. He knew that Ben, a few years back, had messed around with a woman whose house they had installed some smoke detectors in, a woman in the middle of a divorce, on the lookout for an immediate thrill that had materialized in the form of Ben, a decent-looking guy who could turn on a kind of charm that certain women seemed to find irresistible. To expect fidelity from Ben's wife and not from Ben was in some fundamental way unfair, he knew, and yet her violation seemed far more reprehensible than Ben's. Maybe she had known about Ben and the woman and had waited all this time for a chance to get her revenge. But Ben believed that she was unhappy. Why, he didn't seem to know.

Charles got a jackhammer at the rental yard and headed east, turning within the shadow of the elevated freeway onto a street lined nearly solid on either side with men who whistled and waved when they saw his truck, making him feel exposed, as if he were some sort of parade. He drove slowly, looking for two men alone. Men in larger groups stepped off the curb and beckoned aggressively, but Charles kept moving; he knew that if he stopped the men would immediately surround his truck, pound on the windows, and jump uninvited into the back, forcing him to pick out two from a dozen all desperate to be hired without even knowing what they would be asked to do. Finally he saw a pair by themselves, one short and stumplike, the other taller and thinner, with a straw hat shading his face. Charles pulled quickly to the curb, gestured with his head, and the men climbed into the back of his truck without the exchange of a single word. He swerved back into the traffic as others ran, shouting and waving their arms, toward him.

At the first stoplight the man with the hat leaned close to the open driver's window and said, "How much you pay?" He had to say it three times before Charles understood.

"Five," called Charles over his shoulder. "*Cinco.*"

The man said nothing further, but then, heading into the cool shade of the canyon, Charles heard voices, and laughter, and he thought that things were askew, these men whose lives were surely fraught with hardship laughing together while he and Ben moped and sulked like adolescents who have every conceivable comfort but nevertheless decide that life is miserable and unfair. He tried to imagine getting up each morning to stand on the street with hundreds of other men, hoping against all odds to be noticed and hired to dig a ditch. With family, wife, and children, thousands of miles away. I'm lucky, he told himself. I'm doing what I want to do. I'm happy. It's just that sometimes nothing goes right. And this business of Ben and his wife had unsettled him, made him feel that everything he assumed to be predictable was suddenly up in the air, subject to the vagaries of chance, as in an earthquake, when the ground that everyone has always believed to be solid, immutable, begins to quiver and shake.

He showed the men how to run the jackhammer. With a shovel he drew a line in the dust. He knew only a smattering of Spanish, but communication on this level was a simple matter of handing over the shovel, pointing, and saying, "*Aquí.*" He penciled a mark on a scrap of wood, showing how deep he wanted them to go. Eighteen inches. He was right. He began to think that Ben wasn't really holding up his end of the business, but then he stopped himself, he didn't want to feel disgruntled, disappointed in anyone. Not in Ben, who had the ability to keep track of thirty circuits in his head, who could always say with utter confidence which wires were neutral and which were hot, who could gaze upon the total chaos of an unwired panel and see all the circuit breakers in place, neatly labeled, doing their job. With all the conduits in, with all the wire pulled and the ends twisted and spliced inside the boxes, Charles would be able to stand in a room and see a kind of elegant simplicity and inevitability in the path the conduits took through the studs and joists, a reflection of an idea that had never existed on paper, only in Ben's mind. To the owner of the house, of course, and to the architect, even to the general contractor, what mattered was not the craft or art of the work but the fact that a particular light go on when a certain switch was flicked, that current flow from an outlet to an appliance, that the job be finished without delay, without any extra charges.

Charles thought of an old man in the union, a foreman for whom he and Ben had worked, first as apprentices, then as journeymen, abiding his temperament because they had known, Charles guessed, that he had something important to teach them. "You don't be sloppy," the old man had said. "You don't cut corners just because your work is going to be covered up. You be even more careful, because you are the only ones who know what you have done."

They ate lunch outside, in the back, sitting on brittle yellow grass beside the crater that would become the pool. Charles had driven back down the canyon to the minimarket to buy burritos for the laborers. The clerk with the pretty black eyes had smiled at him, causing a little bump in his throat that seemed to sink down through his body on the way back to the house and became a leaden lump of dismay. Already they had fallen behind, at least half a day, and at the pace they were going they wouldn't get done for another week and a half and would be lucky if the money they got was enough to cover their labor and the materials.

Charles glanced at Ben, who had that look again, as if he were watching a movie inside his head. "We've got to pick it up," Charles said, uneasy, aware that Ben might lose his temper, start up his truck the way he had done on Monday after getting into an argument with Shultz and the architect, roar out in a storm of dust, and disappear. Charles looked at the laborers, dozing in a wedge of shade cast by a deck that cantilevered at an angle from the second floor of the house. "The son of a bitch changed the contract. I ought to call a lawyer," he said.

"You signed it," Ben said, in the flat, dry tone that he seemed to have adopted for the day.

"Yeah. He's still a son of a bitch."

"Read before you sign."

"You're telling me."

"How much?" They both looked at Kevin, stretched out in the sun asleep. He stayed out too late at night, drank too much beer, Charles guessed. But so did he, at that age. Who am I to judge? he thought. Kevin. Ben's wife. Anybody.

"Ninety for the jackhammer," he said. "Eighty for the laborers. If they get it done."

"They won't." In four hours, perhaps a third of the trench had been dug. The flaky ground was getting harder, too, the closer they got to the pool.

"Three fifty," said Charles.

"Your time," Ben said. "And gas."

"Four hundred." Charles felt irritation like sweat itching on his skin. He got up and went over to the jackhammer, which lay beside the trench in the thick, grainy dust that coated everything. He picked it up and squeezed the trigger, giving off a burst of noise that made the laborers sit up straight, blinking. He let the jackhammer drop and turned to see Kevin, still dead to the world, and Ben standing above him, foot drawn back as if to deliver a kick to the ribs. Christ, said Charles to himself, at the same time he heard Ben's low voice say, "Get up, asshole."

It was just a matter of time, Charles knew, until Kevin quit. Kevin was a decent kid, despite his flaws, but he would never be able to grasp the importance of something that would end up being hidden inside the walls. What did it matter if you had one too many bends in the conduit? At the worst you would have to pull a little harder to get the wire through. Why did it matter that all of the conduits going into a box were lined up side by side and not crossing over one another? Why was it such a big deal if a home run took a few more feet to get the panel than it needed to? Why was it so important that the boxes were all straight, level, set at exactly the right depth in the wall? Didn't the drywall crew come along and knock everything out of whack, anyway? Who cares about something nobody can see, as long as it works?

Charles followed Ben into the house, hearing voices in Spanish, then the rattle of the jackhammer. He could smell the yellow dust. If Kevin quit in the middle of the job they were screwed. He found Ben in the kitchen, staring in distaste at the wall where the plumbing for the sink was roughed in, where they would have to put in circuits for the garbage disposal and the dishwasher.

"Plumbers," Ben said, the word like something sour he was about to spit out on the floor. "How are we supposed to get in there?"

"What's new?" said Charles. So the plumbers didn't give a crap about the electricians. Neither did the heating men, the carpenters, the cement men—nobody seemed to give a crap about anyone else. It wasn't always this way, Charles said to himself. Things used to be different, didn't they? With a clarity abrupt and startling he saw in his mind his mother, in a housedress, standing beside the young man who had lived next door, a young man who never seemed to wear a shirt, not even on the coldest winter days. He saw his mother and the shirtless young man in the kitchen of his parents' house, standing a little too close to one another. Charles blinked. Was this a memory, or just a piece of fiction floating up out of the feverish matter in his head? His father and mother had always seemed to love each other, in a reserved, undemonstrative way. He looked at Ben. If it wasn't for Ben's predicament he wouldn't have had such a repellent fantasy. They wouldn't be standing there, staring at the sloppy plumbing, unhappy with each other, with everything.

"You've got to lighten up," said Charles, feeling rushed, wanting to get past this scene and whatever was likely to follow. "He's just a damn kid."

"I don't care," said Ben.

"What do you mean?" Charles saw that the plumbers had

notched a stud so deeply that it was nearly severed, no longer able to support anything. The building inspector would jump on that in a second. It's not my problem, he thought, I'm not going to say anything to Shultz. But it will hold things up, become an excuse to delay a payment. "What do you mean, you don't care?"

"I don't give a shit about anything," Ben said, in a low voice that made Charles think of the noise a tomcat makes in prelude to a fight.

"Yeah," said Charles. He was no longer willing to pussyfoot around; things had gone too far now, they had to come to a head. "Well, do something about it then. Kick her out and get it over with." He didn't want to look directly into Ben's face. His eyes followed the black pipe up the wall to where it disappeared through another sloppy notch in the two-by-four plates. "Or tell her you want to go to a marriage counselor. It's not the end of the world. I mean, it happens. You still love her, tell her whatever's wrong you want to figure it out, get past it. Don't take it out on Kevin. It's not his fault."

"She said she stopped."

"Huh?" Charles heard an acquiescent, possibly defeated tone in Ben's voice. I don't want this kind of thing in my life, he said to himself, I want us to grow old together, have grandchildren, buy a camper and travel around without any baggage or clouds from the past hanging over us.

"She said last night that she stopped. That she wasn't going to see him again."

"You believe her?" Charles wondered if *he* did.

"Yeah."

"Well . . ." Charles felt the swollen atmosphere around them suddenly deflate, but it didn't necessarily feel like a relief. It was too inconclusive. Ben would forgive her, everything would go back to being the way it was before—was that the end result of all this turmoil? He listened for sounds to indicate that Kevin had taken the initiative to do something without being told, but all he could hear was the sound of the jackhammer echoing slightly through the unfinished rooms. He grinned at Ben, feeling for some reason embarrassed. "Well," he said, "I guess you're happy."

"About what?" said Ben.

Yeah, thought Charles, about what?

"What do I do?" Ben went on, in a voice with all the previous menace drained away.

"Do about what?" said Charles.

"I walk out of the house and there he is, across the street. I want to kill him, buddy, I really do."

"Don't do that," said Charles, with a stir of panic that brought again a glimpse of the electrocuted man. "That would be really stupid. You have to forget about it."

"You're shittin' me."

"Listen, Ben." Charles felt as if he were talking to Kevin, not quite able to get through the invisible howl of guitars and thrash of drums. "You want to stay at the house for a few days? Let things cool off? You can sleep in the den."

"A man has a right to defend his honor," Ben said.

"Jesus, Ben." Charles thought with dull resignation that they might as well roll it up, call it a day; whatever they had accomplished to this point would probably be wrong and have to be torn out and done over in the morning.

"A man has a legal right," said Ben.

"To kill somebody? Come on."

"You catch your wife and somebody in the act, you have the right to do whatever you want. To both of them."

"Where did you hear that?" Charles observed with unease that Ben's body had begun to sway, that his eyes had begun to roll back and forth like loose green marbles. In his imagination Ben fell to the floor and foamed at the mouth, his legs drawn up and arms disarranged like those of the electrocuted man. How do I deal with this? he thought. Would he have to call the police? Go to the kid, warn him that his life was in danger? Tell Ben's wife to get away? Perfectly normal people went crazy. You could read about it from time to time, somebody running amuck, shooting people, wives, kids, strangers. Was Ben going crazy? How could he tell?

"Come stay at the house," he said. He decided that it was his imagination, not Ben, that had run beyond the bounds of reality. "As long as you want." He took his eyes off Ben and saw a plume of black from a point where the plumbers had nearly set fire to a stud with their soldering torch. "If she says she's not going to see this kid anymore, then it means she wants you to stay together. She wants to work it out."

"Why couldn't it have been you?" he said.

"Me?" Charles was startled. He got along all right with Ben's wife, but she was a little loud, a little aggressive for his taste. She tended to treat Ben like one of her kids. The only time Charles had ever thought anything at all about her was the first time the four of them had gotten into Ben's new hot tub without their clothes, a moment in which alcohol and a few puffs on a joint had combined to afflict him with an adolescent lust. He wondered what Ben was trying to suggest.

"I get up early and sneak out of the house," Ben went on, in an injured, lugubrious tone. "I don't want anybody to see me."

"Sure," said Charles. "That's understandable." He heard Kevin, the shuffle of feet in their direction. They had to wrap this up. "Just don't take it out on Kevin, okay? You can stay at the house. Let things cool off. Get this job wrapped up." He saw Kevin's lop-sided grin between two studs, his head nodding to the concealed cacophony of sound. "We've got to get this job done, Ben. We've all got to hold up our end. You, me, Kevin."

At the sound of his name Kevin grinned, clapped and then joined his hands and shook them as if in self-congratulation. "I picked up the nails," he said, the tone of his voice suggesting unqualified happiness. "What's up now? What happens next?"

At five o'clock, in the fading light of dusk, Charles went outside and saw that the trench had nearly reached the pool. "You finish," he said slowly, emphatically, "I pay ten dollars more." The man in the straw hat nodded and said, "*Sí. Está bien.*" The other man said something that Charles did not understand. He headed back to the house where Kevin was rolling up the cords and putting the drills back into their cases. He would have to take the men back, and then the jackhammer, and it would probably be seven o'clock before he got home. This was the only bone of contention between himself and his wife, his spending so much time on work, getting home and having to shower and make telephone calls and attend to matters of business just when their daughter was wanting to be read a story before going to bed. He had promised more than once that things would change, that having Ben as a partner would take off some of the load, but nothing had changed, not really, except that so many people had gotten into the business, foreigners, fly-by-nighters, guys without the proper license, without insurance, bidding low, trying to get a piece of the business that was booming because it seemed that everybody had decided to build, to remodel, to put up something on every vacant lot, on every acre of empty land.

He thought about asking Ben to take the jackhammer back, but decided not to rock the boat. Ben had worked hard all afternoon, had seemed to get his focus back where it belonged, on the complex scheme of the wiring that he carried inside his head. Ben had even left Kevin alone. He told Charles that if they all worked Saturday they could get the conduit in and that on Monday Charles could pick up the wire. "Let me know," Charles had said again, "if you want to stay at the house." Ben had nodded, but said nothing.

Now Charles watched Ben's truck bounce over the ruts and onto the asphalt of the twisting canyon road. Kevin had already left, burning rubber, going too fast for the road. He was okay, though, a decent kid when all was said and done. Ben, too. He was okay. A good guy. He wouldn't hurt anybody, not deliberately. Charles gestured to the men to put the jackhammer in the truck. The rental yard closed at six and he would have to hustle. He didn't like to speed on the canyon road. Some idiot could come flying around a corner on the wrong side, or back out of a driveway, and he wouldn't be able to stop the truck. Why are you so nervous? he asked himself. So worried about things that are unlikely, matters of pure chance?

He could hear the men in the back of the truck, their voices muffled by the glass of the window that he had rolled up against a chill that descended when the sun went down. In a week it would be Thanksgiving. Then Christmas. He wanted to get his daughter a bike for Christmas. And a rocking horse for the baby. He could still remember the rocking horse he had when he was a little kid and what a thrill it had been the first few times he had gotten on it. He thought about the men in the back. He regretted the fact that he couldn't speak their language and therefore ask them about themselves, about their families, whether they had wives, children. Probably they did, he thought. Still in Mexico. Or somewhere else. El Salvador. Guatemala. Places he had never been and wouldn't be likely to go. He had given each of them fifty dollars, seeing in his mind the money as a bite out of an apple that was the profit deserved by himself and Ben. He had resented giving the men the hundred dollars, and then he had felt ungenerous. It wasn't their fault that he hadn't read the contract after Shultz had given it back to him. Shultz made money because he was smart, he didn't have any obligation to tell Charles that he had crossed out the word "others" and typed "subcontractor" above it. That was the way business was done now, and Charles would have to learn the rules of this game.

The two men in the back of the truck had worked without a single break after lunch, and he wished, briefly, that he could pay them even more. What kind of Christmas would they have? he wondered. Ben had said that these men didn't have it so hard because a lot of them lived together and sent most of what they made to Mexico so that when they went back they would be rich, because of the fact that dollars could be exchanged for so many pesos. Rich? He somehow doubted it. And what kind of life could it be, living so far from your family, crowded with a bunch of others into a place meant for two or three, standing on the street every day, trying to attract the attention of someone like himself, who had a dirty, tedious job, a ditch to dig?

He turned onto Sawtelle, saw the deserted sidewalks littered with wrappers, cans, things that men had earlier dropped there. He pulled to the curb. The truck bounced as the men got out and he rolled down the window.

"*Gracias,*" he called, aware of some deficiency in his pronunciation.

"*Más trabajo?*" the man in the straw hat said. "Tomorrow?"

Charles recognized only "Tomorrow?" He shook his head. "No. Sorry."

"Okay," said the man, with a smile. The short man smiled, too; they waved and drifted into the night, becoming shadows beyond the greenish glow of the streetlights. I ought to have asked them where they live, thought Charles, maybe I could have dropped them off closer to home. He had no idea where such men lived. And he wouldn't have known how to ask this question. At the stoplight he looked at his watch. It was after six. He would have to return the jackhammer in the morning and pay for an extra day. He should have asked Ben to return it, because he had just thrown away ninety dollars, just like that, like trash into a can.

He turned in the direction of his house. The ninety dollars would eat at him, along with his failure to notice that Shultz had altered the contract, and the knowledge that if Ben did something crazy he would be responsible, because he hadn't warned the neighbor kid, or Ben's wife, or the police. But he was sure that Ben wouldn't do anything crazy. It was entirely possible to talk about blowing someone away in the emotion of hurt and jealousy without ever having the intention or inclination to do so. Charles knew that if he caught his wife in bed with somebody he wouldn't go into the den and get his shotgun out of the gun safe and start blowing heads off; he would possibly threaten or even want to do so but that would just be emotion, the terrific hurt of betrayal by somebody he had always trusted. What would he do, though?

He pushed the truck to fifteen miles an hour above the limit, feeling a sudden, panicky desire to get home and see his wife, kiss her and tell her that he loved her; kiss the baby, too, and hug his daughter, tell them how much he cared about them. They might wonder what was going on, but that was okay. He was lucky, he realized, thinking of the men with their wives and children in Mexico or some other country, out of sight, beyond the range of touch, of love. He just wished that Ben would come to the house, at least for the night. He realized that he hadn't said anything to his wife about this business of Ben's wife and the neighbor kid, and he wondered if she knew. She and Ben's wife weren't really close, but they got together now and then, talked on the phone. He realized that he was in a hurry to get home to tell her himself, to put his own interpretation on the situation, before she started thinking that it was all Ben's fault. Maybe Ben hadn't been paying enough attention to his wife. Maybe he didn't listen to her, a complaint that Charles vaguely remembered hearing that night at the restaurant. But how did that justify bedding down with a kid, making a fool out of Ben, screwing up their lives?

He backed the truck into the driveway, up close to the house where thieves or vandals wouldn't be likely to bother it. The windows were lit in the kitchen and living room and when he got out he heard the baby squall. If the baby had been fussy all day his wife would be irritable, and probably have something to say about his being so late again. Then the baby stopped, abruptly, and he heard the distant voice of his wife, calling his daughter's name in a tone that might have been plaintive or simply neutral, he couldn't tell. He had been in such a hurry and now he felt himself dawdle, to delay going inside. The faces of the girl in the 7-Eleven, the young man in the supply house, the laborers, the kid on the Ninja, all appeared in his head and made him feel anxious, as if he was being forced to make some kind of choice. The kitchen window was up a few inches and he heard his wife say clearly, "Your father's home." He checked the lock on the toolbox of the truck and then headed for the side door of the house. "Your father's home." She had said it without any particular emphasis, a matter of fact, and as Charles turned his key in the door he suddenly felt lighter, less anxious, less estranged, more confident of the future, whatever it might turn out to be.

The Chosen

Roberto lives with two of his sisters and their husbands in a house so near the freeway that now and then a bottle thrown from a passing car thumps and spins in the yard or shatters on the driveway. The house of yellow stucco takes up most of the yard that contains a small amount of grass, a visibly leaning garage, and an enormous rubber tree. Roberto sleeps in the living room of the house, on the pillows of the sofa or, if it is late and he has had too much beer, on a mattress in the garage. The garage is cold and the mattress thin. When the wind rises, the heavy leaves of the rubber tree come down with a slap on the roof, and sudden scratchings in the darkness arouse his fear of rats. If not in a stupor he sometimes lies awake the entire night, shivering.

"Roberto!"

His oldest sister, Lupe, bangs the rotten garage door. Through gaps in the boards come daggers of sunlight to stab his half-open eyes. In the hazy hours of the preceding evening he heard his name in this same impatient tone, and the word "drunk," which he has long known to mean *borracho*. He remembers speaking to his younger sister, Patricia, who stared at him with burning eyes, as if his mouth were spouting obscenities. She remains slender and pretty while Lupe grows fat, not just at her stomach but everywhere—under her chin, around her elbows, between the joints of her fingers. Her husband is a hog, a *cochino*.

"Roberto!"

"Go away," he mutters. He must somehow arise and prepare to

work, but the blades of light slash through his brain at the slightest movement of his head. When Lupe's husband comes out of the
bathroom he leaves a ring of scum in the bowl, along with the
black hairs of his beard. Roberto clearly remembers the stinging
soap with which his mother made him scrub his hands, always,
before he was allowed to touch his food. The *cochino* removes the
spark plugs of his car, turning his fingers black, then sits directly at
the table. What is wrong with his sister, marrying such an animal?

All is silent, save for the perpetual tuneless music of rubber from
the freeway and the dull punitive thump inside his skull. He was
supposed to be ready at seven to go with Lupe on the bus to the
house of a lady who will pay him twenty dollars to dig up a banana
tree. The message that finds its way from his brain to his wooden
tongue is an obscenity that everyone could understand, even this
lady. She wants him to cut down the banana tree and dig up the
roots and smooth the ground so that it will look as if nothing ever
grew there. Why does she hate this tree? Lupe took Roberto to
speak to the lady, although the lady did all the speaking while
Roberto stood and shuffled his feet and moved his hands in and
out of his pockets. Before he left he cut with his knife a ripe banana
from a bunch half green and hid the banana under his shirt because he wasn't certain of the propriety of this act. Perhaps the
lady would have had him arrested. He ate the banana on the bus
coming back from the lady's house, and it was firm but sweet.

Lupe goes to the house one day each week to scrub the toilets and wash the laundry and vacuum the floors, and she thinks
that if Roberto does a good job cutting down the banana tree
the lady might hire him to mow the grass and trim the bushes.
No habla Inglés? the lady repeatedly asked Roberto, her speckled
arms sweeping over a bed of flowers, a picket fence, a stone dol-
phin with water bubbling from its mouth. The lady had yellow
hair and was taller than Roberto, a fact that provoked a powerful memory of the school to which he had gone as a child, of the

teachers with voices urgent like that of the lady, but just as devoid of meaning, so that a dreaminess would overtake him, causing him to gaze through the windows and yearn for some magic that would lift him from his seat and carry him away to the distant mountains. As from his teachers, he felt from the lady an unspoken displeasure that he was helpless to deflect or transform. When he said "no" too many times she mimicked him, jutting her chin and repeating "No, no, no, no, no," and from that point on he simply nodded or shook his head in dim comprehension of her exposition, delivered in a mixture of language and gesture so broad that it encompassed not only the banana tree and the many other items of vegetation but the whole earth and sky, the universe.

On his feet at last, Roberto abandons the garage. From an open window come strains of a romantic song, guitar chords, a familiar, nasal voice. The *cochino*. Each step jars Roberto's suffering head and he carefully pulls open a door and enters the cool shadow of the porch where Patricia and her husband Raul sleep. Patricia is gone, to clean some other lady's house; Raul, to his job in the restaurant. The *cochino* sings on certain nights in a nearby *cantina*. He brings home the money he makes, sometimes only a few dollars, and hands it directly to Lupe. He sings of love, this thing with belly concealed imperfectly by a flowing soiled shirt.

Roberto's improbable hope is to wash his face and change his shirt and pants without detection, then leave the house and travel in a circuit that will take him past the apartment of his girlfriend Luisa. He wants to devote his mind to the problem of how to undo the dimly remembered complications of the previous evening. But his fat brother-in-law pounces like a cat upon Roberto's shadow. "How are you?" he asks, in a tone that Roberto interprets as sly, insincere. He would like to pretend that he didn't hear, but instead he grunts, "I am well."

"No work today?"

Roberto doesn't turn to look at his brother-in-law but stands instead like an errant child with eyes affixed to a crack like a river running down the wall. When the silence grows hot he says, "I have work."

"Yes?" says the *cochino*. "Where?"

"In Malibu."

"In Malibu?" The *cochino* pronounces this name slowly, wetly, as if it is fruit in his mouth. The name is the first thing that came into Roberto's aching head, and he begins to feel regret, sadness.

"What is the work?" his brother-in-law persists.

"I don't know."

"You don't know?" He strikes a chord on the guitar that jars Roberto's unsound head. "Why not?"

"There is a lady."

Another chord, slightly off-key. "A lady? What does she want you to do, Roberto?"

Roberto begins to feel voluble, a little dizzy. He giggles.

"She wants me to come into her bedroom. I don't know the reason."

The *cochino* hisses. "You are an idiot!"

"No." Roberto feels his cheeks glow from the heat of this insult. He begins to move toward the bathroom.

"Where is your money?" The *cochino* rakes his fingers across the strings of the guitar, hurting Roberto's head. "Tomorrow we have to pay the landlord."

"I have it," says Roberto.

"Where? Let me see it."

"Tomorrow you will see it." If one more insult comes out of the *cochino*'s mouth, Roberto will beat him with his fists until all of the *cochino*'s blood leaves his body through his mouth and ears and eyes. "Come here," he murmurs, scarcely moving his lips, "and I will kill you." But the brother-in-law has no vigor; in his favorite chair he will sit for hours, singing romantic melodies in his torpid voice.

Roberto slowly straightens his fingers that are swollen and tender from an imperfectly remembered fight. Although he has gazed at his fingers many times, he looks at them now as if they are new and remarkable, fingers that within a few hours will touch Luisa and make music far sweeter than anything that comes from the mouth or guitar of the *cochino*. Inside his swollen head Luisa laughs, and Roberto laughs, aloud, able now to ignore the displeasure that drags down the corners of the *cochino*'s fleshy lips.

Luisa will not be home, but nevertheless Roberto stands outside the curtained window of her apartment. He used to be able to slide between a thick bush of oleander and the stucco wall of the apartment house and tap on the glass of the window, but now there is a fence that he knows has nothing to do with him but still feels like an insult. Luisa lives in the apartment with her cousin, a woman twenty years older than Luisa, a woman whose husband left her and returned to Mexico because he could not abide her tongue. This cousin of Luisa's will not open the door even after Roberto knocks and identifies himself, but puts him into a rage with questions and obstacles. "What do you want? . . . Luisa is sleeping. . . . Why can't you come another time? . . . We are not dressed. . . . You have been drinking."

How can you live with such a person? he asks Luisa. Now he can no longer tap the window glass and avoid humiliation, but must go directly to the door, anger rising in him like the taste of bad food. He wants to marry Luisa. He has brought this subject up and she has said, with great conviction, that first he must have a regular job. Concealed deep within Roberto's heart is the desire to return with her to Mexico, to be married in his pueblo and have his children there—but only two, no more. But what would he do there? They could go to Mexico City, where two of his brothers live, where he once drove a taxi. His cousin Mauricio drives a truck from a factory in the city of Oaxaca across the mountains to Vera Cruz, and Roberto thinks he would like to drive this truck.

He is no *loco* behind the wheel but cautious and responsible, a fact that made him a curiosity among the taxi drivers of Mexico City as well as keeping his pockets empty of pesos, but also a fact that might argue in his favor with the owners of the factory.

He will write a letter to Mauricio this very evening. *There is no work in the United States,* he will write. *This is a great myth. Always you have to watch out for* la migra. *In the* cantina *a bottle of beer costs three dollars. This is seven thousand pesos. Can you believe this? Lupe and Patricia have work, cleaning rich people's houses. Raul removes dishes from the tables in the restaurant. They want another man, but I told Raul, I will go back, I will walk all the way to the* pueblo *before I will remove dishes from the tables in the restaurant. Each week he is paid one hundred and thirty dollars. This is very much, you think. But there is the rent. Eight hundred dollars each month. This is more than two hundred thousand pesos. Even myself, here for almost one year, I find this hard to believe.*

Roberto walks on, aflame with a sudden optimism that muffles the drumbeat of pain in his head. His throat is as dry as the desert and he enters a liquor store to buy a can of soda. *A soda costs more than one thousand pesos,* he writes in the imaginary letter to Mauricio. *Early in the morning I walk from Lupe's house to the street where all the* trabajadores *wait for work. There are a hundred men, several hundred perhaps. There are Mexicans at one spot, and Salvadorans and Guatemalans and Hondurans at another. Some men live close by, but many come on the bus. We wait for the* patróns *to come in their trucks and if one of us is lucky we will be chosen. Sometimes I work one day, sometimes I work for only one hour. One day I was chosen and taken to a rich person's house where there was a trench to dig for a pipe. For three days I dug. The earth was very hard and every night I was so tired I could do nothing, not even go to see my Luisa. On the third day this contractor said he would pay me in the morning, but in the morning he did not come. I have not seen this contractor again. If I see him I will beat him until all of the blood of his body comes out of his eyes.*

On the street where the *trabajadores* wait the sun is high and most of the men who have waited since dawn have disappeared. Those who remain, who whistle and wave at the trucks of contractors and gardeners, hoping to be chosen, are older, darker, thinner, more patient. They know that the gardeners are only going to the nursery to buy bags of fertilizer, and the contractors are merely on their way to the lumberyard to get some two-by-fours, but they also know that one day a truck will pull to the curb and the driver will want two men, and that if they are squatting in the shade with a can of beer between their legs their pockets will be empty at the end of the day. Roberto knows this and yet he doesn't intend to stay for long on the corner where there are familiar faces. He has a dollar bill and some coins in his pocket.

Qué pasa? A man named Francisco has a mouth full of broken teeth and skin red and mottled like old brick. In a voice hot with indignation he tells of being robbed by a group of men he believes to be Salvadorans. He will kill them as soon as he finds them, he promises, with a violent slash of his hand across his throat. The men who come now to the street, the young ones, they are thieves and robbers, Francisco says with great conviction. A second man, named Jose, nods his head in vigorous agreement.

Jose has a long thin jaw and yellow, watery eyes that cause Roberto to suspect that he is ill, perhaps with tuberculosis. These two, Francisco and Jose, sleep in the bushes beneath the freeway that hovers in the air beyond the low roofs of the buildings that line the street. The robbers crept up in the darkness, Francisco says, looking dangerous with his furious eyes and jagged teeth. This is why he doesn't know exactly who they are. There was moonlight, he says, it glinted on their knives.

"How will you find them?" Roberto asks. He has finished the

soda, and yet his throat remains as dry as something abandoned in the sun.

"I will find them," Francisco promises, with a vehement strangling motion of his large, dark hands. "I am like a dog. I will smell them." He imitates the sniffing of a dog with such exaggeration that Roberto and Jose both laugh.

Roberto tells them he has a hangover, that he is going to find a place to sleep.

"I wouldn't leave if I were you," Francisco warns. Their *patrón* is coming to pick them up—for the past two days they have been engaged in the destruction of a perfectly fine house, a house that Roberto would give all his teeth, perhaps a finger and an ear besides, to live in.

"This is true," adds Jose, out of breath. "Perhaps he will need another man."

"How much did this *gavacho* pay?" Roberto asks.

"He has not paid anything." Jose coughs loosely into his hand. "But he is no *ratero*."

"What kind of truck does he come in?"

"A Chevrolet," Francisco answers. "Why do you want to know this?"

"What color is this Chevrolet?"

"It is red," says Jose. "It is very new."

Roberto nods. He has just enough to buy another soda, perhaps even a can of beer, and he imagines finding a place out of the sun to lie down and sleep. He feels nothing, just weariness. Perhaps he will not write Mauricio after all, but suddenly appear one day at Mauricio's door, surprise him out of his skin. His pockets filled with dollars, Luisa at his side, a flower in her hair, wearing a brand-new dress.

A strangled shout from Jose jolts him from this reverie, and he looks up to see a glistening red pickup swerve to the curb, the driver a man with skin like bronze and yellow hair, a man who looks like someone Roberto has seen on Lupe's television, although he knows this can't be true. Jose and Francisco are clambering into the back of the truck and Roberto sees that neither has spoken to the man on his behalf. He doesn't care. He will find a place to drink a can of beer and then lie down to sleep. But before he can turn away, Luisa's voice arises from deep within his brain to accuse him, and he moves suddenly, without reflection, to the edge of the curb.

"You need a man?" He summons in one enormous effort nearly all the English that he knows. "I work good."

The man scowls, blinks his eyes, then leans toward the open passenger window and says something that Roberto fails to comprehend. In the silence that ensues, Roberto feels the dull beat of his heart behind his ear.

"*Tu manos,*" says the man, in strangely accented Spanish. "Let me see your hands."

"*Sí.*" Roberto displays his hands, palms up. This he has been asked to do on other occasions.

The man nods, then leans out the window and gazes at Roberto's feet. If Roberto had worn the shoes he wears to see Luisa, his shiny black shoes, he might have had no chance of being hired. He and the man stare at Roberto's shoes, which are old and dirty. He imagines fleetingly that he is in Vera Cruz, boiling under the sun, staring at the sea that shimmers between the walls of antiquated buildings. The man speaks, now in English, and although Roberto doesn't recognize a single word he nods and says, "Yes." The man then gestures with his head and Roberto climbs into the back of the truck.

Francisco grins with such an expanse of horrible teeth that Roberto is forced to laugh, as the truck swoops like a bird into the traffic, flying north, toward the hazy hills. Facing Roberto, their backs to the cab of the truck, Jose and Francisco chatter. Roberto yawns. His eyelids are heavy, and in a moment he is asleep.

"You better wake up," a distant voice warns. "This *patrón* doesn't want any fooling around."

Roberto blinks. The truck races through broad, cool shadows. Then it turns and rapidly twists up a narrow drive closely bordered by eucalyptus trees. Francisco grins widely, displaying his broken teeth.

"It is Friday? This is true? This is the day we will be paid."

Jose grins also and finally Roberto grins, allowing a coil of pain to unwind upward through his ear and pierce the top of his skull. Someone had hit him at the hinge of his jaw, a fist from nowhere, without warning, knocking him to the floor of the *cantina* where he lay staring upward through a haze of dots and lines and laughing faces. Who was it? He had been talking to the woman, the *puta*. She wanted thirty dollars. Thirty dollars! He coughs, liberating again the pain.

"I will kill him," he says aloud, assembling in his mind a face from fuzzy images—a crooked nose, a mouth of silver teeth, an ear somehow defective in the manner of its folds, a scar, as white as a *gringo*'s skin, below the eye.

"*Sí*," Francisco agrees. "I too will kill. I will kill all of them." With an imaginary knife he disembowels Jose. They laugh. The truck has stopped and the *patrón* is at the back, letting down the tailgate. Inside are shovels, mattocks, sledgehammers. He reaches out to test the muscle in Roberto's arm, and he nods, whether in approval or something else, Roberto doesn't know. The *patrón* pushes the tools into the hands of Jose and Francisco, then leads Roberto to the back of a house that looks like it has been struck by a hurricane, or a tornado. Roberto stops to stare at the house, and the man says something unintelligible in an urgent voice.

"I want to break the concrete," the *patrón* says slowly, lifting a panel on the side of an orange machine that sits at a slant in a patch of sunlight, its rubber wheels blocked against escape by a pair of bricks. The man fiddles with something inside the machine while Roberto stares again at the house, at the roof which is partly torn away, at sections of stucco wall broken open to reveal gray conduits and plumbing pipes and other items that he doesn't recognize. The machine sputters suddenly and roars to life, sending from its exhaust a ribbon of cobalt smoke into the sky. Roberto would like to see what is inside the house, but the interior is too dark to give up any detail. The *patrón* turns a valve and a long brown hose like a snake in the dust stirs itself and stiffens. The engine labors, dies, and the *patrón* swears quietly and repeats the procedure.

"Come here," he says to Roberto, and together they follow the hose past a rubbish container to the back of the house, where there is a doorway, a broad set of steps, and a concrete patio. The hose crosses the patio to a dark, oily jackhammer propped against a wall. The sun has discovered a path through the eucalyptus on this side of the house and its reflection from the concrete glares in Roberto's eyes.

"You can?" says the *patrón*. He points to the jackhammer.

Roberto nods, then says, "*Cómo no.*" He has never done this work before, but has watched others, and therefore believes that he has told the truth. With gesture and Spanish too thick for Roberto to follow, the *patrón* indicates where he should begin. Roberto nods vigorously, hoping the man will not stay to watch him make mistakes. He lifts the jackhammer, surprised by its weight, and drags it to the center of the patio, where he guesses that he is supposed to begin. He squeezes the lever beneath the handles and there is a burst of noise like a machine gun that rattles in the trees. The engine in the distance complains, then eases to an idle as dust from the concrete floats upward through the air. Roberto feels a thrill of anticipation that obscures, for a moment, the relentless beat of pain between his ears.

The sun ascends above the eucalyptus trees and punishes those below. With wrecking bar Francisco attacks the remaining shingles on the roof while Jose stands high on a ladder with a sledgehammer in his hand, destroying more of the stucco on the walls. The *patrón* disappears, then just when Roberto believes he is gone for good reappears to watch and give an order in his flat, strange Spanish. In the beginning, Roberto held the jackhammer at too great an angle and the point skidded across the concrete instead of digging in. The jackhammer was a wild, bucking animal that he despaired of controlling, but the *patrón* corrected his mistake, firmly, without anger. The patio slowly disintegrates into irregular pieces, but the steps are thick and resist the loud, chattering point of the tool. The violence of the jackhammer travels straight up Roberto's arm and enters his head, but gradually his entire body goes numb and a low, steady roar like the sound of the freeway displaces the ache in his skull.

Francisco comes to take his place, but Roberto pushes him away. In faulty Spanish the *patrón* explains that Roberto must rest, that the jackhammer is too much for a single man the entire day, but Roberto feigns ignorance and cuts off further discussion with a burst that shears a corner of the step. Francisco shrugs and returns to the roof. The *patrón* watches in silence, and Roberto swings the jackhammer as if it were a feather, and pieces of the thick step fly.

They eat in the shade, on the north side of the house, near a swimming pool containing a puddle of stagnant water upon which dust and scraps of litter float. They eat the hamburgers and french fries brought by the *patrón,* who sits in the cab of his truck with pencil and papers. Roberto has never developed a taste for such food, but his hunger is so profound that he imagines he is eating thick, juicy *carnitas* in a tortilla with *salsa* so *picante* that his ears are cleared of a lingering, persistent roar.

"Tonight," Francisco says, "I will buy tequila."

"You will be very drunk," Jose agrees.

Roberto looks at them. Dust and sweat form patterns on their faces. Francisco appears to have swum with all his clothes on.

Roberto says, "No tequila for me. No beer. I am going to the house of my girlfriend."

"And what will you do there?" Francisco asks, with a smirk.

Roberto makes a threatening motion with his arm, and Francisco throws up a blackened hand in defense. "Tonight I will find a woman," he says, "and have my pleasure."

"Where will you have this pleasure?" Roberto asks. "In the trees? Beneath the cars?" Francisco swipes at him but Roberto ducks away.

He sleeps briefly, dreaming abstractly of bright colors and geometric shapes, then awakes to hear the phlegmatic voice of Jose, talking of Mexico.

"I will go," Roberto says. "I will get a job driving a truck from the factory in Oaxaca to Vera Cruz. I will get married and have two children. But only two."

"Ha!" Francisco spits into grass that hasn't been watered and is brown and brittle. "You dream. There are no jobs in Mexico."

"My cousin Mauricio drives a truck from a factory in Oaxaca to Vera Cruz," Roberto says, feeling suddenly disconsolate and weary, a heavy weariness that hangs around his neck like a weight on a chain.

"If there are jobs in Mexico, then why have you come here?" Francisco asks. He doesn't wait for an answer. "There are no jobs in Mexico. The jobs are only here. In the United States. In California. Are you so stupid not to know this?"

"I am not stupid," Roberto says, nevertheless feeling his mental powers somehow impeded, as he felt sometimes in the school in his village, when the teacher would ask him this very question. *Are you so stupid not to know this?* The sound of a door, the door of the *patrón*'s truck, echoes in the trees. Roberto turns upon Francisco, stares into his dark stained face, grasps his wet and wrinkled shirt. "This is not the job I want. To wait on the street. To wait for someone to come with a shovel and take me to dig a hole."

Francisco pushes his ugly face close to Roberto's, surrounding the younger man with the odor of his sweat, and his breath, which smells like the wood in Lupe's garage. "Is it better in Mexico? Tell me this, my friend. Is it better?"

The *patrón* approaches, in long strides devoid of any deviation or uncertainty, and Roberto, Francisco, and Jose wad up the detritus of their lunch and get to their feet.

"Time to work. You finish today. Understand?"

The words flutter like birds past Roberto's brain, but he understands that it is better to nod and say yes or even *si* than to shake his head and say no as he did in response to the lady who wanted him to cut down the banana tree. He considers the various truths, half-truths, and outright fabrications with which Lupe might explain his failure to appear. As he gathers his strength to lift again the jackhammer he sees the house of his parents, the house of two rooms in which eight children were born and grew to be adults, all married or otherwise dispersed, and then Lupe's house, which by contrast is a palace but for some reason doesn't feel like a palace at all but a jail.

In the United States a person is not restricted but can do what they want, Lupe wrote in her philosophical way when Roberto still lived in his parents' house, idling away his time. *There is nothing to keep a person back if that person is willing to work,* she wrote, causing Roberto to feel a few pangs of guilt.

He recalls the day he left, standing at the side of the highway, awaiting the arrival of the bus. His father stood at his side, repeating every few minutes that Roberto must not forget to send money. The bus arrived, and through the grainy window he watched his father's face grow smaller and smaller and finally disappear. He felt both eager and afraid. As the bus lurched and jolted through the day and into night he dozed and dreamed in pictures from the television flickering in a corner of his father's house: tall girls cavorting on a beach in scanty swimsuits, smiles of invitation upon

their faces. Two of his brothers met him in Mexico City and he was
amazed by the casual way they carried themselves in the streets
that were more chaotic than anything he could have imagined. The
oldest, Pedro, wore expensive clothes, a gold watch and rings on
his fingers. He scoffed at Roberto's plan to continue north. As for
himself, he had spent a day and a night, a few years earlier, in San
Diego, before being caught and returned to Mexico.

"You will be hungry," Pedro said. "Always. And hiding from
la migra. They are everywhere. And there is no work. This is a
great myth."

"Lupe says there is work," Roberto said stubbornly.

"Lupe is cleaning toilets," said Bernardo, the younger of the
brothers. "Do you want to clean toilets?"

He had intended to stay in Mexico City for only twenty-four
hours, but the time lengthened to a week, and among the *cantinas*
and *cine* and a night with a *puta* his money was scattered like ashes
in the wind. He slept in a blanket on the floor of Pedro's room and
when he awoke to find his pockets empty of all but a few pesos
he raged against an imaginary thief until his brother threatened to
beat him if he didn't shut his mouth.

"I have a friend who drives a taxi. He can get you a job. It is
not hard work, and the pay is good."

Pedro was not precisely a liar, Roberto decided later, but his
words could not always be trusted. Driving the taxi caused
Roberto's head to pound and his stomach to churn, and there was
never an extra peso to save for the trip to California. Then one
day Roberto was drawn into a dispute with another driver who
produced a gun which he aimed at Roberto's heart, and Roberto
quit, packed his things into a suitcase, borrowed all the pesos he
could from Pedro and a few thousand more from Bernardo, and
got on a bus that rattled interminably through day and night and
finally left him, in the hot dust of midday, in Tiajuana. Without
sleep or food he waited for darkness and then, with two men he

had met on the bus and another to whom he paid nearly all of his pesos, he crossed the border and found himself, to his amazement, in the United States.

"Hey!" The *patrón* claps his hands, the sound reverberating in the eucalyptus above. "No sleep. Let's go."

The imprecision of the *patrón*'s Spanish causes Roberto to smile. He remembers a long arc of searching light, the barking of dogs, thick vegetation that tore at his skin and clothing. He remembers trying and failing to sleep in rain beneath a torn sheet of plastic. He remembers arriving, finally, in Los Angeles, where, to his further amazement, he found his sisters and their husbands living in a house with four rooms, a bathroom and a shower, and in the driveway, a car that if not new was certainly newer than anything he had ever driven. On the first night, he remembers, Lupe made a bed for him on the sofa and after a long period of wakefulness he fell asleep and dreamed the most fantastic dreams.

Abruptly he feels elated, like a balloon cut free to rise into the sky. He swings the jackhammer like a toy. He calls to Francisco, who straddles a rafter, and to Jose, who swings his hammer against the house as if the effort contains every particle of his energy. The sun punishes them through the tent of dust that Roberto's jackhammer raises above their heads.

At five o'clock the last of the concrete is broken, loaded into a wheelbarrow, and transported to the rubbish container. The orange machine is finally silent, the hose coiled, and the jackhammer stored away. Roberto feels as he imagines a ghost must feel, his hands detached and floating in front of his eyes. When he removes his shirt to splash water over his head and chest he has to concentrate, to tell his arms what movements to undertake. The silence roars like a fire in his ears, yet he feels acutely aware and alert. With a little smile he imagines kissing Luisa.

He rolls his wet, soiled shirt and stuffs it under his arm. He notices that the *patrón* is watching him.

"You like work?" says the *patrón*, in Spanish.

"Yes," Roberto answers, without knowing precisely what is meant by the question.

"I like your work." The *patrón* offers Roberto a can of beer from a little cooler on the seat of his truck.

"No thank you," Roberto says, in English.

"Don't drink beer?"

"Yes," Roberto answers, embarrassed.

"You are intelligent." The *patrón* gazes at Roberto with an attitude of patience, as if he recognizes the possibility of confusion.

"I have much work. You have telephone?"

"Yes."

"Put the number." From a pocket he produces a pencil and a notebook. "I have much work. Other houses."

Roberto complies, writing Lupe's number with the thick, oddly shaped pencil.

"I pay fifty dollars. For one day. For good men."

"I will work," says Roberto, unsure of exactly what the man has proposed.

"Tomorrow? You can?"

"Yes."

"I don't want *them*." He nods toward Francisco and Jose, who stand at the back of the truck, waiting, apparently, for permission to climb aboard.

"You come at seven." The *patrón* names the intersection of two streets and Roberto says yes, it is possible, he will be there, at seven o'clock. The *patrón* stares intently at Roberto, as if in judgment of the honesty of this answer, then reaches into a pocket and hands Roberto a fifty-dollar bill.

The light has softened and faded into dusk when Roberto reaches the apartment of Luisa. If he weren't so tired the cool air that moves across his arms and chest would be invigorating. He plans to go to Lupe's house, put on a clean shirt and pants and the black and shiny shoes. But first he will have a word with Luisa.

He knocks on the door.

"Who is there?"

With relief he hears, not the querulous tone of the cousin, but the soft, shy voice of his Luisa.

"It is Roberto. Open the door."

She obeys, but only to the extent that he can see between the door and jamb a portion of her face, her soft mouth and black eyes. "What do you want?"

"I want to come inside. I am cold." He feels exposed and in some kind of unstated danger, without his shirt, in the courtyard of the apartment house where strangers may observe and hear him.

"You can't come in," she says. Her eyes are completely dark and her mouth set in a firm, hard line.

Anger flares in Roberto's weary chest. "Open the door!" He pushes with a hand but the door does not give, it is held with the chain. He curses, something he cannot help but knows that he will surely regret.

"Go away," Luisa says. "I do not want to see you."

Wanting desperately to believe that she is joking, he peers closely into her face, trying to see a sparkle of humor in her black eyes. He tries to look beyond her, to see if the bitch, her cousin, is behind her, causing her to say these things. He steps back, grins and then guffaws, showing her that he recognizes how she is having fun by teasing him. He brays like an ass, holding his belly. The door clicks shut.

"Luisa!"

He kicks the door. A window in an adjacent apartment rattles and a woman's head appears. The woman speaks in agitated English. Roberto stares at her. She is the landlady, an old woman with a plastic cap that conceals the hair on her head. The woman's face is the color of flour. Roberto ignores her, beats upon Luisa's door with his fists until it cracks open.

"She will call the police!" Luisa speaks in a violent whisper. "Last night you awakened her. You awakened everybody!" Her eyes look glassy now, her lips twisted and swollen, making her ugly.

"I will go to change these clothes," Roberto says, breathing slowly, measuring out his words. "And then I will return. Today I had work. I have money." He produces the fifty-dollar bill, holds it up close to the crack in the door.

"I don't want you to come," Luisa whispers furiously. "I don't want to see you. You make my life a misery."

"I have work!" Roberto cries in frustration. "A man who builds houses. He wants me to work, every day." .

"Do you remember?"

"What?"

"You came last night. You were drunk. You told me you were not going to drink anymore, but last night you were drunk again. I don't want to see you, Roberto. Never again."

"I don't remember." Chaotic images fight to the surface of Roberto's mind. Hazy memories swirl, making him dizzy. He feels sickness in his stomach. Again the door has closed. The old woman's head still protrudes from the window and Roberto looks around until he sees a small stone that he picks up and heaves at her. The stone narrowly misses the old woman's plastic skull, ricochets off the glass, and strikes an iron clothesline pole with a loud, bright ping. He laughs at the sight of the woman's startled mouth, in the moment before she jerks her head inside and brings the window down with a clatter. Then Roberto runs. He runs down an alley, dodging children playing a game, and in the distance he hears a siren. The siren could not be for him and yet a terror seizes him and he runs like a wild, terrified animal. He runs until a fire rages in his chest, and still he runs until he knows that he must either stop or die.

Roberto smokes. He never smokes, only when he is *borracho*, and thus his lungs rebel, making his body double with a spasm. Someone laughs. Laughs and then coughs, a deep sinister cough, full of disease.

"Jose." Roberto allows his tongue to work without the direction of conscious thought. "You are my friend, yes?"

The darkness is like a blanket close around them, the only light the ember of the cigarette, reddening and waning as Jose puffs. Nearby but invisible, Francisco snores. The bottle sits between Roberto's thighs. He raises the bottle, finds his lips. It tastes like nothing. Once the contents of the bottle were warm and glowed in his throat but now it might be water, or Coca-Cola, or something that would repulse him if he could see it or knew what it was. This latter notion causes him to laugh, a loose wet sound, then cough.

He wears the shirt that he wore to work, but it does not exactly fit him anymore; perhaps the buttons have not discovered their proper holes. Another hilarious notion that he proposes aloud but which finds no audience, brings no response save the unceasing drone of traffic directly above his head. Since there is no one to hear him he allows himself to slowly slide toward the oblivion of sleep, where the roar of a diesel truck above transforms into a dream of travel, of roads that curl and dip and rise through a landscape devoid of cars and trucks and buses, a landscape entirely barren, empty of a single living thing.

Previous winners of

The Flannery O'Connor Award

for Short Fiction

David Walton, *Evening Out*

Leigh Allison Wilson, *From the Bottom Up*

Sandra Thompson, *Close-Ups*

Susan Neville, *The Invention of Flight*

Mary Hood, *How Far She Went*

François Camoin, *Why Men Are Afraid of Women*

Molly Giles, *Rough Translations*

Daniel Curley, *Living with Snakes*

Peter Meinke, *The Piano Tuner*

Tony Ardizzone, *The Evening News*

Salvatore La Puma, *The Boys of Bensonhurst*

Melissa Pritchard, *Spirit Seizures*

Philip F. Deaver, *Silent Retreats*

Gail Galloway Adams, *The Purchase of Order*

Carole L. Glickfeld, *Useful Gifts*

Antonya Nelson, *The Expendables*

Nancy Zafris, *The People I Know*

Debra Monroe, *The Source of Trouble*

Robert H. Abel, *Ghost Traps*

T. M. McNally, *Low Flying Aircraft*

Alfred DePew, *The Melancholy of Departure*